LOYAL 2 DA HOOD

LOYAL 2 DA HOOD

**M
I
Z
R
O
K**

Library of Congress Control Number:		2014921404
ISBN:	Hardcover	978-1-5035-2156-8
	Softcover	978-1-5035-2157-5
	eBook	978-1-5035-2155-1

Print information available on the last page.

Rev. date: 07/08/2020

To order additional copies of this book, contact:
Xlibris
1-888-795-4274
www.Xlibris.com
Orders@Xlibris.com
635496

Illmatik Creations
www.illmatikcreations.com
info@illmatikcreations.com

CONTENTS

MY ACKNOWLEDGMENTS

First and foremost, I would like to thank the Almighty Father for his guidance in helping me achieve such a goal. I never understood the hard work and determination that it takes to actually write a book. I send my love and respect to all of the authors working hard on their projects. To those that have enjoyed my first street fiction novel, wait until you read the sequel:

STILL
LOYAL 2 DA HOOD

God bless my beautiful grandmother. Te amo, Abuela! When life seems like it is coming to an end, you always find a way to uplift me with the strength that I never knew that I had. You are truly one of God's angels.

I send my undying love and loyalty to my hardworking mother that struggled through life to raise two sons and a daughter. Mami, I love you! I know that I have not been a perfect son, but my love for you is unconditional.

Uncle Felix, you are the father that I never had. I trust you with my life. Now that you are home, I no longer have to worry about movements being stagnated. Si tú sufres, yo sufro, si tú lloras, yo lloró, si tú botas sangre, yo boto sangre, somos uno!

Titi Maggie, I love you with all of my heart. You have always been there for me through good and bad situations. You are a beautiful person.

Danny, never forget that I will die for you. You are my brother, my nigga, and my blood. Death before dishonor.

I am proud of you, Priscilla. Continue in your positive direction. You are my baby sister. I love you!

Uncle Eli, though we are not tight, I will never forget about your sacrifices to get me out of jams. Family over everything. My love and respect!

Toma tú bandera, toma tú machete, vamos a seguir peleando para la liberación nacional de Puerto Rico! With love and respect to my grandfather, Norberto Claudio Gonzalez, a true revolutionist.

One love to my nigga Azibo Aquart, who is sitting on death row up in USP Terre Haute, Indiana. You kept me focused on writing this book while we sat in the hole speaking through sink pipes. You're a real nigga and I fuck with you. There isn't too many of us around anymore. Real recognize real!

Angel, I cannot believe that you are graduating high school this year. You are a very smart young man. You have been getting in the honor roll since the first grade. You earned that Presidential Award from President Obama. You have an excellent mother, who would sacrifice her life for you. I miss you, Angel. My firstborn. Never doubt that your father loves you! I know that you are disappointed in me for the life that I have chosen to live, but I hope that you do not judge me for my mistakes. I wish that I were home to watch the Patriots kick ass this year with you, but soon enough, we will sit down together and enjoy each other's company.

Jaiden, I love you son. Continue to focus on school and writing rhymes. You are a very intelligent young man that can accomplish anything that you set your mind to. Follow your dreams and never give up. Take care of your twin sisters and good-hearted mother. Te amo!

Anaya, my beautiful daughter, you know that your father loves you, even though your mother purposely keeps us apart. I miss you! I miss watching cartoons with you and watching you grabbing a million toys in the toy store.

Mizhai, you are my baby, my youngest. It kills me to see you through a glass, but you give me the motivation and strength that I need to fight my way out of the belly of the beast. Remember, you only have one father—me. No-one can ever take my position. I look forward to seeing you at our next visit. Duérmete niño mió, que sueñes con los angelitos. Te quiero con todo mi corazón y que Dios te bendiga.

-REST IN PEACE-
TO ALL OF MY BROTHERS AND SISTERS
WHO HAVE FALLEN IN THE
STRUGGLE

CHAPTER 1

JUDGMENT DAY
MIZERY

I t's May 31, 2012. I am nervously pacing back and forth inside of a holding cell at the John Joseph Moakley Federal Courthouse, which is located in Boston, Massachusetts. After three-years-and-seven-months of preparing for trial, judgment day is only minutes away. My lawyer, Attorney Joseph Machera, a short and thin tanskinned Italian man with a pushback hairstyle, just enlightened me that our jury, during a four-hour deliberation, had finally reached a verdict.

Trial commenced on May 21 and concluded ten long stressful days later. I am defying a fifteen-year minimum mandatory sentence, plus a maximum of life, pertaining to three counts of Felon in Possession of a Firearm and Ammunition, in violation of 18 § 922(g)(1). These weapon charges triggered the Armed Career Criminal Act, due to six prior convictions being used as predicates, although Congress only requires government prosecutors to be in need of three. Predicates are prior convictions for either a violent felony or a serious drug offense or a combination thereof. Joining those matters is Dealing in Firearms and Aiding and Abetting, in violation of 922(a)(2)(A) and 18 USC § 2. The charge in the name of Distribution of More Than Fifty Grams of Cocaine Base, in violation of 21 USC § 841(a)(1), enhanced me as a Career Offender because of two predicates. But right before jury selection, a sexy prosecutor walked pompously before the court and filed a notice of a prior felony conviction under 21 USC § 851, doubling my guideline imprisonment range to 360 months to life.

As I reminisced about everything that went down, it was frustrating to understand how the team and I had been so sloppy. We allowed a cooperating witness to infiltrate our circle throughout an eighteen-month investigation disclosed as *Operation Royal Ruin*. A rat-ass nigga named Teddy Bear became an Unknown (UK) in Walpole State Prison, where this traitorous coward embraced our impeccable love. You know what's fucked up? That I got real close with this fuzz, so close, that I honored him to be my son's godfather ahead of Mizhai actually being born. What a true bitch! He deserves an award for his Oscar-winning performance. Trust me, that cheese-eating faggot would have even fooled you.

I remember on a few occasions when we robbed and shot niggaz, but of course, the jury, at no time, would hear about such things, since snitching is forbidden in my way of life. I know that I'm probably—not by any chance—ever going to see Mr. Teddy Bear again. He testified how government officials issued him a new identity and padded his wire-wearing ass in a hidden witness protection program somewhere in another state. On the other hand, I am pretty sure that federal authorities are still utilizing their source in order to set up more targets in other investigations.

"Rodriguez! Rodriguez!" a baldheaded court officer yelled out for me. "Are you ready?" he added.

"I think that I'm ready," I answered, while shambling out of the holding cell.

Mr. Clean handcuffed one and the other hand behind one's back; locked shackles around both of my ankles; and then led me into an awaiting elevator. Our ride down seemed like a lifetime. When we finally exited elevator number one, he and I started footing it down a narrow basement underpass, which had been equipped with visual cameras that were recording everything inescapable. The tunnel reminded your boy of that motion picture titled *Swat*—when some prisoner got escorted through a similar-looking passageway on his way to be transferred. We were moving in silence, hearing the clinking sounds of shackles click-clacking together. I was dripping in sweat, trying to ignore a pounding heart at the point of us stepping onto another elevator that immediately ascended. As those metal doors opened back up, two different court officers suddenly appeared, vigorously sticking me inside of a tiny holding cell where they removed all of the restraints.

After about five minutes of impatiently waiting, both of the COs attended a defendant into a populace courtroom, where it was all eyes on me. I had on a crispy Polo white long-sleeved shirt. On top of it, sat a brand-new, sky-blue cashmere sweater vest that had blue lining and white diamonds across the front, which was manufactured by Russell Simmon's American Classics. I freaked it with a solid blue Pierre Cardin tie in a big knot! In case niggaz don't know, that's that fly shit. This simple outfit came along with some plain black Guess slacks. The creases were ironed into these pants so sharp, that it made one scared to rub one's fingers alongside of them and get cut. Making sure that there were no flaws, on my feet, flashed a pair of black ostrich above-the-ankle Stacey Adams shoes having hard bottoms. The man looked fresh. I can't help it that I'm a sexy chubby nigga. My counsel and I occupied our defense table while Honorable Judge Zobella presided on her bench. She then called in a diverse jury.

"Has the jury reached its verdict?" Honorable Judge Zobella queried.

"Yes we have, Your Honor," replied an old black foreman.

"What say you the jury?" Honorable Judge Zobella requested their verdict.

I peered at the foreman and gave audience as he began reading from a verdict form, "Count one, for Distribution of More Than Fifty Grams of Cocaine Base, we find the defendant, not guilty! Count two, for Felon in Possession of a Tec9 semiautomatic pistol, a .40 caliber handgun, and ammunition, we find the defendant, not guilty! Count three, for Felon in Possession of two .380 caliber handguns and ammunition, we find the defendant, not guilty! Count four, for Felon in Possession of a .22 caliber handgun, a nine-millimeter pistol, and ammunition, we find the defendant, not guilty! Count five, for Dealing in Firearms and Aiding and Abetting, we find the defendant, not guilty!

Grateful eyes closed, giving thanks to the Supreme Soul. Locking gazes with Attorney Machera spoke for itself. He was definitely going to cash in on a bonus. I, Mizery, was free to go, so I headed toward my grandmother, uncle, and aunt that were all on their feet positioned in the closest row to the defense table smiling at me. This heart of mine belongs to them. They have always stood by one's side through times of trials and tribulations. Now that's a real family.

Before FBI agents took hostage this lion, I had everything, or at least I thought that I did. When our indictment came down, only a few of my team members were arrested, so the others continued to get money and hold it down for UK. I guess it is true what people say, 'Out of sight, out of mind,' because during my incarceration of awaiting trial, these so-called brothers of mine never showed me any love. But it is, what it is, and one can only charge it to the game.

As for my wifey, Maliya, and my son, Mizhai, well, I don't even know where to begin to explain it. Mizhai could have only been a month old when the alphabet boyz stormed into this king's castle and kidnapped me. Remembering the day of his birth—September 26, 2008. Maliya and I had been arguing that whole week. The lady of pleasure decided to go crash at her mommy's house in Lynn. It is a fact that wifey's pregnancy drove that young girl to act out of order, but Mrs. Mouthy's beak did not know when to shut up. Anyways, this Latin long stroker had been sprawled out on this female's comforter, trying to get some bomb sloppy, when a phone text came into view from Maliya. A close-up of our newborn son appeared on a Verizon cell phone screen. That stunt that this sneak pulled killed a newly parent mentally and emotionally. I really wanted to be there to welcome Mizhai enter this beautiful world. Then shorty with the mean head game put a fucked up assumption in one's consciousness about what Maliya had just did. This little jumpoff spat out, that in an obvious opinion, Maliya did not know who the daddy was, so the swindler played it safe.

For the first three months of being caged up, wifey faithfully visited me, bringing along Mizhai. She wrote, sent money for commissary, and deposited funds into a phone account in order to accept collect calls. Maliya gave her sacred word to hold one down as my ryde-or-die bitch, but deep down inside, I knew that gimmy-beaver wouldn't last long. The broad can't be blamed in a way. Maliya was very young, which is one of many excuses that this hurting has fashioned for one's ex. Nonetheless, reality came to be that big Mizery fell in love with an eighteen-year-old Dominican dime, someone trusted and adored. Maliya beguiled an attracted man into believing that we were beyond compare, a Jay-Z and Beyoncé, fun-loving couple that had been living in a dream house away from the hood.

My wifey pushed her own purple Range Rover, which had been sitting on twenty-six-inch Giovanna rims. The interior model was black and purple with purple lights. The system composed of a Sony Xplod radio, entailing sub control, two fifteen-inch square Kicker L7 subwoofers, plus a 1,000 x 1 JL Audio amplifier. Maliya used to think that she looked cute lamping in that SUV.

We shared a family Escalade truck carrying TVs and a Play Station 2. The rest of that big boy remained factory. Our getaway vehicle had only been driven when we felt like disappearing and doing us. Maliya and I went everywhere in that truck, including Disney World in Orlando, Florida, Disneyland in Anaheim, California, and anywhere else you can think of—we've been there.

You should have seen the motorcycles that Maliya and I were riding around on. I had a new Kawasaki Ninja Zx14R, the Ninja of all Ninjas. It got named Beast. My bike stayed spicy, comprising fresh fully gold plated paint. The windshield blinged gold with a black crown in the upper left-hand corner. It also brandished black and chrome Kawasaki Ninja labels. The kickstand, clutch, rear set, brake kit, exhaust pipe, and extended swing arm were all nickel-plated. Even my chain gleamed nickel-plated! The leather seat, along with both tires, was brown and gold, exposing custom Louis Vuitton logos. Beast's 300 Fatboy back tire encircled a twenty-inch solid chrome five-star rim. Both of the rims had been custom patterned by D'Vinci. I know that you're feeling my shit, but I'm not even finished yet. Beast had an automatic stage 3 jet kit, that when kicked in, especially on the highway, it made this mind-blowing bike turn up, as if someone shot a gold bullet, anytime the clutch recoiled. Everyone used to love watching the xenon strobe light, which posed in the center headlamp, go crazy. The Ninja of all Ninjas stood so powerful, that it had to be stretched an extra twelve inches, and then conserved by a fat tire, because of how Beast ended up to be tuned up so tight. Whenever the clutch sprung out, in any gear but first, it would respond by trying to rise and shine. In spite of making an attempt to do so or not, that monster took to the air on its own.

When Maliya found out about the motorcycle that my peoples were fabricating, she begged me to order her one. Therefore, you already know, I held my wifey down and copped that spoiled girl a baby Ninja, the Kawasaki Ninja Zx250R. The bike toned candy-coated purple paint, encompassing mad finish, always resembling wet and clean, despite when it's dirty. The windshield had purple tint, illustrating a black crown in the lower left-hand corner. Black and chrome Kawasaki Ninja labels also highlighted on the windshield. The bike settled on black and chrome Wired windmill rims, which embraced Pirelli tires. Never failing that bitch, an extended chrome swing arm solidified baby Beast, so babygirl didn't fly up in the air, if she, by any chance, ever drove reckless one day. A GPS screen had been custom-built on the gas tank, so when baby-momma rode, Mrs. Rodriguez would perpetually be on point of that female's whereabouts. On wifey's leather seat, *Maliya* got stitched in purple cursive. That heartbreaker's baby Ninja couldn't be fucked with! It was brand-new and hooked up, better than anything on the streets. You wouldn't even know that this bike claimed a 250 when hearing that Vancen & Hines pipe. To top it all off, I had Ricky Gadson, an official leader of the international Team Green, sign both Kawasaki Ninjas.

One thing is free from doubt; nothing can stack up against my baby Midnight, a 5-Series BMW. She was jet-black and had matching ostrich interior. The dark limo tints, together with those twenty-two-inch ADR chrome rims, killed it! Cousin Fat Joshua fastened black-on-black five-point crowns that bubbled out on all four of the headrests. Televisions had been installed throughout the vehicle. A seven-inch touch screen Boss radio sat pretty, controlling Midnight's system. The inside Audio Pipe speakers screamed from an Alpine voice amplifier. All trunk booming sounds originated out of a wooden box that held three twelve-inch square L7 subwoofers, which generated power from two 2,000 x 1 JL Audio amplifiers. Everything was connected to a Kicker crossover for clear listening. That system knocked. But peep what it put on show under the hood. The engine boasted a V10, increased by 10 horsepower, including updates. It used to get up from zero to sixty-two miles per hour in three point seven seconds. If one is nice with the stick, one can push her to two hundred and two miles per hour. You can compare that to any Italian sports car. Midnight sat low to the ground because of its lowered suspension. What sent that beamer over the edge on piff status were those fiber vents and panels.

I remember one day, when I recorded a track with Max B, before he got caught up for that body case. Fat Joe and Birdman were also in the studio. They were trying to outbid each other on who would buy Midnight. Fat Joe offered me seventy-five thousand dollars, but then Birdman forced it, by proffering one hundred and seventy-five thousand dollars. I laughed, and told those niggaz that your boy was good. As you can see, this UK Gangsta had been doing all right for himself. I stashed over one hundred thousand dollars in case times got rough. When those cuffs locked around both of my wrists, Maliya had firsthand availability to that greenback, this way, the family did not need for anything.

It's distressing doing one's best trying to forget what a nigga went through when Maliya left me for dead. The letters, visits, money, plus the collect calls came to an end. Calling Mrs. Wifey about thirty times a day to let it be known that Mr. Husband still thought the world of her, always resulted negatively, because of course, she would hang up without accepting the collect calls. What tore this noble man up mostly was the woman's unsympathetic decision to remove the prince from his father's life. Sometimes, Maliya would empower, in a notarized affidavit, under the authority of my grandmother and aunt, for them to take along Mizhai on scheduled visits whenever they caught a break. But nothing would ever be the same. The trust had been betrayed. And beyond that, big Mizery felt excruciated during those lonesome days in a cell, abstracted in the brainwork of the inexplicable. Finally, the facts were accepted and this dog's concentration fell upon the upcoming court procedures, because crying over spilled milk is senseless.

Grandma, Aunt Maggie, and Uncle Felix preached nonstop from the word go on this entire ride to Chelsea. Auntie Maggie is an all-around appealing woman that seems to never age. She is 5'6", light-skinned, shapely, and has shoulder-length dark hair. Everyone loves her charming personality. Somewhere down the line, after she gave birth to Daniel and Steven, a change of interest occurred. Auntie Maggie divulged desirability for other women.

Uncle Felix is an old-timer that has been around the block a few times. He is a short and stocky light-brown-skinned guy trending a pushback hairdo. The man has a sincere heart. Before him and Aunt Michelle, a nice-looking Italian woman, got divorced years ago, I would frequently be over their house in Revere watching athletic events on Pay Per View. My Cousins Alexander, Adriana, and Xavier were children back then.

Grandma looks great for her age. The woman is always in high spirits. However, it makes me sad thinking of the day that I will have to say goodbye. My grandmother hit the kitchen as soon as we entered the tiny apartment. She prepared arroz blanco, beans on the side, fried plátanos, and fried chuletas. You know, that bomb-ass Puerto Rican food. Following that delicious dinner, Titi, who is Auntie Maggie, announced a sudden departure because of an engagement to wake up extra early for work in the morning. Titi Maggie handed over twenty dollars and one of those cheap Metro PCS cell phones. It's still in a box. I brushed through the user's information, which was obviously a fake name, and seen that next month's bill is due on the tenth. I thanked Titi Maggie with a kiss. Once that one's relatives had left, it called for Grandma to lay down the house rules. The golden ager is a church person, one of God's angels. Therefore, I already knew that they were going to be strict canons.

"Abuela?" I called my grandmother in Spanish. "Have you seen Maliya and Mizhai?" her grandson asked.

"Mirar hijo, leave that little girl alone. When you went to jail, Maliya just up and disappeared. I only seen my great-grandson on those few occasions that we drove him to go spend time with you. Maggie is associated more in your son's life than I am. Maliya sold your house, motorcycle, truck, and car. She has a new boyfriend, and is so fascinated by this person, that Mizhai addresses the man as Daddy. The family didn't want to mention any of this in the act of you preparing for trial, since our direct attention was on a not-guilty verdict," Abuela explained in detail with concern written all over her face.

"Yo entiendo, Abuela," I prevaricated, while truthfully steaming inside. Even so, I didn't want my grandmother noticing, for the reason that it's a botheration envisioning her ill at ease, so it was decided for a troop to Store 24. But first, a quick switch up from court clothes to some archaic shit.

Abuela lives on Chestnut Street in Chelsea, Massachusetts. It's right in the hood, my hood. Chelsea is a small city located outside of Boston, directly across the Mystic River. Even though Chelsea is Suffolk County, has a 617 area code, it'll never be officially considered Boston. But don't get it fucked up, we body shit in ChelRok. At one time, the city of Boston took over Chelsea because the city went broke. They attempted to restyle our city's name on a West Boston wave. But fuck that! The people of Chelsea protested and the name remained the same. Welcome to ChelRok, aka Crack City, which is underneath the notorious Tobin Bridge. A place branded as the Unknowns' nativeland, where niggaz love to bang and get money! It is never going to change!

As soon as I stepped foot on my block, the feeling of being home zestfully washed away some agony. It was a warm night out; moreover, you could easily behold a pack of lions up and down the street knee-deep in that gold. A deep and rowdy clique made up of crack dealers were huddled up at the corner linking Chestnut Street and Fifth Street. About four bud sellers were postured on a set of stairs over from little-ass Cisco Park. But more than that, you had those young gunclappers eager to put in that work surrounding the already G-Fived heads. Of course, hoodrat bitches and as well as random niggaz were out there too—you know, like any other hood. This is one of the Unknowns' territories in Chelsea.

You know a UK Gangsta on site. Black bandanna and hat swagging to the left, plus always Five poppin' instantaneously upon acknowledgment of each other. Walking down Chestnut Street placed me at the center of attention. I did not recognize anyone; they were all new faces, Baby Unknowns. Observing had to be big Mizery's choice for now, before exposing myself to potential informants. In the act of traveling on foot, one eagle-eyed a jillion head-turning ho'z, but with this beat-down gear on my body, who would have the nerve to holla at a shorty? I banged a right at Fifth Street and kept it moving, until taking a left on Broadway, in the direction of Store 24. Once inside of the semi-crowded store, I hopped in line.

While waiting, this white girl passed me talking on a cell phone. The pretty girl rubbernecked the kid, as if she had seen a ghost, and, unaccompanied, continued walking up the aisle deeply involved in her conversation. Shorty had a fatty for a snowbunny. I stepped up and set down a twenty-dollar bill on the counter, in order to purchase two packs of Newport's, along with this cool lighter disporting a sticker of some vicious roaring alpha lion on it.

It felt good smoking freely without worrying about being snagged by correctional officers that stay hating. As I was openly standing outside enjoying a Cancer stick, that snowbunny that caught a nigga's eye exited the store. She audaciously tramped right up on this UK Gangsta, smack-dab in my face.

"You don't remember me, huh?" the pretty white girl stated more than asked, while staring into my eyes.

"Am I suppose to? I have been locked up three-and-a-half-years. You're probably confusing me with someone else," I looked fixedly back into her eyes, all through responding.

"Damn Mizery, you're an asshole! Isn't this the tightest pussy that you have ever had? You were worthy of my virginity. Amandria!" she softly punched me on the shoulder, showing a hint of hurt in her voice.

"Oh shit! What's good, babygirl? How have you been? I didn't even recognize you because of your red hair. How are Ma and Rachelle doing?" I uttered in a shocked tone.

It was surely godsending to encounter Amandria at this time; it is felt that our feelings are ditto. We perceived the happiness. Amandria is an ex-girlfriend. People misconstrue her of being Spanish, but she is strictly Caucasian, although when our beings first met, Ms. Fabulist fibbed about being mulatto. Babygirl's sexy green eyes, thick body, lovely wide smile with exceptional white teeth, and wet-looking hairstyle permanently has an enchanting effect on me. Though this woman is a bit taller than I am, I believe that the two of us make an excellent twosome. Amandria is whom I characterize as my junior wifey. These lovebirds gave and took one another's virginity at a young age. Amandria will forevermore be that first female that I have ever French-kissed, loved, fucked, lived with, and lost one's heart to. Amandria and I have not laid eyes on each other in about seven years. Last time that shorty and I spent a night together, if this mind's eye serves one right, it had to be at the Red Roof Inn on Route I in Saugus. The duo wined, dined, drank, smoked, popped X, and sexed. The next day, at the Chelsea District Courthouse, I had been sentenced to eighteen months for a probation violation, which had to be served in the Suffolk County House of Corrections, better known as South Bay.

South Bay is a wild county jail located at 20 Bradston Street in the city of Boston, where you have people from every project and hood from Suffolk County, and the whole shooting match of nation gangs all cramped up together in overpopulated units. So imagine how much drama pops off? The 3-Building units consist of over one hundred and fifty convicts per unit. You have three niggaz breathing in one undersized cell sharing a television. The 4-Building is almost no different, except that these units are smaller and connected. Three televisions sit in segregated rooms put down for African-American, Caucasian, Asian, Cape Verdean, and Spanish dogz. Even the correctional officers swear up and down that their hard. Those panic-button-hitting pigs have been under a superabundance of investigations on behalf of questionable deaths, reported as suicides, overdoses, and justified force. Yet, we all know what it is.

After being released from South Bay, Amandria and I never had the opening to recapitulate where our affair left off. And before long, ultimately, I met Maliya. Yet, here we are today, exchanging our cell phone numbers, similarly looking forward to catching up on old times. My junior wifey let it be known that she had to setoff because her son was waiting in the car. *Amandria? A kid?* That shit baffled me for a quick second, but it has been seven years since our last run-in, so a lot can eventuate in such a long period of time. Amandria pecked an old friend on the cheek and along came a tight hug. My dick instantly got hard as a rock. The chemistry is undeniable; I am definitely going to smash that again.

On the way back to Abuela's house, a right was taken at Fifth Street, exactly when this black hatchie, tinted the fuck out, came slowly creeping beside me. The passenger side window went halfway down, just as an alien rocking a grey hoodie over its head, revealing two grey bandannas covering every bit of facial skin, threw up that bullshit 'R', and then shouted, "Us Niggaz Love Violence!"

Out of nowhere, two people wearing black bandannas tied around their faces ran out of the Cherry Street alleyway shooting shit up. I heard the sounds of bullets smacking off the car's frame, together with glass shattering onto the concrete. I cautiously broke camp, cutting and running back up Fifth Street, but instead of bending left on Broadway, it was a precipitated right, now dogtrottin', until turning right at the Chelsea Walk, a small brick pathway. I ended up in the middle of Cherry Street, give or take a few feet away from my grandmother's backyard.

As soon as I got in, Abuela was on me. "Tu oísteis esos tiros?" she worriedly inquested.

"Si, Abuela. I became aware of it while inside of Broadway's Chinese store, the one across the street from that new computer place," I responded, even though that's on the other side of Broadway. I am not pleased by lying to my grandmother, but like-minded, as I have said previously, her grandson gets disturbed anytime that she is beside herself.

As Abuela plodded nearing her bedroom, God's angel uttered, "Por favor, ten cuidado. These bloody streets have only gotten worse since you have been gone. Oh, I almost forgot, Maliya llamo. She is expecting you to return her phone call. Now don't go cuckoo, fighting and arguing. Accept the things that one cannot change, but more importantly, establish a friendship with Maliya in consideration of your son. I wrote the number down; it's over there on the telephone stand."

"Bendición, Abuelita," I showed one's respect, and then cruised over to my grandmother and kissed her goodnight.

"Dios te bendiga," she retorted, unveiling a ravishing smile.

I wasn't sure how this phone discussion would play out, but I knew that I did not have a yen to wild out. A part of me has an aversion apropos of her merciless deliverance that crushed a good heart. Nonetheless, this trickster captivates the other half. Maliya was my ryde-or-die bitch ahead of what went down. At most, all the smoke arose a month after Mizhai's birth, so in a way, it is understandable. They were alone, but at least she should have shown baby-daddy some moral support as a friend. Fuck that! I'm sick of bringing about cleanups for that smut. I picked up Abuela's house phone and called her.

"Hello," Maliya answered in a normal expression.

"What's good, Black Widow?" I couldn't help it, I had to say some fly shit.

"Are you going to start talking shit already? There is no time for games. Your situation split us apart and I moved on. It's that simple. Now here is a proposition," she was beyond heartless, as her cold words stabbed my spirit.

"I'm all ears," I rejoined in a low laid-back tone, not wanting Maliya to hang up on me.

"I know that you just touched down and don't have any paper, so we are prepared to hand over triple beam grams if you allow my fiancé and I to change Mizhai's last name to his on the birth certificate. Besides,

Mizhai loves the only father that he knows," Maliya spoke in a hateful manner.

This bitch is forcing it! I gripped the phone so hard, that one could hear the plastic cracking, as I was being attentive to this dumb-sounding birdbrain speak. "Are you fucking crazy or just fucking stupid? Tell your fucking fiancé that—" I started wilding out, before her ill-bred ass cut me off.

"Don't yell at me, nigga! I am not the one to tolerate it. Think this over and get back to me," Maliya suggested smoothly, as if she had a car for sale.

"Can I please kick it with Mizhai?" I asked at a standstill.

"No! He doesn't even know who you are," Maliya blurted out, in front of hanging up the phone in my face.

"This fucking sleazy ho has the audacity to treat me treacherous!" I barked, and then threw Abuela's house phone across the room.

"Cálmate, Miguel Angel. Do not end up behind those walls again over that piggish little girl. She is not worth it. You are going to fall in with a more fitting woman than her. Then Maliya will be the one to regret hurting you," my grandmother moralized, which somewhat calmed me down.

"Esta bien, Abuela. I am going to turn on the TV and call it a night. Te amo," I expressed, as my grandmother hobbled back into her bedroom with that uneasy poker face that only I could recognize.

In the fourth quarter of a Boston Celtics basketball game, my jeans started vibrating. "What the fuck!" was my brief startled blurt, until it registered about the Metro PCS cell phone that Auntie Maggie had given me. Alizé popped up on the surface. That's Amandria's new nickname.

"What's up, babygirl?" spoken like a true pimp.

"Are you still awake? I was lying in bed watching television and you came to mind, so I am checking on you, hoping that a man of your character would like to come over to keep an old friend company? We can smoke a few blunts of some Purple Haze and have a couple of drinks?" Amandria sounded sexy as she seduced me.

It's clearly evident what it is—the time was now to go beat that pussy up. I've always had a soft spot for Amandria, even when we found ourselves with other companions through life's mysterious ways. She insisted that I jump in a cab and took the initiative to pay for it.

Less than fifteen minutes later, I pulled up at the Commandant's Way condominiums in Admiral's Hill, where my mother resided right before the dreadful incident had occurred. Alizé, waiting outside beforehand, paid an Irish cab driver and wasted no time taking me into those gladsome arms. This caring person squeezed one's hand at the exact moment that we went through both of the lobby doors. Simultaneously, I pictured Mami smiling down on me. Even though the two of us were not very close, she is forever in her son's left-titty as the queen that gave one life. Many folks have mistaken Mami for being a girlfriend or little sister in my early teen days because of Ms. Gonzalez's petite frame, long-flowing dark hair, and pretty young-looking features. I really miss Momdukes, a hardworking woman that managed two jobs in order to support three children. This soul's creator passed away by cause of a fatal car accident during a time that little fat Miguel had been committed to the Department of Youth Services (DYS).

Amandria snapped me out of my trance with her liquor-smelling whisper, "Don't worry beloved, your mother is in a better place. Just know that she misses you too."

Upon entrance to her apartment, I was flat-out amazed on how up-to-date Alizé financed it. All-white puffy couches, a sixty-two-inch plasma flat screen, and an enormous fish tank, involving glow-in-the-dark fishes, stylishly sat in a cushy-sized living room. Shorty had the spot looking spiffy. Meanwhile, I made myself at home, side-by-side Amandria on a loveseat, while scoping that loud that she twisted and lit. Alizé passed it to me, after only taking a few pulls, and without warning, jumped up, precisely heading into the kitchen in order to fetch us two shot glasses with an exclusive bottle of White Hennessy. As I banged on that purp, instantly smoke hit my brain.

When Amandria returned, bottle and glasses in hand, kindly she filled our glassware. My junior wifey lifted her shot and articulated, "A toast to a positive future." We gently tapped the shot glasses before chugging them down. Amandria snatched the blunt out of one's fingertips in a playful manner, and at that instant, flounced an erotic body until reaching a bedroom door. I just kept guzzling shot after shot.

Shortly after that milf ducked out, Alizé reappeared looking pornographic. She wore a pink half shirt, pink booty spandex shorts, and her hair was pulled back in a bun. My eyes were glued on the bubbles of that meaty butt and full titties, just as shorty seductively approached me, ready to fuck.

"Do you think that you can handle this?" she teased me in the most provocative way. Her pretty green eyes witnessed the growth begging for attention.

"You already know," I replied in a gangsta tone, hoping that she would suck a nigga's dick, which was throbbing in anticipation. This dog stood up and began kissing his playmate. Then the half shirt came off as my left hand massaged her pussy. Next were the spandex shorts and panties.

"Strip!" Amandria commanded me to do so, right before she grounded onto her knees.

The 5ive Jungle jeans slid off, as speedily as can do. Single-handedly, shorty wasted not one tick on the clock stuffing this dick into an accepting mouth. Big Mizery was so lost in the moment that I didn't even realize that junior wifey used those pink glossy lips to stretch a condom over minime. *David Copperfield's successor!* Alizé astonished me with such a nifty little trick. However, nothing can bear comparison to the warm and tender feeling from Amandria's mouth gliding on this pole. Even though the Trojan prevented actual contact, my lion head roared, as she did the tornado on it, slowed down, and then deep throated very slow.

"That's right, at your tempo," I encouraged her, while holding back, trying to avoid cumming too fast. Pounding that pussy in a doggie-style position came next. After all of these years, Amandria is still tight and crazy wet, just how papi Mizery relishes it.

"Fuck me, Mizery! Oh yeah! Harder! Make this pussy cum! Faster! Yeah, right there!" she ordered, taking every inch of dick thrusted her way.

Shorty loved it. We switched positions and Amandria ended up on top; riding me backwards. I finger-fucked her asshole with my thumb, using pussy wetness for lubrication. Something about watching Alizé get aroused in both holes drove an atingled man crazy. *Babygirl's wet-wet is right.* I thought to myself, as I began to ram all seven inches of this curving mini bat deep inside of that soft place.

After about five minutes of junior wifey's rodeo show, she decided to rearrange our bodies again. This time, her fading pink glossy lips landed back on my dick, behind pulling off the slimy condom. It didn't take long for me to bust. That freaky bitch let it skeet all over a pleasure-loving face.

The following morning, Amandria woke me up with soft words, "I have to go pick up my son from Ma's house.

I forgot that she had a child. "How old is your son?" I questioned, while in the verge of heading into her bedroom bathroom.

"My baby? He is almost six-and-a-half-years-old. An admirable kid that gets excellent grades in school and is very athletic. He's protective of his mommy too," Amandria spoke about her son and then laughed at what she had considered a joke.

"What's his name?" I curiously asked through the door.

"Angel. Well, are you all set to vamoose? I know that I'm a silly bitch, but not as amusing as this car of mine. So where is your destination?" she inquired, as soon as I stepped out of the bathroom and faced her.

Damn, she just diverged from our exchange of words real quick. I ignored my half-baked brainchildren, not even entertaining the odds. "I'm going to go ahead and tour the pith of Chelsea. I am feeling confident that I will bump into some plugged in cats that owe me some bread. But thanks anyways," I declined the offer, preferring the exercise to fool's paradise.

Without asking, Amandria handed me two hundred dollars and then stated, "Get some clothes, you look a mess." In addition, at that moment, she caressed my lips.

I laughed to myself. *What some good dick will do for a nigga.* We parted ways on the journey to Jack's Men Shop, which is scened at the Chelsea Square on Broadway, in order to buy this season's black Timberland boots, a pair of black Polo jeans, four different color T-shirts, socks, boxers, and one black du-rag. Jack, the owner, sacrificed any choice of a free fitted hat and welcomed me home. Jack has known little fat Miguel since my pamper days. Without a doubt, the black-on-black Utah Jazz fitted hat with the big 'U' in the front had been tossed in its own bag to be kept clean. As I slipped out of Jack's Men Shop, with paraphernalia in one's hands, three young-looking Puerto Rican kids approached me. They were flagged up with black bandannas.

"Hey homey, what do you rep? Why do you have that five-point star next to your eye? Are you Peoples?" the tall and skinny white-skinned kid that paraded two long braids did his best to G-check me.

I released all four bags while backing up in a boxer's stance and uttered, "I'm a UK Gangsta! What's poppin'? Niggaz got drama? The kid has been locked up for three-and-a-half-years and niggaz done forgot that I'm Boss One around this bitch!"

"Boss One? Our Boss One is in a federal detention facility warring against a life sentence. His name is Mizery," the same fearless individual responded.

I gave a smug look-see, in conjunction with declaring, "I am Mizery. That's the problem, if you brothers would have maintained communication and held me down like y'all was suppose to, instead of leaving a nigga for dead, then it would have been known, that Mizery—me—got exonerated at trial yesterday. But it's all good. What it is?"

"Okay, Mizery! Respect, my brother. Welcome home. The hood name is Gambino," the courageous one identified himself.

Before long, I got introduced to Loski, this short and stocky white-skinned brother that could be Popeye's impersonator. Homeboy had those homicidal eyes that would make your loved ones cry if you crossed him. Loski popped the Five with me, by and by cocking a white and black Boston Red Sox fitted hat on a finball slant. Gambino also opened this OG up to Firu, an extremely short and slim brown-skinned kid that was drooping braids. He appeared to be still in those puberty days. Manito kept playing with his waistline, indicating that he's hammered-up.

"So how is business in the hood? I hope that our family still has shit in a headlock? Before Teddy Bear directed his movie, every drug in ChelRok, Revere, East Boston, Everett, Somerville, Malden, Medford, Saugus, and even some hoods in Boston were coming from us," I pointed out something that was already known.

Firu countered with energy, "Ain't shit poppin' out here! This cat named Don Cuba has everything on murder. The man's little team is supplying everybody. We don't have a solid connect hitting us with that fire, so our dynasty roams the jungle without food. Grove Street belongs to those Roach niggaz now. There was no purpose of being out there with no twork, so they ended up taking over."

"But don't get it fucked up, we out here bangin'! Roachkilla!" Loski let it be known.

"Look, give me a few days to get right. Networking with official people is the goal. We will soon after regulate figures to how they were," I assured my bloodline.

We exchanged math and thenceforth popped the Fives with each other. The goons went down Broadway toward Fifth Street, but I locomoted opposite of them, in order to avoid those hot-ass streets where that shooting occurred last night. It was in all likelihood those lynch men on the money. They were presumably on their investigating shit, checking to see if I'm a snitch or an enemy.

While promenading past World Line Computers, I made eye contact with an attractive Asian woman. She had fairly long silky hair and nice sized breast, which accompanied a perfect petite body. Her golden-brown skin color and flawless face mesmerized me. She said, "Hi." and after that expressed tenderness.

The sexy chubby nigga beamed back at the goddess, although I continued walking till hitting a right at the corner of Fourth Street. I did not think that I could magnetize a professional-type woman such as her. She has the presentation as owner of that computer store, egotistically in a Michael Kors business suit. Ms. Professional is definitely salacious and all of the above. Ideations of being with an Asian gentlewoman have never crossed my mind, not because I don't find them alluring, it's just that the opportunity has yet to present itself. Gossip had it as a young buck that all Asian pussy was slanted to the side comparable to their eyes. I admittedly believed that dumb shit like an idiot. The impulse of circling back to spit game swiftly faded away when reality settled in about my fuzzy braids and sex-smelling clothes. One day it will happen—maybe not today—but I promise that I'm returning for Ms. Professional.

CHAPTER 2

WORKING HARD
LAYA

I am scrolling down some spreadsheets under the power of Microsoft Excel on my Voodoo computer screen; while all along enjoying a fresh cup of coffee. It is only a matter of time before World Line Computers finds itself jam-packed with merchandizing. On Fridays, everything in our store is half off, from computers to programs, office supplies to electronic devices, and as well as Boost Mobile phone plans. Leaving me opened-mouthed, Mr. Irksome Don Cuba managed to mosey rudely into an uninhabited office, intruding one's piece of mind.

"Ms. Lee, can I holla at you for a minute?" Mr. Don Cuba whined, his voice barely above a squeak as he stood defiantly before my desk.

"May I assist you with anything, Mr. Don Cuba?" I asked, as politely as I could possibly muster, after sliding aside the computer mouse. I was wishfully hoping that this unwanted pop in ends shortly.

"Ms. Lee, it's good to see you. Have you given our last conversation any thought? My state of mind has not changed. You are definitely the sexiest Asian chick ever to be in one's presence. I would leave Maliya in a heartbeat and your sexy-ass would never have to work another day. I'll take an oath," shadowing these words, Mr. Don Cuba leered at me with those creepy, narrow, finely pampered eyes of his.

Illmatik Creations

Mr. Don Cuba is not a bad looking guy. His medium height, dark skin complexion, clean baldhead, and in shape body gives him a handsome effect. However, the philanderer's bamboozling character would turn anyone off.

"So is it a yes or a no?" his pushy question agitated me, to where my facial expression made it clearly apparent to the eye.

Wow! I see that there is no end to this skirt chaser's undesired advances. "Mr. Don Cuba, I am very busy today. I have no time for your playboy talk. But maybe your wife does, who happens to be heading right this way," my sudden announcement changed his relaxed posture into a nervous one.

Lord Jesus, how I resent this womanizer's unending attempts at being a player. And just that fast, God unchained me from Mr. Don Cuba's omitted sexual overture by the angelic voice of his son, Mizhai. The little boy babbled out, anxiously toddling a pair of blue and black teensy-weensy Jordan's into a methodized office ahead of the child's mother, Maliya. "La-a, La-a," Mizhai struggled verbalizing my name. He reached out to me with his ants-in-pants, bitty hands.

"Hey cutie," I replied, reaching to snag up a full jar of gummy bears that was sitting on my desk. It had become our own little tradition: Mizhai taking off like lightening into the office while attempting to vocalize 'Laya,' as best as he could. Me, scooping the boy up and resultantly awarding him with a handful of chewy colorful creatures. "Mizhai, I know what you want. Here, have some candy," at that split second that I had offered and spread out to him in my hands, red, yellow, and green gummy bears, his miserable mother loudly chimed in.

"Do not give him any candy!" Maliya ordered, her voice tight and forced with authority. "He's hyped up enough as it is!" she added to her madness.

I just brushed my shoulders off, alternatively relinquishing the candy to his mother, over the boy's letdown ruckus. All you could hear was the tot's boohooing throughout the office as they left. I then took a load off on a specialized Office Max desk. *Why me? Did I really cope with six strenuous years of college, just to find myself ready to jump on hoodrats like Maliya?* And with that, I had been drawn into a thought-provoking daydream, optics hermetically sealed against the reality of one's position as half owner to these always-packed computer stores.

The Lee family used to live out West, just on the outskirts of sunny Anaheim, California. I had unfailingly been an excellent student all through kindergarten and middle school, not to mention when I moved to Massachusetts and graduated from Lynn Classical High School. If my deceased parents taught me anything, it was how to be a studious, assiduous scholar. Dad became a biochemist; he had been the first post doctorate professor from UCLA's Hallowed Halls to receive tenure there in his first year of teaching. Mom's academic example did not lag far behind her husband's.

My mom, who the woman's daughter adored like no-one else, had come a long way from the humble beginnings in deepest, darkest Cambodia, growing up in the small village jungles. Mom had achieved a great deal, since day one that she arrived in America, wide-eyed and at the heels of her new husband. At first, this eager to learn pupil strained to commit in memory, the confusing, foreign English language, involving all of its similar-sounding words and grammatical rules. It was hard at first, but beautiful, naïve Mrs. Lee, with such long-flowing black hair and pretty petite features refused to give up. Succeeding earning a GED at night school, this graduate had tackled the Bachelor's Program in Nursing at simple Beach Bay College, representing lonely Bayside, California. After that though, the determined seeker did not stop there. With a BA now in hand, this young mother-to-be, next, challenged the Master's Program in Nursing Sciences and Management at prestigious USC, neighboring Downtown Los Angeles. Though things didn't come easy, my mother had triumphed at the end.

Thinking of my scrupulous, yet humble parents, always brought a proud flush to their daughter's eyes. If only Mommy and Papa were still alive, they would have been highly pleased with one's accomplishments. I finished high school by means of a perfect 4.0 GPA, thenceforth, accepting a full-ride scholarship at UMass. Thenafter, I obtained a BA in accounting. Yes, following their footsteps, a well-raised daughter furthered her education at Boston College. From there, I received my Masters in Business Administration. I nodded to myself, deeply immersed in memories of better times.

Not that this was any walk in the park. There had been plenty of studying, of that no-one can doubt. I despised those long hours huddled in the cramped college library. In spite of this, at college, I began to find myself, but not in ways that my parents would have approved of. On many occasions, I had abandoned the books for full-house late-night binge drinking among a few cute, giggly sorority sisters at Bloody Aces Bar & Grill. Many steamy sexual encounters will never be forgotten in the snowy winter days of Boston. I fully explored one's emerging sexuality equally between various boyfriends and female lovers. Awkward at first, I found myself virtually burning with lust and intoxicated with newfound desires.

Now fondly, I recall the first real boyfriend of mine, Jose Santiago. Timid at first, Jose took control. Plastered to his hard, in shape body, is how I had lost my virginity at Hampton Beach in New Hampshire as a birthday gift. Pleasure quickly washing away the brief pain of this first romantic experience.

With stunning Shy, I was the aggressor; though that thought still made me blush even today. It had started innocently enough, some drunken tickling in Shy's dorm room. We were both drinking—I, my favorite, Southern Comfort. Shy, because she was a bit squeamish about hard liquor, Amoretto, a mild brandy. Then, more on blind curiosity than anything, I kissed Shy, surprising the two of us. A quick butterfly had led to a hungry exchange of eager tongues. From that, a pair of hornballs fumbled getting each other's clothes off. Her and me settled into a long night of kissing, touching, and more until finally collapsing together in a heap, sweaty and flushed with the other's juices dripping from one another's moist lips. I have never endured such deep pleasure, at least not while in college.

The decision to be with a woman had broken Jose's heart, and in turn, Shy had broken mine. There were other lovers from there on, but none as exciting as the first two. After earning my MBA, one's business mind quickly advanced into a postgraduate career. What followed was a hurried rush through the new and scary world of job seeking, a dark and intimidating place for a naïve young woman like myself. Eventually, I had struck gold, or thought so at the time by securing a manager's position at World Line Computers in Dorchester, one of seven franchise stores across the state of Massachusetts. Ulteriorly, given my no-nonsense approach and seeming passion for business, the boss, now partner, Carlos Gomez, offered me a partnership to the company,

World Line Computers. A dream of owning an establishment that nowadays seemed to be turning into a private nightmare.

After what felt like hours of living in the past, I was agonizingly brought back to our real world, when an irritating phone forced me into consciousness. "Ms. Lee," words softly escaped one's sleepy lips with a quick glimpse at a white Hermes watch, which affirmed that it had only been a matter of nine minutes since I drifted off to la-la land.

"Ms. Lee, I am sorry to disturb you, but one of our customers is demanding your presence. The lady simply refuses to take no for an answer. Mr. Don Cuba's wife claims to be entitled to a new laptop, even though she declined to pay for a warranty from over twenty-four months ago," my broad-shouldered, incessantly serious, butch secretary explained.

"Okay, Ms. Damaso. Give me a couple of minutes and I'll be right out," I told her, and then shook my head in undeniable vexation.

I then headed to the Customer Service Department, where Mrs. Queen Bitch stood, laptop in hand. I was in no mood for a public confrontation, so I okayed this replacement without reason. Right at that moment, Maliya glared at me, threatening, "That's right, bitch!"

I had to practically bite through my tongue, stopping myself from kablooeying on the cruel cunt. She doesn't even know that I will smash her ugly, big-nose face, by means of that laptop computer. As an alternative, I backed the mutt down with an icy stare of my own. I am far too much of a professional to stoop to such childish ways.

By then, I was beyond angry and aggravated, so the decision is to leave work early. TGIF! Thank God It's Friday. With jingling car keys in one hand, and a Hermes clutch purse in the other, a knowing-look had been directed at Ms. Damaso, signalizing for her to lock up at closing time. The plan got quickly established mentally to go grab a horror movie at Blockbuster, and then relax, while eating my regular microwave lunch of Lean Cuisine Shrimp Scampi.

Once outside of the store, my attention kicked around over to that man from yesterday, the interesting one with the tattoo next to his eye. Today, the individual looked good, good enough to warrant a long sexy look, in order to let him know that this pretty lonely attractive woman was attracted. Last time that we saw each other, he must have been coming out of work, because the man looked a mess, begging for a makeover. However, at this moment, Mr. Intriguing had a clean lineup with fresh braids tucked under a du-rag and hat. The cornrows reached the middle of that wide back. He's 5'9", chubby, light-skinned, and has sexy chinky light-brown bedroom eyes. The guy is Spanish, but it's hard to tell exactly what nationality. This oncoming person must have noticed that troubled guise while approaching me.

"Hello, mi amor. Why is a beautiful lady like yourself looking so sad?" this newfound acquaintance pumped, and thereafter leaned closer to me. "If you a need a shoulder to drown your tears on, I'm right here," he stared at me, with those calling eyes of his, awaiting my response.

Instantly smiling at his funny, yet corny line, there was no doubt that he had brightened this dismal excuse for a day. "It's just one of those god-awful days, so I'm making a getaway to my apartment, in hopes to simmer down by watching a movie," I vented out to this stranger.

"Am I invited to come over and enjoy that flick with you? I'll bring some caramel popcorn," a cute smile broke across his cheeky face, behind a suave attempt to come to my home.

"Slow down, lover boy," was my reply, expressing friendliness at this curious admirer of mine. "How can you assure me that you're not some serial killer or something?" I further added. It's true; I don't know anything about this guy, not even his name.

"I'm just playing, sexy," this mystery man answered. "But let me have your cell phone number, so at least we can get to know each other? Maybe go to dinner and end up spending a weekend at the Foxwoods Casino? You might even have a nice time," as he flirted, Casanova confidently pulled out his cheap, all-white Metro PCS cell phone.

I quickly shot back with a nice tingle dancing between my legs, "How about I take yours, and then, if you happen to come to mind, those digits will be dialed." I was teasing though. He and I both know that I am going to reach out to him. Why wouldn't I? This guy definitely captured my interest.

"My name is Mizery," he stated, with a voice full of bravado and confidence. I giggled at the first mention of his name.

"What type of name is Mizery?" I kidded around, trying hard to suppress a full-out laugh. Not even waiting for his reply, solicitous hands speedily snapped out the new, hot-pink Gaga cell phone. "The name is Laya," I threw out there in my sexiest voice. "What's your cell phone number?"

After logging in his information, I turned around and started navigating toward a 2008 Nissan Maxima, while all along noticing how Mizery continued to stare hard at me, looking like he had been sexing one's soul through the Chanel outfit. Once this exhausted body made it to the car, I couldn't help but to smile at a dozen white roses that were neatly placed on the windshield. *Aw, how cute.* My body purred, blushing like the red bloom on a newly exposed rose. Attached to the outside paper was a tiny card that read:

.....If you're not in a relationship.....
—Look Back—

For some reason, I was stuck on stupid. *This isn't me, who does this?* On its own, an impressed woman's head just turned, eyeing Mizery, who flashed a phone gesture with his hand, ahead of coolly walking away. Okay, I admit it. He melted one's heart. Even so, it did not stop there. Upon sitting behind the steering wheel and turning over the ignition, one could smell a mixed scent of admirable roses, together with winning cologne. Instantly splitting my sides.

CHAPTER 3

PLAYBOY
DON CUBA

Y ou already know that Maliya is my other half, but Ms. Lee, she's that bitch. Every time that we jive at the computer store, it makes it harder and harder to ignore this vanquishing attraction concerning her. The professionalism is amorous. I would deep-six Maliya in a heartbeat if Ms. Lee would put the Don Cuba ring on. Maliya knows that I am trying to bag Ms. Lee, because whenever I need to get up and go hit World Line Computers, Maliya invites herself or the pest kicks off bullshit. Only a softhearted nigga would trust that tightfisted woman. It's obvious that Maliya is all about that bread. Even so, I still have affection for this broad to an extent. We have been together now for three years. I am essentially raising little man since his father is locked up. I love Mizhai, as if my own, he so much as calls me Daddy. Maliya can be distempering sometimes, yet at the end of a good day, that head game makes up for it.

Answering my phone—"What's up, Hitman? Are you ready for a few more thangz?" I asked.

Hitman is a black young soldier that holds that name because the dog earned it by way of his serious gun game. This twenty-year-old killer looks older, due to a 6'1" skinny frame, charcoal skin color, and shoulder-length cornrows. To keep it one hundred, he's my right-hand man. I certainly do not confide in anyone else. Word has it that Hitman used to be nice playing basketball, preceding a shootout contra Boston Police officers, which left homeboy's brother Bugzy and cousin General dead on Lucerne Street in murderous Dorchester. Hitman was shot in the spine and ended up in a wheelchair. Doctors were decisive that the nigga would nevermore stand on his own, but homey contended and refused to accept that defeat. Now the young gunclapper is jumping out of flashy whips and getting money real hard. This little animal even accepted the limp and cane, realistically believing that the ho'z dig it.

"What's good, Don Cuba? You know that Mizery is home, right? The hood is rumoring that on his first night out, him and those UK niggaz shot up some UNLV kids," Hitman disclosed.

That's why Hitman got stripes on my team. He's always on point. Not to mention that he has never failed me when ordered to execute someone.

"Oh, yeah! That nigga wilding. Mizery must of beat'em in the head at trial. He is one lucky motherfucker. It is not a secret how the federal government rarely loses. But if he wants to bang, let'em all continue bangin'. Fuck the Unknowns and the UNLV Rebels! Fuck that gang shit! If it don't make dollars, it don't make sense. As long as they aren't fucking with my dough, who cares about those clowns? Keep your eyes open on Mizery and posted on his every move," it needs to be ascertained that Hitman understands the seriousness to this situation, so I put forth precise objectives.

"Without question, big homey. Listen, I'm trying to come see you for five more of those thangz? The kid is down to one joint," Hitman requested, with money in his voice.

"Aight, I got you in a few hours. First, my fiancée and I have to speak, before we leave to go buy Mizhai a pair of sneakers," our talk was consummated by an understanding.

"Maliya! Maliya! Come here for a second!" all one could hear, were the sounds of Burberry heels tapping stair by stair on her way down, after I shouted Maliya's name a couple of times.

"What, baby? Why are you screaming?" I knew for certain that she was nervous with her uneasy answering.

"Tell me that you don't know that Mizhai's father touched down?" I basically dared her to be untruthful.

"Baby, it slipped one's mind to let you know that we spoke two days ago. His grandmother told me that her grandson had been found not guilty at trial. She then fished for my number. In spite of this, the point of calling was about Mizhai. When Mizery rang me back, our discussion ended rather quickly with a dial tone. He went berserk when I adduced to the fatso to accept our offer to change Mizhai's last name to yours on the birth certificate. Your fiancée even denied him permission for a heart-to-heart with Mizhai when the little dick nigga begged if he could. Don't worry about me being unfaithful. This pussy is nothing but loyal to you. You're the only man that I love," funny bitch, she was now suspect with her little play-acting.

"It's all good, if my dulce held me down like that. Whenever you talk to Mizery just let it be known. Have some respect. It would be a sad thing if our relationship went sour now that Mizhai's father came back into the picture," I expressed concern for our relationship.

"Papi, I swear to God that this won't happen again. Now let us forget that this ever occurred and move on. There's no need to be dwelling on nonsense. I am going to go get Mizhai geared up, so we can head out shopping for a pair of black Air Forces. Also, Lady Roam described this outfit that I must get from Neiman Marcus," Maliya kept the ball rolling on one hundred other things that she thirsted to acquire.

"Not today. Daddy has too much business to attend to when we rebound from buying Mizhai's kicks," I explicated. There's no ifs ands or buts about it; I am not hiking it up and down a store looking at clothes and shoes all day.

CHAPTER 4

LET'S GET IT
MIZERY

It has been two weeks since the jury returned a not-guilty determination, and I am stone broke, still nesting in Abuela's apartment. I have been lingering around, intellectualizing about what I'm going to do with myself. Something got to give, those pesos keep calling me. It's time to holla at my brother Projekt, an Unknown from the Cathedral Projects, which is located in the South End of Boston. He was also swept up in Operation Royal Ruin. The same weasel roped us all in. The morning that law enforcement raided our homes by way of federal tactical teams, helicopters, and local police, it had exposed the squealer's identity.

Bless, Jon-Jon, and Trizsmacks are my unfailing assassins from ChelRok. We have been bangin' hard for our squad for years. Canito, Chunky, Redstar, and Projekt represent the same menacing projects. Introduction was simple, a gangsta stare with the Fives poppin'. As I explained formerly, you can identify a UK Gangsta when you see one. The awkward silence in that cell clearly demonstrated everyone's wariness of each other, primarily not knowing if anyone had intensions of turning stool pigeon in order to inherit a lighter sentence. After being guarded into a heavily populated courtroom by extra-tough court officers and marshals, we were then individually arraigned in front of a magistrate judge. Unsurprisingly, the racist bastard held us all without bail. The federal system is designed to bury people with criminal records underneath their jails. Our government has no mercy for those who they prosecute.

Shackled and box-cuffed is how all eight of us arrived at Wyatt Detention Facility in Central Falls, Rhode Island. We were all housed inside of a gang unit referred to as H-Pod, in Sector III, which divided the Unknowns from other gangs that were inhabitants to the other secluded sectors. Shit was fruitless and did not make any sense, because if we really wanted to get at each other, it could have happened. One day, Projekt got into it with a Spanish CO. The situation panned out with him smacking flame and smoke out of that coward. Comedy central. Projekt had been extracted straight to G-Pod, a lockdown unit. Wyatt's administration classified him to a max custody status—in other words, it intrinsically means that you are stuck like Chuck and get a bullshit review every thirty days.

Living that box life is a changeless routine every day. You wake up to breakfast being served through a cell trap. Following chow comes an hour of recreation in a cage similar to one of those Michael Vick dog kennels. Then comes my favorite part of the day, an untimely shower, where I make dirty love to those Curve and Latina magazine ho'z. Any convict's meaningful movement has to be when quartered in a small locked room, labeled the law library, which incorporates a typewriter, plus a computer with the LexisNexis program. Because in order to understand our government's position, one must get in tune with the language of the courts, so researching controlling cases comparable to yours is extremely important. On Tuesdays and Fridays, you are allowed to make personal phone calls. If your clout is up, a respected gangsta can keep the phone hostage in your cell for hours. At least that's what I do. Visits are also conducted in the law library through a video monitor and phone seven days a week. It's better than nothing.

Eventually, I ended up in G-Pod for knocking out some white boy over the television. The institutional board classed me on max custody as well. Despite everything, we had it made in segregation. Sergeant Kloud provided us with official bud from the world under a little racket agreement. One of Projekt's bitches would pay him eight hundred dollars for an ounce of exotic loud, like some Purple Haze, Sour Deez, Mango Piña, Grand Daddy Purp, or any of that good-good that he could get. Blowing it down in those rec cages were part of our typical day too. It used to be priceless when caseworker Miss Dee came gating out into the recreation area, which would be clouded from marijuana smoke. She knew what it was, but kept her workface efficient and held us down with institutional needs. A cute face, a little overweight, yet at that time, I would have dicked that shorty down.

Dog, the two of us even had a handful of jakes making deliveries throughout the jail for us. Sergeant Spraycan and CO Coyote would drop off the bud to our clientele and then bring back the large bags of commissary. CO Woody and CO G were two other correctional officers that alerted the G-Pod population in relation to all shakedowns being lead by those bigheaded twin sergeants known as the Bushwhackers. This way, we had all of the contraband stashed.

For the next nineteen months in seg, Projekt and I became close like real brothers. We used to confer through the cell vents and doors about all in all. He even helped me get over Maliya breaking my heart. Dialogues consisted of organizing our teams and investing in legal businesses. But fast-forwarding, one day, unexpectedly, Projekt got habed into court and never came back. Real talk, your boy started stressing. Then again, don't get it fucked up—his brother was happy for him. I just missed the nigga.

About two weeks later, a missive slid underneath my cell door from a Nicki Minaj. Laughter came automatic, because right away, I knew who it was. Projekt repeatedly head tripped about fucking Nicki Minaj's sensuous-ass. I unfolded the letter and read it:

Mizery,   Another Day Ready

Loyalty is everything, twin! The day that I went to court, my case got dismissed for false testimony in front of the Grand Jury, because the government could not produce the alleged evidence that they claimed to be in possession of. I am already doing the one-two, so when you touch down, I will put you on, bro. We are going to do everything that niggaz planned. I put $500 on your books. Check your account. Fuck all of this letter shit. Put this number on your phone list and get at your boy!!!!!

PS. #857-249-5509

One Love,
Projekt
UK

Projekt held me down all through trial. He even gave Tio, Uncle Felix, some dough, in order to buy your boy two flaming-ass suits. That was some real live dog shit. Not too many niggaz keep it one hundred like that. The only reason that manito wasn't actually present at one's trial had been because I did not want any hooligans there. This would prevent giving the jury the wrong impression. I finally dug out my cell phone and hit up Projekt.

"Damn nigga, you have been out on the bricks for over two weeks and you are just now calling me! What's good with that?" Projekt was not feeling the situation.

"My fault comrade, it isn't anything but a dog trying to get his mindset balanced. I've been considering studying at Bunker Hill Community College to achieve a trade in electricity," on the up-and-up, I was really contemplating what I just explained to him.

"Fuck all of that! Where you at?" he burst out, and totally ignored my positive intentions.

"I'm on the Nut," I revealed, as if he knew where it was.

"What the fuck is a Nut? Give me Abuela's address, so I can enter it into my GPS. This Beantown gangsta doesn't know anything concerning little-ass Chelsea," Projekt wisecracked as always.

After rendering him my grandmother's information, it was off to the backyard to smoke a Kush-Blunt. As that fuego filled a nigga's lungs, Laya's office number vibrated the jack. We have been kicking it a lot lately; I just have not had an opportunity to make plans for a date. I am constantly trying to figure out a way to pop up at Ms. Professional's store, in order to surprise her, but how can someone trump up an awe-inspiring image being broke?

My piece of shit cell phone rang again, but this time it was Projekt. "Come out front, nigga!" Projekt articulated hyped up.

Once outside, you could hear the music thumping out of an all-white 2009 Acura TL, which included leather seats the color of dandruff, three TVs, and some official chrome rims. His whip was fire. Projekt exited the TL and popped Fives with me. He opened a car door and bared several bags of clothing, plus four boxes of footwear. We carried everything into Abuela's crash pad.

"Yo Mizery, in one of those Timberland boxes there's a whole brick. That's that UK love. It's the takeover, my nigga! The prices out here are crazy, and this coke isn't pure, but it's what I'm working with right now," Projekt stated, and then peeled off two crispy hundred-dollar bills, which he then handed to me.

"The love is real. I'll die for you, twin!" I placed the Five on my heart, signifying one's willingness to shed blood for him, behind one's acclamation.

"You already know. Now let's go celebrate," he returned the love, by doing the same, after agreeing that the feelings were mutual.

The two of us decided to go get bent at King Author's, a strip club in ChelRok. It was elbow-to-elbow populating pimps, tricks, crooks, pushers, undercovers, gangstaz, and working girls pitching for a money dick to suck. I even seen Loski, Firu, and Gambino making it rain on some ho'z that were freaking the poles on stage. They showed their Boss One some love by handing me two bottles of Rosè Moët and Bombay. I directed my brothers to set up a meeting for tomorrow at five p.m. and introduced Projekt. Everybody else rolled out a red carpet for Crack City's finest with drinks and blunts. The best part of the night had to be when I got some head by this Brazilian stripper named Fatima in the Champagne Room. That bitch is fly and has a pretty pussy, but tonight, it was all throat.

Then drama popped off, like eight Roaches blitz inside of the club clapping shit up. Loski whipped out and started firing back with a rusty .38 revolver. The crowd went into pandemonium. When the shooting let up, we all bounced, bypassing the boyz. Rumormongers propagated how nobody had gotten shot, but that one of those KA dancers was grazed in her neck by a bullet. From today on, I pledged to never get caught sleeping again.

It had to be like four-in-the-morning when Projekt dropped me off at Abuela's apartment, totally fucked up from all of the alcohol consumed and weed smoke inhaled. The buzzer was buzzing for ten minutes straight before Grandma finally buzzed me in. When I came stumbling inside, my grandmother went bonkers, "Tu no tienes respecto! You have been out of jail for two weeks now and I've yet to see anything forward-looking. You're either going to end up back in prison or dead. I am trying to conserve an unhealthy heart and will not let you kill me softly. Miguel Angel, gather your things and get the fuck out!"

"Abuelita! Abuelita!" I tried to plead, only for God's angel to give me the cold-shoulder by closing her bedroom door. My grandmother had to be extremely pissed off, because for Grandma to swear, as dedicated to the Catholic Religion as she is, beyond any doubt was solidity. The mixture of substances took over, and with all of my belongings, I headed to Amandria's condominiums in a taxi.

This older lady held both of the lobby doors open for me as she witnessed my drunken self struggling to carry bags in. The cab driver remained parked out front, while waiting to be paid, but I kept it moving onto an elevator. Drunkenly, this drunk continuously knocked on Amandria's door until it opened to some degree.

"Its six-in-the-morning! What's up, are you all right?" a concerned woman asked.

"Papi's home," I slurred.

"Home? You got a nerve. Last time that I checked, no dick has touched my bed since two weeks ago, even though I have been waiting," it was clear that she felt hurt from her unmoved words.

"I'm sorry, babygirl. Is there anyway that I can make it up to you? It's not about another female if that's what you are thinking. A nigga was just trying to get focus, but nothing had come together, until today that is. Incredible Mizery has officially turned green. I'm smarter, more thorough-going, and destined to blow-up," I kicked my best game to Amandria.

"Weren't you living at your grandmother's house rent-free?" she cross-examined me, knowing something had happened.

"Yeah, but never mind all of that. You know how Abuela is. Plus, for the past two weeks, all this gangsta has been thinking of is what it would be like to hit that sweet, nasty, gushy stuff one more time," both of my hands slid into her robe, as the liquor aggregated words together. "Now wipe that confused look. Don't act like picturing this hard dick sliding inside of you doesn't turn you on," the two of us laughed at one's jocularity, and then Amandria made way. *Got'em coach!* I thought to myself, as I hoisted umpteen bags inside. "Good, now bring that million-dollar cookie over here and make me rich," I uttered self-assuredly.

"Mizery, stop teasing me," she yanked me close to her by my shirt collar, in back of flirting with the kid.

"So you want some more of this dick, huh?" I toyed back, in front of getting it kracking by unbuckling my Dsquared² jeans.

"Of course, why do you think that I let you in, silly?" she jested, ahead of tossing a blue robe to the carpet floor, which followed with her moving a pair of light-blue DKNY panties to the side, revealing a clean-shaven wet pussy.

"Damn baby, you have a pretty-ass pink panther," I admired her, as my pole got stupid hard.

After gently setting down a lusting body on the kitchen tiles, and removing all clothing, my mouth and teeth began nibbling on desirous pussy lips. Following that, came massaging an extremely soaked clit with this hurricane tongue. Two of my fingers went deep into that wet cave until I found the G-spot. Amandria tried to squirm away as soon as she sensed that perfect touch. "Oh, shit! Oh, shit! Mizery! Baby! Oh, shit! Stop! I'm going to cum! Don't stop! Stop! Oh, shit!" she moaned, as my fingers got drenched with Amandria's cum dripping down them. I do not think that I have ever seen a girl get confused from busting a nut. Alizé turned over now, yearning for some pounding from behind. The pussy tips were swollen from a stupefying orgasm, so she felt even tighter than the last time. As this jackhammer pulverized her kitty cat, the more my sperm craved to come out, and when it did, the explosion shot out all over junior wifey's fat ass.

I woke up at eleven a.m. and today is going to be a very busy day. My first goal is to call Maliya. I was optimistic that she might be inclined into letting me see Mizhai. The attempts to do so are guaranteed to never stop. Even if it meant requesting visitation rights from Family Court, but hopefully Maliya will stop playing her little-kid games and just allow a concerned parent to be a father to our son. Scrolling down to Cumguzzler on one's Metro PCS cell phone screen had this grouchy morning person snickering to myself.

"Hello ... Hello ... Hold on. Yeah, hello," Maliya answered.

"Maliya, don't hang up. Please, hear me out? Let us act as if we never had the first conversation. Don't you think that Mizhai has a right to know who his real papi is? Our personal relationship can be left in the past, but as two adults, shouldn't the two of us establish a healthy friendship or some type of understanding? Why be enemies?" I meant what was propounded.

"Okay, Mizery. You get one chance. Do not fuck it up or I promise that papi will kiss Mizhai goodbye forever. Meet me at Chuck E.

Cheese around one p.m... Don't be late because you'll be eating pizza by yourself," she adamantly voiced, right before the call ended.

You already know that there wasn't any time to waste. I had so much to do in such little time. A jubilant man took a shower, got fresh, and was off to Toys "R" Us.

While roaming the vacuous store, scrutinizing for something to buy my son, I saw these two little black kids racing remote-control cars down an aisle. I'm glad that Projekt gave me two hundred dollars last night, because the Grasshopper came up to one hundred and eighty dollars in total.

It's twelve forty-five p.m. and one could see a swarm of kids inside of Chuck E. Cheese's through the outside window. I smoked a few Newport cigarettes while anticipating their arrival. *How will Mizhai act toward me? Moreover, what should I expect from Maliya?* I was being hopeful that this visit would not end up turning into a mess. The fire almost touched another cigarette, when Maliya, holding hands with my little man, came into view. As soon as they reached me, Maliya said, "You have thirty minutes. I got shit to do."

My son definitely did not know who his father was, even though that I explained in Spanish over one hundred times who Papi is. He loved the remote-control car and would not put it down. When our visit had been cut short, the little nigga gave me a hug. Minime is mad cute. Mizhai had his hair braided and was fly from head-to-toe in Jordan gear. Maliya attained some respect; our son looked right. During the visit, Maliya and I did not even interact. In addition, when they left, she did not so much as say goodbye. The bitch just kept it moving. But it ain't about nothing; I no longer felt love for her.

Thank the All-knowing that Amandria let me use her hooptie for the day while at work doing a double, because with that shit that Projekt gave me, I knew exactly what the kid needed. The chef had to set up a quick drug lab, fast and for cheap. Therefore, it looks like Wal-Mart is the destination.

First thing on the list must be a digital meat scale that comes with a tray. It cost thirty-five dollars but on sale for half off. The next item was a one-quart Pyrex pitcher without a lid for one dollar and twenty cents. Right beside it, they were advertising big boxes of baking soda, which were also on sale for ninety-nine cents. You know what's crazy— for some reason, Wal-Mart always has the big boxes of baking soda priced dirt-cheap. *I wonder why?* As I advanced over to a second-string utensil department, instantly the variety of spoons and strainers caught this money hungry individual's attention. Yet, when these chinky eyes landed on a little steel kitchen hammer, I knew that I had to get it. With only twenty dollars, a nigga had to disregard those spoons and strainers and slide that little steel kitchen hammer inside of one's pocket. This thief then jaunted up to a black lady cashier and placed the digital meat scale, Pyrex pitcher, and box of baking soda on her counter. Shorty stared at me like she's hip. It came up to nineteen dollars and sixty-nine cents with some tax. One's right hand reached into a pocket to my Double RL jeans and went around that three-dollar little steel kitchen hammer that I swiped, to pull out the only twenty dollars that I had, and then happily handed it over, drug lab complete. On the way out of Wal-Mart, one last thing needed sat right there to the left, a stack of Wal-Mart advertisements.

Amandria is still at work and Angel was cooling at his grandmother's house. I had the crib all to myself. I found a glass pot that Amandria uses to boil eggs in, and it is definitely big enough for me to put the Pyrex pitcher in, move that shit around, and thenafter take it out. Big chef dog filled Alizé's glass pot halfway with water and added salt, so the water would burn hotter. After removing the tray off the digital meat scale, I divided this kilo of powdered cocaine into thirds, each weighing three hundred and thirty-three grams. The point of my method is to see how much would be diminished when cooked-up. Three hundred and thirty-three grams of powdered cocaine went into Crack Pyrex, along with thirty grams of baking soda. A cup of water had been poured into that same Pyrex pitcher and mixed all around, applying one of Amandria's spoons. Crack Pyrex at that point rested in the middle of Money Pot. I watched the water in Crack Pyrex and around Money Pot boil at the same time. As it boiled, big Mizery hawked what began to rise to the top, but it was too white, so you could tell that the crack wasn't done yet. Another one of Amandria's spoons got utilized by scooping up boiling salt water from the sides of Money Pot, in order to drop it entirely over what rose in Crack Pyrex. As this transpired, all that could be seen was the garbage in the powdered cocaine break away from a rock that formed. It's ready! My chubby-ass hopped over to the freezer; captured an ice tray; turned around; and thenceforward threw on a thick oven mitt. I then took out Crack Pyrex, which by now had to be bubbling like crazy. I set it inside of the sink and added three cubes of ice. When they disappeared, three more were affixed. Accordingly, my wrist work had been put into play. Everything in Crack Pyrex locked up, except for some baking soda, shake, and some strange shit sitting down low. I poured all the excess water out of Crack Pyrex down the drain. I then laid and spread the crack onto some Wal-Mart advertisements to dry.

While puffing on a Newport cigarette, thoughts entered one's mind about how important batch number one is. I am going to be able to judge what can or can't be done to this coke. My cell phone displayed that it was two forty-nine p.m., indubitably enough time to freak this twork before our meeting. I parked the dried crack onto Wal-Mart's digital meat scale as my heart skipped a beat. The numbers blinked and finally read three hundred grams. This twork is trash, but I can fuck with it.

The chef went back to work by turning on a burner on high. While waiting for what is left of the salt water in Money Pot to boil, I dumped thirty grams of baking soda and three hundred and thirty-three grams of powdered cocaine into Crack Pyrex. Next, a cup of regular hot water from Amandria's sink got tilted inside of Crack Pyrex, and with a spoon, I commenced synthesizing it. Succeeding that, Crack Pyrex had gotten arranged in Money Pot, which was surrounded by boiling water, until what cooked inside of Crack Pyrex started foaming up like cappuccino. Now came spooning some salt water into Crack Pyrex to watch it burn down the cream. Suddenly, Crack Pyrex's water became clear. You could see the powdered cocaine at the bottom burning into pure base. It began converting from cream, to tan, to finally light-brown oil. When it settled, Crack Pyrex was taken out of Money Pot and thence a lot of ice cubes were unloaded inside of it. When that oil turned hard and the excess water had gotten poured out, I floored an oversized caramel cookie onto some more Wal-Mart advertisements until moistureless.

I am going to do things a little different to this last batch. The salt water in Money Pot was emptied out and replaced with fresh water. As it began to heat up, that dried-up caramel cookie had gotten weighed. The digital meat scale declared two hundred and sixty grams of some raw, so now my objective is to make up for all of the losses. The chef proceeded by pouring fresh water into Crack Pyrex, and all at once, located it into Money Pot until both of the gadgets had boiling water. I removed Crack Pyrex and set it aside, in order to spurt hot water as needed. Off went the stove, because there wasn't going to be any more heat used for this one. Naturally flowing, one hundred and thirty-six grams of baking soda had been weighed; right after, one hundred and sixteen grams of powdered cocaine got tipped within Money Pot. A couple of ounces of hot water from Crack Pyrex went into Money Pot as well, just enough to wet all of the powdered cocaine. As soon as I did this, it set out by snapping at me, as it began transforming yellow. It commenced melting the powdered cocaine. The chef promptly threw half of the baking soda inside of Money Pot and thenafter stirred it with a spoon to help calm down the powdered cocaine. This is what you call a shock treatment; its sort-of like scrambling eggs. I placed a rubber stopper in Amandria's sink, in order to fill it with cold water, so it could cool down Money Pot when that point came. I am still scrambling, looking for any moisture, because wherever there is dampness, one has to sprinkle a little bit of baking soda to soak it up. Now it's timely to rest Money Pot in the cold water. I smattered the rest of the powdered cocaine on top of a layer that already existed while jumbling the wet powder around. The hot Pyrex is in the other hand, adding drops of water to make what's in Money Pot melt again. By now, you should know what steps are coming next. The chef patted all of the remaining grams of baking soda on wherever it looked wet, and then I returned to clambering it. Lastly, two ice trays were discarded, ringing Money Pot.

Meanwhile, while an anxious man stood there waiting for that smacked-up twork to cool down, my ambition pushed me to inspect Amandria's kitchen cabinets, to the point where one found what I had been searching for, a big box of Ziploc freezer bags. The Wal-Mart advertisements that contained two hundred and sixty grams of pure solid base were folded up forthwith and thenceforth beat with the stolen little steel kitchen hammer, until it smashed up into tiny rocks and fine powder. Everything in Money Pot calmed down, so you know what followed—onto more Wal-Mart advertisements to parch. Finally, I finished using Amandria's kitchen, so it called for a swift cleanup. Her apartment smelled like straight crack, even with wide-open windows. It's now three fifty-nine p.m. and time was running out.

After what had been cheffed up dehumidified, it got spotted on the digital meat scale, which read exactly what one expected, four hundred and forty grams of blown-up crack. I transferred it into a big Ziploc freezer bag and included the two hundred and sixty grams of straightdrop. Now it demonstrated seven hundred grams of some crackhead surprise. With the three hundred grams of some decent, I had a bird, a kilo, a brick, a whole fucking joint! In case you non-hustling niggaz were lost in the movement, let me break it down to you in lamest terms. In batch number one, your boy suffered a casualty of thirty-three grams, clearly manifesting that this coke was trash. Nonetheless, here is where you separate a rookie from a pro. The professional knows how to freestyle to finagle a whole thang. In the second batch, seventy-three grams of cocaine had been purposely abated by burning it down to its oil in order to manufacture base. In batch number three, I blew it up with one hundred and thirty-six grams of baking soda, which made up for all of my losses. Well, enough of Crack 101—let's get money!

It was four forty-nine p.m. when Boss One drove up on Cottage Street. Gambino, Loski, and Firu guided their newfound brother as to where to park. I then followed them down a flight of stairs into a dim basement, where around thirty-eight Unknowns stood in silence. They introduced me to Bloodychino, Shine, Lucky, Babyface, Born, Ghost, Spooky, Kaos, Blackrob, Mecca, Chino★Scarface, Koka, Fever, four-Five-six, Chi-Chi, Rizzo, Big Ark, Lady Roam, Preme, Dready, Pluto, Quest, Wolf, K-Rock, Malcria, Leesy, RayDog, Gladiator, Maniak, Eks, Pretty Flako, Ricknice, Izzy, Mexicano, Emo, Dago, Blockhead, and LB. I already knew some of these family members.

"Okay, now let's get down to business. Starting today, our family will head in a new direction. We shall move as one. Every hood is going to be appointed a connect, better known as a Horseman. Everybody must buy off said Horseman and they have to buy directly from me. The Four Horsemen are promised to be given two hundred and fifty grams of crack on consignment, which stands in as a startup package. Every three days, I am coming to collect ninety-three hundred dollars from all four trusted Horsemen. Each Horseman is guaranteed to profit twenty-four hundred dollars selling their ounces at twenty-eight grams for thirteen hundred dollars each. I capitalize on seventy-two hundred dollars, since I am paying thirty thousand dollars a joint right now. It's time to get rich! Anyone who violates this chain of command is sure to be dealt with for disrespecting the powers that be of the UK family," I declared as Boss one.

"Wolf?" I called him out as the first appointed Horseman. My dog is a loyal brother that has been around for years. He's a well-built Puerto Rican man that stands at 5'8" with brown skin color and shoulder-length braids.

"What's good, comrade?" he came forward, after emphasizing his words.

"You got Chestnut Street. Here is two hundred and fifty grams. You're officially a member of the Four Horsemen," I broadcasted, before tossing him the twork.

"Dready?" I called forth another loyal brother whose gangsta I respect. He is Jamaican, 5'11", dark-brown-skinned, medium built, and sports lengthy dreads.

"You already know. It's the Jamaican rattlesnake," everyone was laughing at his humor, as he two-stepped into our circle.

"You got Cottage Street. Here is two hundred and fifty grams. You're also officially a member of the Four Horsemen," I made known, ahead of tossing him the twork as well.

"Gambino?" I selected him because of his aspiration.

"Bang! Bang! Roachkilla Gang!" the young nigga voiced, and then after he went around the circle poppin' Fives with everybody.

"You got Hawthorne Street. Here is two hundred and fifty grams. You're the youngest member of the Four Horsemen," I vocalized, as one put the twork in his hands, and then gave him a gangsta stare, letting him know not to let me down.

"Gladiator?" I brought out a straight gunner. My nigga stands at 5'8", is medium built, light-colored, has short braids, and is one hundred percent Puerto Rican.

"A loyal lion over here," he asserted, in advance of walking into the middle of our body showing no emotions.

"You got Grove Street. Here is two hundred and fifty grams. You're officially a member of the Four Horsemen too," I made a sagacious edict, and thence handed him the twork while feeling his fidelity.

"My brother, the family lost Grove Street to those Roaches. We need to exterminate. Their connect is Don Cuba, some scram-ass nigga that got them eating real heavy," Gladiator informed me.

"I don't give a fuck about Don Cuba or any Roach! Take our hood back by any means necessary!" I demanded.

"Say no more," Gladiator assured me with murder in his eyes.

Our meeting went as planned and unity within our people developed. It felt good to see four-Five-six up and functioning, because my last mental picture of him was in a hospital bed almost dead from a .22 Ruger bullet to the brain. That little nigga is a dog for overcoming such a dreadful occurrence. The young gunner is white-skinned, Puerto Rican, skinny, sports a short cut, and always thirsty to let his gun spit.

Kicking it with Eks about some throwback females that we knew from Malden had me dying. My hitter just touched down from Ray Brook, a federal correctional institution in Otisville, New York, and the nigga jumped right back on the bullshit. He is Honduran, average-height, very thin, keeps his long black hair in a ponytail, has light-brown skin color, and looks like the singer J. Holiday's twin. We popped the Fives, and then afterward I moved away and called Projekt, in order to make sure that things in Boston were on the same page.

"What's poppin', Five?" Projekt uttered, but I could hardly hear him.

"Is everything Gucci?" I implored.

"Do you hear all of these UK Gangstaz? There are about twenty loyal warriors over here," I could tell that Projekt was amped in his reply.

"Projekt, we have to get a better connect. You lose way too much with this twork," I had to be honest with my dog.

"I know, Mizery. But just have patience. Everything will fall into its rightful place. If niggaz start rushing things, then we are going to slip and end up back at the Boston Moakley Federal Courthouse. Bottom line, those alphabet boyz are still and all watching us. Don't be stunned if they throw another Teddy Bear our way, if they haven't already!" Projekt yelled, because of all of the noise that was being made around him.

"I'm hip manito, but with a bird plug of some raw and the right price, we'll fly them away with ease. The squad is official and our hoods are begging. However, your cautiousness is respected. If a nigga even looks like a rat, he is going to disappear. I am not retracting, ya-dig? It's about wrapping rubber bands and going legal. That's our plan. Whoever attempts to stop that will for sure feel the wrath of the Unknowns!" I stated with truth behind it.

CHAPTER 5

TAKE OVER
GLADIATOR

"Rebel Gang!" Baby Yak yelped, behind taking a sip from a bottle of E&J Brandy on Grove Street, which is also known as San Andreas. It was named after the video game *Grand Theft Auto*. Ugly, Fat Cheese, and Problem were on the block serving crackheads. Surrounding them were several individuals flagged up with grey bandannas and red hats flourishing *UNLV Runnin' Rebels*. Though the majority of these dudes are Asians, you will find different nationalities among'em.

"Yo, y'all ready to re-up? I'm heading to meet up with Don Cuba in ten minutes!" Fat Cheese shouted, a short and fat, golden-brown-skinned, El Salvadorian kid with a bald fade, who claims to be the leader of the UNLV Rebels.

Problem responded, "Here's twelve hundred dollars for an onion."

Problem is from East Boston, but makes his money in Chelsea. *BORICUA* can be seen tatted on the man's forearm. He is a whitish individual who stands at 5'7" and rocks a low fade. Dude formed a little size to himself while bidding at Middleton Jail.

"I'm cool," Ugly replied.

Ugly wanted to become an Unknown at one point of time, but never got G-Fived, because instead he pledged devotion to the Rebel's grey flag. Originally, the kid is from Franklin Hill Projects in Dorchester. One might misread him for being African-American due to the mocha skin color. However, this tall and heavyset Puerto Rican cat that maintains a low cut with a taper could easily demonstrate his Latin decent upon hearing the Spanish accent.

Fat Cheese rushed into his yellow Lexus and sped away. Him and Don Cuba are on good standings, but Fat Cheese had been plotting on robbing the nigga in due time. He recently started hating on Don Cuba in view of himself speculating that Don Cuba purposely did not want to upgrade their currency matters for personal reasons. The truth behind this was a smart hustler's decision. Don Cuba wanted to elevate the fat nigga to a whole man, but those UNLV kids at most have two blocks— San Andreas and Shurtleff Street—so Don Cuba didn't visualize any dollar signs in doing so. I feel'em. The Rebels only took over San Andreas when Mizery and his team were swept up in their indictment three-and-a-half-years ago. Don Cuba simply gives Fat Cheese a half of a joint weekly on I-owe-you status. Nonetheless, homeboy is avaricious and hungers for more than all of them can maneuver.

A few minutes after Fat Cheese left, two Puerto Rican girls came rambling up the block. The tall and chubby, light-colored chick with shoulder-length brown hair grandstanded a set of Playboy titties and wore a pair of PZI shorts that made her ass stick out real ill. A pierced tongue had been sucking and teasing a lollipop. Shorty's sidekick was a short and thick, pulchritudinous butter-pecan Rican with short black hair, who modeled PZI shorts as well. Yet, her's were so skimpy and tight, that one could get a load of the bottom of those plumpy ass cheeks. They walked by the Roaches smiling. Lady Roam and Kaos knew that boys would be boys and holla.

Problem jumped down off a dope fiend's steps. "Come here, nena. Yeah, you. The one shaking that fatty," he rhapsodized to Kaos, while Ugly grabbed Lady Roam's right hand and pulled her close. "What's good, ma?" he tried to get some play.

Okay, that's our cue to ambush. I stepped on the gas on my way through those short Bellingham Street backyards aiming two .40 cals on rapid fire. Babyface unconcealed a chrome sawed-off 12-gauge and Born gripped a fifty-shot Tec9 as they skulked out of the Marlboro Street cut. It was redrum. I ran up on Problem, shooting him twice in the chest. Somehow or another, he scraped by and got safeguarded in a hallway. I fired nine shots through the door, hoping to hit that bitch-ass nigga's head. Babyface wild out with the shotty. At close range, he blew Ugly's face off. You could see his brain matter dripping off a fire hydrant. Born let off that whole fifty-shot clip at anyone that even looked like a Roach. I clocked a few drop. It's surprising to grasp how manito's Tec9 did not jam, because according to hood tales, those thangz love to malfunction at the wrong time. We all hopped over a Bellingham Street fence, where LB had been waiting in a stolen Office Max work van.

Later that night, a band of Roaches was hanging out at Fat Cheese's house on Shurtleff Street, grieving Ugly's death. Problem laid in Boston Medical Center in critical condition, and as well as a few other UNLV niggaz that suffered from gunshot wounds. As Fat Cheese broke down the half-kilo of crack that he scored earlier, and taking in everything that just went down, someone knocked on the door.

"Fat Cheese, open the door!" a female voice cried out.

"Ma, is that you?" Fat Cheese thought that he was hearing shit, as the words came out of his mouth.

Fat Cheese gestured for his Asian boy Sok, some short and slim baldheaded nigga to open it, merely to catch sight of Gambino holding a terrified mother by the hair with a .380 automatic handgun pressed up against her temple. Gambino marked out, "Open the fucking back door before I wig this bitch!" Sok complied, only to eyeball Loski holding Fat Cheese's sister in a light dope-fiend, while pointing that same rusty-ass .38 revolver that he was clapping in the club to a teenager's right cheek. At that moment, Gambino tossed a throwaway cell phone to Fat Cheese.

"What's good, papa? It's simple, San Andreas is ours again. Next time that the guerillas show up, there's no more talking!" I gave my solemn word and ended the call.

Gambino casted loose the old lady, but sprightly leveled the burner at Fat Cheese and harangued, "Oh, you trying to get money, huh?" when spotting the half-kilo. "Good looking out for bagging this shit up, you fucking bitch!" Gambino grabbed the bag of crack, while all along keeping his angle on Fat Cheese, and then slowly scuffed the stairs as he walked backwards.

In the process of backing up and still grasping shorty in a chokehold from behind, Loski specified, "When we're safe, I'll let this bitch go!" At that exact moment, Dready drove up in a Yukon truck to scoop them up. Mission Takeover accomplished!

CHAPTER 6

I'M FEELING HIM
LAYA

What a frazzling day! Too many complaints, too much paperwork, and not enough finances being generated. My desk, disheveled to its capacity. It's been hours of typing business proposals to Voodoo, Alienware, Apple, Dell, and a few other computer companies regarding their most recent products that have not hit the market yet. I'm tired of rubbing burning eyes and loosening up aching fingers. Instinctively, I reached for an empty pack of chocolate chip cookies for the third time, but stopped short upon realizing it. Hunger is unquestionably distracting one's mind. During some thoughts of mine, the sounds of someone entering a widespread office became the point of convergence.

"May I help you?" in an uninterested way I asked, while all along reviewing the printed out documents.

"Special delivery," a deep voice vocalized.

I snooped up to make out that it was Mizery. At once, for the second time, he brightened up my gloomy mood. We'd been chatting on our cell phones for about a month now. However, this come around, beyond the shadow of a doubt is a big surprise. Today, this unpredictable friend of mine had been dressed sophisticated with his braids in a ponytail. Dolce & Gabbana cologne blessed the atmosphere as plumpish fingers handed me five pink roses.

Illmatik Creations

"These are to make you aware that my friendship would like to advance deeper," Mizery gave me a hug and kiss on the cheek, following his annunciation of how he felt toward me.

All I could do was smile. "Thank you," was my sincere utterance.

"Well, it's almost time for lunch. I brought us something to eat from Tito's Bakery," his smooth approach turned me on, as he began transforming my workplace into a cute little inside picnic.

"Sure, sounds good," I retorted. It was that easy with him. He made me feel so comfortable.

After about a couple of minutes of us savoring our food, which consisted of Cuban sandwiches, plantain chips, and Morir Soñando drinks, I broke the ice, "So, Mr. Miz, confess a little bit about yourself?"

"My story isn't anything special. Grandma, Auntie Maggie, and Uncle Felix raised the black sheep of the family. Sadly, Mami passed away in a horrible car accident. Our relationship had been distant. We were always bumping heads. I hypothesized that she despised me because one's gangsta ways brought remembrance of Popdukes, but I am not resentful at that awesome woman for this unascertained opinion. I love my mother. When the Most Highest yowls for this soul, I want to be buried right next to her. They say little fat Miguel was an out-of-control teenager, whereas at fifteen-years-old, a Middlesex Superior Court judge committed a juvenile delinquent to the Department of Youth Services, a jail for minors, until the age of eighteen. Charges were in regards to shooting at these older white people in a party. No-one got shot. Nonetheless, when the cops showed up, those white boys identified the only Spanish person there as the culprit for gunnin' at them. After a quick struggle with local police officers, they found the gun stuck in-between the bars to a sewer drain only a few feet away from us. DYS wasn't so bad; I had fun in a way. The only thing that one desires is the girls; at least that's the viewpoint that I have. Shortly upon being released from DYS, the UK family introduced their frontrunner to the crack game. I fell in love with it. Just recently, a jury auspiciously found this sought-after FBI target not guilty after awaiting trial for three-and-a-half-years on federal charges, which pertained to firearms and narcotics," he gave a brief summary of his life.

"Wow, did you learn your lesson?" I respected his uprightness, as this inquisitorial fancier continued with my interest. Mizery wasn't hiding who he is or was.

"Honestly, I am really not trying to go back to jail. That's why you see me dressed up today in one of the suits that my brother Projekt bought for trial purposes. Well, he actually paid for them and Tio Felix was the buyer who went to Men's Wearhouse, where you buy two suits and get one free. Today, the choice was that free suit, since the rest of them make this righteous civilian stand in as an official drug lord. Only our Almighty Father knows how the jury reached a not-guilty verdict. People are probably thinking that this guy is forcing it with a suit, but you would too, if one was a big nigga blazing a five-point star on your face. Putting on a bullshit grey tie is crazy; one's being feels malice against that gay-ass color. I actually been out all morning looking for a job by filling out applications, and after our lunch date, I'm going to pursue mission impossible," Mizery unraveled his job-seeking plans, while all along looking extremely handsome in the mix of trying to be professional.

"So this is a date, huh?" I flirted, being gracious. "That's good that you're staying positive. One can only truly value that. Do you have any children?" my liking in him was apparent.

"As a matter-of-fact I do. Mizhai is three-and-a-half-years-old. My little man's blessing event came around a month before this last incarceration. His mother Maliya abruptly ended our relationship when I needed her most. My ex-love did one dirty and broke a good heart, but the worst part of it was a fucked up decision to keep our son away from a loving dad. The self-seeking broad even sold the house and vehicles. Now Mizhai thinks that someone else is daddy," as Mizery vented, it's obvious that he spoke of Don Cuba's family. Curiosity got the best of me.

"Mizery, can I ask you a personal question?" I pried into, momentarily playing with a straw in my fruity drink.

"Of course ma, we are carrying on conversation," Mizery conformed, and at that instant, swiveled toward my office door as if he had sensed somebody making an intrusion. But when apprehending that it was just a figment of his imagination, Mizery simply returned to our luncheon.

"Are you familiar with someone named Don Cuba?" I asked, and thenceforth took another sip of my exotic juice.

"I don't think so, that name is unheard-of. Why?" he replied, and then gawked at me puzzled.

"There is this guy, Don Cuba, who has a fiancée, Maliya, and they have a three, or four-year-old son named Mizhai. The couple is my store's biggest clients. Moreover, Mizhai is a unique nomenclature. Now that I analyze the names, it makes sense. Mizhai, Mizery," I narrated, as if I had solved a mystery.

"Yeah, that's them. It has to be," Mizery confirmed it with sadness in his voice.

"Your son is at the computer store at least once a week. He's so cute with those long braids, but I cannot stand Maliya. The snob really thinks that she's God's gift. She is always lugging a stank-ass attitude. Her fiancé Don Cuba perpetually makes passes at me every time that the woman isn't around. He acts like an old dirty man," we both shared a laugh at my drollness.

"You don't have to say anymore, she was my girl at one time. I could easily sit here and tell you one hundred stories about her ignorance, but it's not worth any of our time," he aired, understanding the reasons in not liking Maliya.

"Have you gotten the opportunity to spend time with your son since being released?" I poked my nose into this with another meaningful probe.

"I got to see Mizhai once. Maliya is making it difficult to establish a relationship with him, but I am not giving up. I'll play by her rules in order to continue to see my son. What's up with you? Can I get to know a little bit about your beautiful self?" he changed up our ventilation and now put me on the spot, trailing his responses to the twenty-one inquests.

"You can say that it had been a rough childhood—well, not exactly a rough childhood—but at young ages, JB and I witnessed our father shoot and murder our mother, and then in return, shoot himself. We were placed into a foster home for the next five years. At ten-years-old, and JB was fifteen-years-old, a lady social worker, one day, unexpectedly, explained that they were going to relocate us into separate foster homes the following week. That same night, JB packed up everything possible so that we could run away to Lynn, Massachusetts from Anaheim, California. Uncle Chan Lee, along with Cousin Han welcomed their family members. JB made sure that I graduated high school. He also pushed his baby sister through college, wanting nothing but the best for me in life. I love JB. He's my world," I gave Mizery the short version.

For the next hour, we ate, laughed, and joked. I like Mizery. He has a good heart. I cannot wait to kiss his sexy fat lips. My feelings for him are creeping slowly into love.

CHAPTER 7

TIME TO REGULATE
DON CUBA

"What's up, Hitman?" I yakkety-yakked into my cell phone, while trying not to choke on this PR-80. It's the Rolls-Royce of marijuana.

"Shit is crazy in the hood. Those UK niggaz killed two of your UNLV soldiers. Ugly got his brains blown out and Problem died in ICU from two gunshots to the chest. A few other Rebels were hit up as well, but nothing that serious. Later that night, two Unknowns invaded Fat Cheese's home with his mother and sister hostage at gunpoint. Gladiator forewarned Fat Cheese that San Andreas is their hood again, and on their way out, Gambino took his product. They're wilding out!" Hitman explicated.

"Hold up! San Andreas is ours! I allowed those bitch-ass Rebel kids to make money over there with an understanding that they see me for the product! Now those UK pussy niggaz are crossing the line by fucking with my chips! Hitman, get your team together and do what you do best! No-one is going to be on San Andreas unless I'm their re-up man!" I exclaimed, and then watched one's phone smash into pieces as it hit the floor.

I know that those motherfuckers don't want a real life goon to summons an official hitsquad from Cuba. I'll have their families wiped out in a snap of a finger, and then the next day, these natural born killers will disappear. Matter-of-fact; let me ring up Diamond, so that she's on deck. The Angels are known and feared as dangerous assassins in Cuba. You hear about them in fictitious terms all over urban novels by great authors, who actually base their stories on the rumored murders from the aforementioned coldblooded executioners. I gripped the other cell phone and dialed away.

"Cuba!" Diamond yammered, already well-informed that it was I by DC exposing on her cell phone screen.

"I'm just calling to put you on point that your brother might need the team," I let her know ahead of time.

"You all right, bro? We'll leave right now; exclusively, just say the word?" she sounded fearful with her immediate response to accommodate me.

"Todo esta bien. This is wholly to make you aware just in case. How's everything out there?" I asked, missing my country.

"Lo mismo. Same shit, different toilet," my sister is always bywording something stupefied that makes me die laughing.

After our discussion, it felt like the right time to have a little chat with none other than Mrs. Maliya. The bitch thinks that she's slick. It's palpable that her and my son have been creeping to see Mizery. Let's see how real this sneaky ho is.

"Maliya, let's parley for a second?" I struck as being untroubled.

She was on Facebook blabbing away with a million people, when her focused eyeballs turned to me and spoke, "Yeah, baby?"

"Do you have anything to bring to light? And do not play brainless! Because I ought to be cognizant on why our son is running around this house calling his remote-control car Papi, when he addresses me as Daddy! Who taught him how to say papi?" I was heated, and she felt it in my loudness.

Maliya knew that she fucked up again. The bitch stuttered in her response, "Miz-Miz-Mizery did. It is only rightful that he spends time with Mizhai. And the remote-control car came from him. I'm sorry that I didn't tell you."

"This is the second time that I've had to check you on this. If your trifling-ass wants to be with him, then take your son and be off this!" quickly regretting said utterance that was stated out of anger, my art-of-war instincts kicked in and remixed the situation. She could be easy access to Mizery if I ever need to put the nigga's lights out. "Matter-of-fact baby, I'm sorry. I am over-exaggerating. You know how jealous I can get, plus, Mizery is Mizhai's father. It would be selfish of me to take him away from the child's father, but shouldn't an engaged woman be honest, instead of having her fiancé cerebrating that his fiancée is two-timing with another dude? I love you, and would hate for our relationship to fall apart over nothing," I prevaricated, softening Maliya up in such a convincing way.

"I'm sorry, papi. I will be straightforward from now on. I would never cheat. You are my heart. How many times do I have to explain this? Now let me make it up to you," from out of left field, after sincerely apologizing, that Dominican ho licked those candy apple-coated lips and got down on both knees right there in the living room. Maliya began by washing the head of a full-grown dick in slow circular motions. As it grew harder, Superhead sped up. She deep throated the snake and wild out like a porno star. *Look ma, no hands!* I was guffawing to myself, as Maliya did her thing, but after today, even a twerp would not sleep on this bitch. It is unmistakable that this trick cannot be unsuspicious.

CHAPTER 8

CASH RULES
MIZERY

Amandria breezed by from showering hardly covered in a peach Louis Vuitton underset. She went straight into our messy kitchen on a wild-goose chase for a ringing cell phone. This UK Gangsta snuck up behind her, startlingly pinning a sexy woman against the sink. Thereupon, osculating a pretty neck. Something about wet hair arouses me. I slipped shorty's thong off, and almost simultaneously, I turned Alizé around and lifted my bitch up on the counter. I wasted no time tasting pussy.

"Damn, Mizery! I love it!" Amandria cried out through clenched teeth, while pulling on the kid's braids. She excitedly came, and thenafter nimbly hopped down to bend over. Your boy was in that. Ruthlessly tearing it up. "Mizery, fuck me harder! Yeah, baby!" Alizé had this animal going harder and harder the more noise that her inner self made.

Seductively, behind ejaculating together, Amandria plays fiddle with an enticing thong, although waggling it up a pair of thick thighs. Basically teasing me, gesturing for seconds. But she knows, and I know, that there isn't any time. In mid sentence of spilling nasty slurs, fingers were raised silencing my words. Catching on to her concerns, Angel's facial expression unveiled a boy that perceived an eyeful. Not knowing how long he has been standing there, I playfully lashed out, "Hey, little monster. What's up?" washing away his star struck manner.

"Nothing," Angel simply responded, before dashing into his room to play the Xbox 360, which he had just received as a gift from me a couple of days ago.

"Baby, I'm going to take another shower," Amandria made known, as she closed the bathroom door.

I almost followed her inside of the bathroom, but Angel's sudden outburst caught me off-balance. "I'll fucking kill you, bitch! Come out and play, nigga! All you do is talk shit and hide!" he rapped out.

Once behind Angel, laughter came automatic. Angel had on a pair of headsets, while competing with a few online friends playing Modern Warfare. Still, I had to be an adult and correct the little nigga.

"Angel?" I called his name.

"What!" he barked.

"Stop swearing. I can hear you throughout the house. If your mother hears you, she is going to flip out," I said, approaching this situation as a friend.

"All right, Mizery. I will not swear again. I promise. Now help me kick some butt," Angel respected my wishes, and thenceforward invited a well-thought-of grownup to play video games with him.

For a quick second, conceptions of Angel being mine crossed my mind. It's like staring at the mirror when I was that age. He is a healthy-looking boy with a bald fade, styling a tail that starts from the top of the back of his head. It's that Boricua shit! Not to mention that gangsta swag that he's developing as of lately.

Angel and I attempted to outkill these online gamers, but they were too good. In fact, while wearing the headsets, it became as plain as the nose on one's face, that Angel's friends were middle school kids. Eventually though, Madden came into play. *Now we're talking.* I'm nice with it. I blew Angel out three games in a row. From this day forth, the two of us pledged war.

Later that evening, Dready had been the first Horseman available with my bread on deck. The nigga requested that I acquire ameliorated product in powder so that dynamo could Chef Boyardee for greater profit. Also, Dready invited me to his birthday party next month, which will be hosted at King Author's. I promised to turn up and pop a few bottles. In addition, the brother was apprised about the two-fifty package being delivered shortly. Gambino's linkup became of in nothing flat. The little nigga stayed on point. He's money hungry; it's visible in manito's desire to gain five hundred grams on this heyday, even though it couldn't be supplied yet. Gladiator stood ready as usual. He handed over the bands and requisitioned to move up as well. However, the circumstances were not any different for him. Gladiator imparted that since Mission Takeover those Roaches haven't tried to retaliate. I advised the loyal lion to keep our watchful eye open. In the ten minutes that we were posted up on San Andreas, the traffic proved to be self-evident that this block does not stop rumping. There wasn't any need to get up with Wolf because homey dropped off the paper last night. Therefore, the time came to double up.

"What's good, Fatboy?" Projekt japed, as he spoke into his Sprint cell phone.

"On your word, I'm coming through, Porkchop," I jested back, but at the same time, I was hoping that I didn't have to wait all day.

"I'm picking up right now. Meet me in my bricks," is all he had to say.

The rented Lancer whipped on our way to the Cathedral Projects. Amandria trailed, eating dust in that poor excuse for a car. I'll be damned if I get caught trafficking white. Amandria is a white girl, so the boyz won't fuck with shorty. My junior wifey was instructed to sit tight in that beat-down station wagon until she received notification on how to proceed. Four of Projekt's soldiers were heretofore on standby as I walked inside of the projects.

ChelRok's realist popped the Fives with Young Gunna, Shizauto, Freddie, and Pito. We kept on truckin'—-there were over fifteen heads that were spotted throughout the concrete jungle. Nothing but undying love and loyalty from JP, 357, Stiz, Jungle, Eddito, Yayo Al, Frost, Kan-Kan, Chikitin, Klover, Gato, and Tizzy. I even had seen a few other brothers roofing it on their security shit. The sworn protectors shepherded me inside of a project building, where fiends were lying on newspapers, entertaining the expectations to use their crack pipes and needles. Trash, used condoms, and cigar guts that were scattered in all directions, only added to the urine-smelling hallway. Shit was your ordinary fucked up projects. Just how I love it!

"Loyalty is everything, twin," Projekt expressed, as I entered his spot.

"Vice versa, comrade. Swing two of those thangz. Here's your money," I haughtily beseeched with respect, and then flung him a backpack having sixty stacks in it.

"Okay, balla. I see you! My twin is on the same shit that I'm on," Projekt vocalized, ahead of unmasking two bricks, as if he had predicted the move.

"My hood is booming and the brothers be getting aggravated having to wait around till I get right. So fuck it, I'm snatching up two, in order to keep the system rotating," a nigga stated, barely checking out those birds, which were certainly the same stepped-on shit.

"Pito, bring this bag out front to Mizery's shorty," Projekt ordered him to do so.

"Say no more," Pito assented, following his command.

I left nearly an hour after Amandria made it home safe. Shorty rode dirty without me, so she had been awarded with money for her and Angel to go shopping. I was proud of my junior wifey. Now it's time to hit the kitchen and chef these thangz up. By now, the drug lab had newfangled, updated equipment. The chef no longer toiled on a twenty-dollar budget. The whip game hasn't change. I put it down like the first time—you know—Crack 101—how your boy showed you step-by-step.

When the crack caked up, the Four Horsemen coincidentally crossed my threshold to pick up their twork. They were elucidated relative to that brick on deck, in case niggaz sold out, there wouldn't be any more downtime. The progress was respected.

While sitting on the couch wrapping rubber bands around each rack, suddenly, this urge to phone Maliya lit upon me. I uplifted one's new Verizon cell phone and spieled to myself, "Here we go with the bullshit." It had been forwarded undeviatingly to voicemail, roughly after four rings. *Is this relentless bitch giving a nigga the fuck-you button?* Behind almost five more minutes of nonstop ringing, her voice sang and danced by way of a speaker.

"What do you want, Mizery?" she rudely wailed.

"Bitch, you know exactly what it is! I want to see my son!" I roared.

"Who the fuck do you think that you're talking to like that? I am not one of your little ho'z!" she snapped at me.

"Why do we have to verbally fight, Maliya? I just wish to see Mizhai," I bantered, in the manner of a straight sucker.

"Real talk, Mizery I cannot fucking stand you. The only reason that I am willing to let you see him is because Mizhai keeps referring to the remote-control car as Papi, so it is self-explanatory that he is burning to lay eyes on his father. I'll be in Friendly's at the Northgate Mall in forty-five minutes," she specified with an altitude. *This heathenish girl better stop completely hanging up on me.*

Minutes were ticking, giving me no clock room to stick around for Angel and Amandria. I glutted two stacks into one of my Levi jean pockets and reserved the rubber-banded dough in a safe. Thenafter, I stashed the twork inside of a teddy bear.

While back in Enterprise's Lancer, my initial stop was at Jack Men's Shop, where two Leonardo Parrot outfits with matching Timberland boots were chosen. I also snatched up a Tom Brady jersey. Forwardly, I stripped off again, as fast as a rabbit braking in front of Game Stop to buy a Play Station 3 with eight games. At the cash register, I purchased three posters of the Ninja Turtles.

As this dog trekked inside of Friendly's, Maliya ogled a new and improved Mizery on some, 'Oh, this nigga is worth a million now.' Tilted left, an official black Boston Bruins fitted hat, jazzing a yellow B and brim, had been sitting fresh on one's dome. It's raining out, so you already know, 617 swag—a black Champion hoodie trending the yellow Champion sign underneath an all-black leather Moncler jacket was the choice. The white, black, and yellow Flights, inclusive of the black laces that I laced up, were spic-and-span out of its box. With every step that this sexy chubby nigga took, my two-sided, yellow and white gold, Cuban Link chain, plus an icy AK-47 medallion, swung side to side, giving one that shiny UK Gangsta look. As soon as Mizhai saw me, he recognized his father.

"Pa ... Pa ... Papi!" Mizhai movingly tried to recite one's name, as he extended his miniature arms for me to pick him up, which took place following a kiss. The child was all smiles. We sat at a small table with Mizhai on my lap. I watched him run over the gifts and also kept busting Maliya checking out papi Mizery, but fuck that meretricious fallen woman, it's all about Mizhai. But don't get it fucked up, Maliya's actualization actually spellbinded a longing man for a quick second. She flossed some Frankie B jeans that showed off a cuffed round ass. Her long dark hair appeared wet, exactly how I like it. Maliya's Dominican tropical skin color, medium-height, wine-bottle figure, and fuck-me-hard face almost persuaded a tempted being to invite the leech on a date that would have ended up in a telly. It is prominent that Maliya still loves a nigga; you can identify it through the eyes. I really wanted to inquire if *Mizery* tattooed on baby-momma's stomach had survived. That shit vanguished stupid big. For the next three hours, we ate, talked, and most importantly, Mizhai and I bonded.

CHAPTER 9

RYDE OR DIE
AMANDRIA

Lately, this bitch Maliya has been allowing Mizery to spend time with Mizhai. I am happy about the situation, but mindful of ex-wifey trying to reconcile their differences. Although there is not an actual commitment between us, I'm the wife. Mizery's family is right here. We have touched on this subject many of times, always deciding at the end to remain as fucking-friends. Angel loves him. For the first time in his life, he has a man to idolize. It brings a smile to my face when they hang out together. Just the other day, Mizery and Angel made a bet on who could run faster. A race around our condo ended shortly, when Mr. Olympia fell out gasping for air. Angel won fifty dollars and bragging rights.

"Babygirl, can you do me a favor? Bring this bag to Gambino and he is going to give you a few dollars. I can't make it, because I promised Angel to take him to the mall and buy that spoiled brat those new Timberland boots that just came out," Mizery explained.

"No problem, my love," I assured him. Mizery was talking to me as if this mule wasn't about to supervise a drug transaction.

Illmatik Creations

An hour later, while coming to a halt at the Chelsea Public Library, I felt it in one's bones that something was completely wrong, but went against a gut feeling and scooted pass an entrance. Gambino remained seated at a table skimming through a BITT magazine. Right away, he looked up, nonchalantly pointing his head toward three detectives that were sitting at another table resembling a conference. In spite of this, it didn't cause discontinuation from me strolling over to Gambino and doing my thing.

"Baby, let's go. We have to pick up the kids," Gambino opened his eyes wide at my unexpected communication, and then got up and followed me out.

"Good looking out, Amandria! You seen a nigga shook right, right? The four-pound was bulging out, I have ninety-three hundred dollars on me, and I'm on probation! I owe you!" Gambino vowed, as he had been astonished at how that predicament played out.

"Yeah, you were sweating bullets over there," I vouched, expressing amusement. "Here," I put into words. We did the exchange in my car and thenafter Gambino was dropped off at the McDonald's in Prattville.

Back at my place, I explicated to Mizery what happened, plus, Gambino, before now, had called and gave an account of his version. Mizery reacted impressed, and commended his girl by saying, "That was some smooth thinking. Let me find out that you're a natural hustler." He flashed a sexy smile, letting me know that I had passed the test. We celebrated with wild sex. Two G-Bitch ecstasy pills energized this body to fuck Mizery really good. It had a horny female sucking that desirable dick all night. Every time that it popped up, my lips and throat were on it.

CHAPTER 10

DON'T UNDERESTIMATE ME
LAYA

While getting dressed, I peeked out of the window and took notice of a tiny car trembling the entire neighborhood with rap music blaring. Like a bat out of hell, I slid on a matching underwear set made by Victoria Secret; threw on an Etro outfit; clicked in a pair of Sharon Khazzam earrings; fastened on a Cartier watch; squirted on some Boss perfume; and thenceforward I snatched up my new Gucci purse and raced out of the front door. We had reservations at a restaurant.

I observed that Mizery was driving a different car. This one had an Alpine touch screen radio, televisions custom-built in the headrests, and the system is so loud that I can feel it in my chest. Shiny rims and tinted windows on a gold Honda Accord look nice. Nevertheless, the observations did not stop there. Mizery's chain resembled the ones that you extend credit to in music videos. A wide smile came from a cute vampire with diamond fangs and neatly braided hair. Not to mention the sparkly ears that blinged like his watch and rings. The man had been wearing a graphic print shirt by Roberto Cavalli and a pair of Burberry charcoal relaxed pleated trousers. Black porno paisley-lasered velvet Jimmy Choo Sloane slipper shoes sealed the deal on Mr. Construction Worker.

"I didn't know that we were attending the BET Awards?" I facetiously asked.

"The sky is the limit for you," Mizery japed back, and thenceforth he planted a kiss on my right hand like a gentleman.

Undeniably, he is selling drugs. On the way to the restaurant, one's concern for him grew meaningful, not wanting to see my newly found boyfriend go back to jail, or worse be killed. Mizery could not afford any of these possessions without a good paying job. Even if it is true about the man's claim to be working off and on as a laborer for a construction company, those thingamajigs are way out of his league—something is up.

A stunning pair arrived at Kowloon's on Route I in Saugus and optimistically entered the beautiful restaurant. The atmosphere had been quiet and dim as the chef cooked the food right in front of us. When she finished, the tiny Asian woman plunked down a Pu-Pu Platter with fire flaming within on a perfectly neat table. It turned romantic in a way, as this in love couple ate, talked, and flirted. I really like Mizery. This is another special day with him and me spending time together. Our kissing episodes are so intense, although we have not had sex yet. My last relationship was four years ago. I seldom have any time for anything, being so devoted to a career as mine, but slowly though, I am letting Mizery in. No matter what the conversation came about, worrisome thoughts kept drifting off to the drug selling. I had to bring it up.

"Mizery, can I pop a question?" it was flapped with sincerity. "But please be outspoken?" I added.

"Baby, seek your answer?" the serious emphasis in his voice assured me that he was going to be truthful.

"Are you selling drugs again? Not to be all up in your biz, but if we are going to be a couplet, everything should be known between us. So please understand?" I squeezed out in an affected way.

"The truth is that I am. Right now there isn't any choice. You have seen me trying to find a job. Nobody wants to hire a nigga with a criminal record like mine. It's crazy sitting around waiting for a call merely when I am needed. Then to bust my ass doing labor, only to be paid between fifty and seventy dollars a day. Life can't cheat a striving person like that," he confirmed it.

"I know that you're attempting to do so. However, you don't want to go back to jail, right? Plus, I can't be implicated in illegal activities, for it would jeopardize my establishment," I explained, hoping that he would understand one's position in this matter.

"It's understood, ma. I promise that in a few months I will stop. My plan is to save up enough money to go legal," he sounded sincere. Honest to God, the man showed no sign of a liar.

On our ride home, I was contemplating if I should introduce him to my brother. JB eats, sleeps, and breathes drugs. Though I am not mixed up with such a lifestyle, at least I'll know that Mizery will be in the right hands. Big bro has been playing this game since we ran away to Lynn. That is how JB afforded to raise me and compensate all of one's college expenses.

"Mizery?" I called him, and then tapped his thigh.

"Yeah," he returned, in the mix of turning the knob to lower the music.

"What if your professional, law-abiding sexy girlfriend, told you that I know somebody that could help get my love in and out of the drug game? Would it catch your interest in meeting this person?" this extraordinary query threw him off guard.

"What are you talking about, ma? There is no need to present me to any one of your ex-boyfriends, better yet; you should not even be taking part in this. God forbid, if things go sour and I fuck up everything that you've worked hard for in your life," he stated, jumping to conclusions.

"Baby, calm down. I am talking about JB and Han. Your girl is not going to be tangled up in anything, just paving the way. If all agree to do business, the connection was deemed right. But if it's not beneficial for neither of you, then shake hands like some gentlemen and have a few drinks," I clarified my idea.

CHAPTER 11

CONNECTION
MIZERY

A few days after our dinner date at Kowloon's, Laya called to break the news that she had spoken to JB and that we were going to be introduced today. Hopefully things work out with him being a suitable connect, and not one of those Asian kids from Shirley Ave in Revere dissevering sixty-two grams, because how the fuck could he possibly help me? Nevertheless, my promise to Laya was to allow her to do the honors, so let's see what's poppin'.

This UK Gangsta got to Laya's apartment in Everett about twenty minutes early and positioned the Honda Accord in front of her driveway. As I had been stepping up a flight of stairs with a black Exemplaire, porous crocodile leather duffle bag in my hand, an all-black Porsche bumping some French Montana pulled up and then parked. Two Asian cats came into view as they were footing it in one's direction. Homeboy that drove was like 5'10", tan-skinned, medium built, had a short light fade, and stepped all cocky-looking, identical to Bruce Lee. The passenger could be no more than 5'5", tan-skinned, plump, and rocked a baldy with a Fu Manchu, Mr. Miyagi's twin. While cracking up mentally at these niggaz, I strutted through an open door sensing them following me.

Laya familiarized us in her elegant living room. We shook hands and remained standing. Three businessmen with money on their minds.

Our toastmistress brought forth shots of Grand Cru and furthermore remarked, "I'll leave you gentlemen to your business." as Laya's sexy body pranced out of the room.

JB shrewdly took control by saying, "Mizery, right? As you know, that is my baby sister. One can only hope that your intensions are sincere. There isn't anything that I wouldn't do for her. I am trusting that you will keep Laya free from danger. She tells me that you are in the business and could use a helping hand. I have three rules: Number one, loyalty. Number two, I deal with you and only you. Number three, never bite for something that you cannot chew on."

I stood quiet for a moment, while taking in everything that he just gave an account of. That's when it became clear, just how serious these Asians are. Mr. Miyagi—I mean Han—had some evil eyes. During our talk, the short guy remained motionless. It is observable to his position as the enforcer. Even so, this dog held one's own by letting them know what it was, "As to Laya, we are very good friends. We're both expecting our relationship to reach a healthy commitment. Over my dead body, will anybody hurt Laya or place her in harm's way. Your rules are respected, for how can one move in opposition?"

JB spoke again, "So now comes the most important question—how much can you dispense?" He subsequently broke the short silence in a serious manner and continued, "Everything that comes from me is one hundred percent pure. I'd rather make fast profit than slow profit. I will give you each kilo at twenty-four thousand dollars. The price is right and the quality is excellent. You can't go wrong. I am willing to cuff you up to ten whole ones."

I was engrossed for a second before answering, "With all due respect, without exception, my money is upfront, although the trust is noted. Here is one hundred and twenty thousand dollars. I need five bricks." The black duffle bag slid toward JB, until it bumped his gator-toe Mauri shoes. With new confidence, my shot got washed down, as the now empty shot glass rested back on the coffee table. *Big-boy time!*

They venerated my movement by perceiving realness in this alliance. The three of us shared a few more drinks, as we kicked it about other things. I found out that JB and Han are part of the Asian Mafia. The two are into all types of shit. Han is an official gun connect. The nigga showed me a fifteen-shot Ak-47 handgun. *Fire!* He broke it down how one other person has this hammer from the Bean, which the dude actually made it hot by jewelling it on an En Tu Caserío hood DVD. I underestimated Laya. She is banded together, but moves in silence. That's when it occurred to me that I wanted to wife her.

The next day, I got up with JB and Han, in order to pick up the commodities. One could smell the coke right through the Adidas gym bag. Plain and simple, the perico was raw. Three birds were dropped off at Amandria's crib, before the don took flight to surprise Projekt. Real niggaz do real things!

As I walked inside of Projekt's spot, as always, all you could smell was that greenery. I tossed JB's gym bag on Projekt's lap, while manito's concentration stayed focus on a flat screen television viewing that throwback movie titled *Juice*. "What the fuck is this?" he mumbled, without even inspecting it.

"Loyalty, my nigga! Here are two bricks of unstepped-on cocaine. The moment that we have both been waiting for," I proclaimed.

I went into detail about all that came into existence. Our conversation then headed over to pricing and organizing. The both of us even talked about opening up legal businesses, which had been premeditated when the team was trapped behind metal. It had been decided that it's now time to go pay Big Fu a visit.

Projekt turned to me and jawed, "Manito, soon I am going to bring closure to a book." while nodding his head up and down. I ignored the weird statement. That nigga be so high sometimes that he just says anything.

CHAPTER 12

IT'S ABOUT TIME

BIG FU

I've been trying to remember why people first started calling me Big Fu and then it hit—in prison was when it had occurred. Thinking back, I blame it on my good friend Mizery. It's that damn tattoo of 'Fuck You' on one's right hand. But it's okay though, it is better than Theodore Roland Velli, surely a tag for a square. Not like, I am not sort-of a nerd. I have always enjoyed studying regardless of what topic it might be. I majored in sociology at the University of Utah. In fact, that is what one obtained his bachelor's degree in. This scholar is fond of deep sociological theory and theorists like Ervin Goffman and Max Weber. Yet, I will read almost anything. And there isn't anything that I cannot do on a computer.

This leads me to the task at hand. It was hard work plying on some businesses for Mizery and Projekt, two high-level shotcallers for the Unknowns. Both of these men are good friends from prison, in which their phone call has been enthusiastically anticipated. My main office is in the back of this establishment, Liberty Loan, which is scened on Broadway in Chelsea. In addition, on said ownership list, it is teamed up with a bar dubbed Paradise and a restaurant designated Big Fu's Steak House. They come in handy for making some extra currency and washing money for those who do not wish to frequent appropriate financial institutions. What's going to take place for the two is a tradeoff, a seventy-five-thousand-dollar production and distribution loan beneficial to an exchange of one hundred thousand dollars in cash. The investment is bogus of course, but it brings about legal protection to their undertakings, specifically for the racket of an escort service, just in case law enforcement happen to come snooping around, investigating where they got the money to open up their organizations. But more than that, I am going to help them lick into shape and card carry conducive to their scheme.

I am digging into the past when we were all in G-Pod on max custody—Mizery and Projekt used to break night airing their layout through the cell doors. So when they recently phoned me and requested an appointment, I was fully aware of what to expect. What my friends did not know is that the whole time that all three of us were sitting up in G-Pod, their subjects had been formulated. Moreover, after Big Fu's release, this quick-witted mind patched up a few loose ends and then sat back awaiting a call from them.

I began outlining the place of business by coming across an abandoned building on Fifth Street, right in the Unknowns' territory. It's a hole in the wall, but with some good help from our buddy Benjamin Franklin, a success can be made. All the more, one of my purchasers for blow, an architect named Bolo, sketched out its inside design, which consists of two showboat rooms and a sizable basement with three cubicles fit for biz.

The barbershop waiting room will frame up three thirty-two-inch flat screens. The middle television shall be inclined to play music videos hooked up to a Pioneer surround sound. To its left, is in contemplation of a Play Station 3 for heads sticking around to be serviced at the hands of a barber or braider. Only sports channels or local games will be viewed on the remaining screen. When it is time for a customer to get their haircut or lineup or braids, one of the working girls cheerfully shaking her ass, will escort one into the active room, where the patron will be seated in one of nine chairs facing a mirrored wall. Diamond Kutz is bringing aboard nothing but the best-known barbers and braiders.

Now the next dirty pool was fun quarterbacking, plus this fat bastard is going to be their number one John. Magik Entertainment is a referral agency for models, dancers, and escorts, which stands lawfully protected with contracts on part of all of the employees and clients. Female or male employees upon being hired are obligated to sign a referral agreement stating that he or she is precluded from having any sexual contact with clientele for a fee, among other rules and regulations. The service agreement befits the public and states similar information with an exception of a credit card extension. Magik Entertainment will have a 1-800 phone line imposing a flat fee of one hundred dollars an hour, in order to provide the earthling a female or male of their liking to the resting place requested. The models, dancers, and escorts work off tips. Get it? Got it! Magik Entertainment accepts Visa and Master Card. A credit card machine has been diagrammed to be located at the office to confirm payments.

Speaking of the office, it has been designed to be stationed in the cave. A backdoor entrance was blueprinted, in order to avoid crowding up the upstairs department. The cubbyhole's desk is decent-sized, but the Lazy Boy leather chair on wheels is comfortable. An updated computer sits comfortably on its own table, alongside of a ledger that will be used to keep records of all appointments made. Basically, it also documents how much each employee owes the company when they sign-off. A model, dancer, or escort signs-on by calling the dispatcher to indicate their availability to apply oneself. Said dispatcher is instructed to login the breadwinner by situating their picture, which contains additional information on an extensive bulletin board. This is for when clients call to live it up with a specific type of person, their desired model, dancer, or escort is brought to light.

The Boom Boom room contains hi-tech video equipment with a king-sized bed, so a model, dancer, or escort can flaunt herself or himself, as they fancy, with a view to be a drawing card on different websites. Magik Entertainment's advertisements will be through the Yellow Pages, Phoenix, Backpage, Craig's List, flyers, business cards, word of mouth, and many other ways. This adventurous project is selectively hiring nothing but flawless models, dancers, and escorts.

Royal Rydes was the easiest out of the three feats to standardize. Projekt and Mizery were reckoning to lease three brand-new, all-black, 2012 Escalade trucks. The cellar's last remaining room is a wide den. A 1-800 number, ledger, desk, Lazy Boy leather chair on wheels, and a thirty-two-inch flat screen will be awaiting a hired dispatcher. Royal Rydes' luxury excursions, and as well as their flat fees, should knock out all of the competition. Furthermore, an egg in one's beer is derived out of Magik Entertainment when a model, dancer, or escort needs a driver for the day.

It was a perfect setup for Projekt and Mizery, and of course, this is only a brief explanation of how I organized these businesses. Speaking of the two men, they just walked inside of my pawnshop. Projekt ran bloodshot eyes over some chains, but showed no emotions of interest. Mizery squinted at a few earrings, until something caught his attention.

"How much for these pair of VVS one-carrot diamond earrings?" Mizery asked Mrs. Johnson, an older woman that manages this pawnshop for me. Without her, my monopoly that I laid the foundation to would not be as prosperous. To be honest, I am attracted to Mrs. Johnson's awesome body.

"They average around six thousand dollars, but I can go in the back and play with those numbers a little. Would you like to purchase them, big guy?" Mrs. Johnson respectfully proposed.

"Please, these earrings are for my son," Mizery explained, as he looked over at Projekt. "Any fly shit over there?" Mizery pumped at Projekt for his opinion.

"I ain't feeling any of these wack-ass chains. They're all too simple," Projekt disapproved the jewelry.

I heard and saw all of this from my suite by virtue of state-of-the-art surveillance equipment. I set up audio and video cameras inside and outside of the pawnshop. As I stomped my four-hundred-pound American ass out of a security cage between the backroom and the showcase room, one could sense the positive energy in the air. The showcase room door was unlocked to welcome the duo with a handshake and a hug of respect. A quick gesture for them to tail me into the office followed, and when we got snug as a bug in a rug, I handed them shots of Jack Daniels.

"Damn Big Fu, you are doing big things around here," one could tell that Mizery was impressed on how he complimented me.

"I'm surviving, my friend," I delivered, sure of myself. "You should see the bar and restaurant. Thank God, for a wise decision to dib and dab with the powder, nothing serious, but enough that it caught one's attention. Dealing with high-class corporate people that pay an arm and a leg for good quality stuff has been de facto profitable," I added.

"Big Fu, how much do you pay for a kilo?" Projekt inquired, hunting for a way in. It was clear as a bell, as to their interest in facilitating me with this fly-by-night operation.

"I'm not investing in big amounts as of right now. It has been five hundred grams for a price of twenty-two thousand dollars from this Dominican guy named Flaco. He's from Roxbury. Our dealings came about after he picked out an engagement ring," I informed Projekt and Mizery.

"Big Fu, you are getting raped! That is way too much! How's the quality?" Mizery popped a question.

"You know that this nerd is naïve to the drug venture. That's why I have been waiting for you guys to contact me. My clients are complaining about the last two batches. They say that it burns their noses. The first batch that Flaco provided everyone loved. Now this third batch is hard to sell. Usually, once a month, I'm phoning Flaco for an additional five hundred grams," I let them know what's what.

"Listen, my nigga. We are going to resolve this problem for you. By what method do you do business with your clients?" Projekt picked at one's brain, as he sparked up a thick blunt.

"My clients bear the expense of two thousand dollars for twenty-eight grams. Is that good?" I made an inquiry.

"What! You're sitting on a gold mine. The only thing that you need to do is feed your people good quality coke and your ass is golden. Since Chelsea is the landing place, you'll be dealing with me. I am going to pass you down a brick for thirty thousand dollars. That is nothing, but eight thousand dollars more than what you have been paying for a half of a kilo. The quality is one hundred percent pure and it's guaranteed that your clients will fall in love. The profit should be forty-two thousand dollars a kilo!" Mizery put this in plain English, but stopped his demonstration when Projekt passed him a burning blunt.

"Thank you, Mizery. Expect a call whenever this non-hustler somehow peddles off this so-called cocaine. Now let us talk about money in my world of business. It's conspicuous that you guys finally made contact with me because the time has come to invest those almighty dollars in the businesses laboriously planned when we were all cooped up in G-Pod, right?" they both acknowledged one's presumption with a nod and remained silent, curious to what was going to be put forth next.

"There is a confession to be made," Projekt and Mizery looked topsy-turvy, as if their presenter's statement was crazy. "While you guys spoke about your future business plans, I had been ear-hustling and took it upon myself to organize and legalize the bigger picture. So when you gentlemen sat in front of me, like right now, all would be at beck and call. The first obligatory element necessitated to legalize your moneymakers is to bring about legal tender, and that is where I come in at with a fraudulent businesslike loan for seventy-five thousand dollars. And in turn, the expenditure is one hundred thousand dollars in cash," I paused my presentation, hit the blunt, passed it to Projekt, and then broke down everything that I already explained about organizing the enterprises.

"That's what the fuck I'm talking about!" Mizery put forth, rendering the air with enthusiasm.

"Tomorrow we'll come through papered up. Tell the architect to meet the team here at this spot so we can take a fresh look at his blueprints. Also, have the realtor on the scene in order to secure that abandoned building. After accomplishing those goals, Chelsea City Hall will be the next objective. Thereupon, we're going to apply for licenses for all three businesses," Projekt verbalized, full of determination to get things done.

"While you guys handle all of that, I'm going to shoot straight to Amandria's bank, where her sister is the branch bank manager. I'll have Rachelle help me open up accounts for each foundation. I am also going to request for a credit card machine and customized checks. When you confirm that we have the keys to our abandoned building, the next move will be to call Verizon to setup business phone lines. By the afternoon, we'll have lunch to catch up on all of our progression. Afterward, the three of us can head toward the Cadillac dealership to autograph some paperwork," Mizery was determined, as he spoke about his projects for tomorrow.

"Okay gentlemen, we're going to have a busy day tomorrow. Projekt, I will be ready in the morning. Please be here by nine a.m. sharp. My only request is that I be the first client to enjoy Magik Entertainment's leisure activities," we all broke out into laughter because of one's jocularity.

"Big Fu, you have my word," Mizery pledged.

We all shook hands before I escorted my friends back into the showroom, where Mrs. Johnson called out to Mizery, "Excuse me, sir. Do you still want these earrings for your son? I wrapped them up for you."

"I'm sorry, mam. My mind is so preoccupied with something else that I completely forgot about the earrings. How much do I owe you?"

Mizery asked, in advance of unfolding three stacks of bills encircled with rubber bands.

"Put that bankroll away. Your greenback is not any good here. Those earrings are a gift from me to Mizhai," I enunciated with love. Mizery and Projekt are my true friends.

The next day went as planned. Projekt was at my pawnshop a half an hour early with the cash as promised. Mizery came and picked up the big wheel check for seventy-five thousand dollars, so that he could open up those potato accounts at his sister-in-law's bank. Projekt and Mr. Serrano buried the hatchet at twenty-five thousand dollars for that pigeonhole formation. They also rubber-stamped the proper paperwork. Mr. Serrano good-heartedly accommodated Projekt by turning over the keys with the proviso that Mizery would transfer said funds into Mr. Serrano's countinghouse, as soon as the fictitious shoestring operation check cleared.

Afterward, came our meeting with an idealist to dicker a bill in pursuance of reconstructing the inner portion within this godforsaken construction. Bolo explicated to Projekt that what they seeked to be prepared would mark at forty thousand dollars. The adjustment on the payment was clinched at half on paper and the other half in ready assets. Bolo assured Projekt that this taskwork would be buttoned up in sixty days.

And before long, the trio headed to Chelsea City Hall. Thereupon, applying toward certification in the names of the referral agency, grooming palace, and chauffeuring service. Everything had been accomplished better than foresighted, but the only kickback was that before any service could be accredited as a bona fide setup, inspectors must canvass the capital asset. It will be sixty days, at least, in expectation to be in receipt of authorization in hand. Projekt, Mizery, and I sewed things up in Chelsea City Hall almost at one forty-five in the afternoon. Thereafter, we were off to Bella Isla, a Spanish restaurant on Fifth Street, where Mizery gave his feet a rest, already chomping away on a piece of fried chicken.

"I opened up the accounts under Royal Rydes, Diamond Kutz, and Magik Entertainment. When Big Fu's check clears, the branch bank manager has been instructed to deposit twenty-three thousand dollars in each account as a startup statement. The leftover one thousand dollars will be divided into thirds, three hundred and thirty-three dollars, and banked into separate balances. Subsequently, the credit card machine and the checks should be willing and able for pickup. Verizon technicians are scheduled to hook up our phone lines sometime next week with the 1-800 phone numbers, three-way calling, call forwarding, call waiting, etc., etc., etc., basically the works," Mizery informed us of his accomplishments for the day.

I was enjoying a plate of arroz con gandules with pernil de lechón and a cold Heineken, while Projekt broke the news to Mizery touching on today's performance on our side of the fence. When the food had been gobbled up, my spacious BMW truck burned us down the road to the Cadillac dealership. Mizery and Projekt put their John Hancock's on documentations, but in place of leasing them and getting fucked in the long run, they financed all three vehicles. The two of them preserved the wheels simple, except for two orders, that the two front side windows come about legally tinted and to limo tint both of the back passenger windows, so that privacy could be respected for their customers. Upon the Cadillac dealership obtaining their down payment, all three trucks will be available. Thereabouts, all and sundry were exhausted from today's errands. Once again, we cross-hearted to assemble tomorrow at the workstation with every intension on brainstorming regarding future advertising. This meant yet one more overworked day.

CHAPTER 13

I'M WIFEY
AMANDRIA

"**D**eeper ma, just like that, nice and slow. I'm cumming!" Mizery gave voice in a sexy way, which made me go harder and faster till he squirted in my mouth.

I love pleasing him. He does so much for Angel and I that wifey cannot complain. My love pays all of the bills and forks over more than ample amounts of money for whatever hankered, but chiefly, Mizery is a father to little man. Since that episode with Gambino, the man started placing confidence in me helping out. Alizé is his delivery girl. Every three days, Mizery bags up two hundred and fifty grams of powder and two hundred and fifty grams of crack all into eightballs and fifties. Two cell phones are full of clientry. Yet, not your normal street customers, these people are hardworking individuals with well-paying careers. In the short time of Mizery's dealings with those Asians, cash has been flowing in like crazy. He's swimming in presidents.

Mizery and Projekt are organizing legal businesses. They have some professional people lending a hand. I overheard them talking about a barbershop, an escort service, and a cab company. Mizery even gifted me the Honda Accord and bought himself a 2008 forest-green Cherokee, in which he kept plain, not wanting to attract any attention with a fancy car. While Mizery chilled in Angel's room playing Madden, I decided to be a nosey bitch and go through his cell phone. I sifted through all of the text messages and saw the following:

Incoming Text: Sexy Laya

> Are we going to Foxwoods this weekend?
> Let me know? So I can get ready after work.
> I promise this weekend will be special.

Incoming Text: Wolf

> Get at me

Incoming Text: Maliya

> Mizhai wants to C u

Incoming Text: Sexy Laya

> I'm thinking about you. I hope that you are thinking of me?

Incoming Text: Gladiator

> I'm ready

Incoming Text: Titi Maggie

> Give me a call?

Incoming Text: 857-233-9009

> Big Fu—new number

Incoming Text: 617-889-4158

Guess Who? ☺

Incoming Text: 857-888-0985

It's Izzy. This is my new number.

Incoming Text: Big Beautiful

Let me get Chi-Chi's new number?

Incoming Text: Emo

Got some ho'z lined up for the weekend...

Incoming Text: Dago

I flamed at some MS-13 kids! I thought that they were Roaches.

Incoming Text: Chi-Chi

Nigga, let me find out that you are fucking with Kelly and I'm cutting you off! That's my little cousin.

Incoming Text: Illmatik Creations

This is a confirmation email for your order of item #28.

Incoming Text: Sexy Laya

I'm leaving work now. Come over. I'll cook.

Incoming Text: Rattlesnake

Paper on deck!

When I read those text messages from this Sexy Laya whore, one's stomach turned in knots. *This is unbelievable—Mizery fucking another bitch? Does he think of me as only his friend still? Should I say something or keep quiet?* However, my anger got the best of me. "Mizery, get out! Go fuck your other bitch!" I screamed like a fruitcake, and then at that moment, aimed a gun at him. With the .357 Magnum trembling in this enraging scorned right hand, I got audacious and yelled, "Who the fuck is Laya? She sounds like a fortune cookie eating chink! I'm serious, leave! Now!"

"You are trippin'! We ain't even together! Our agreement was a friendship with benefits! Now you're coming at me all crazy! Fuck you! You ungrateful, bitch!" Mizery voiced, but never showed any sign of being panicky from this madden woman pointing the pistol at him.

He's pissed. I felt bad, especially for Angel. He cried as Mizery left. Angel really got attached to Mizery. One night, Angel insisted upon calling Mizery Daddy. It had been construed how that's a question for Mizery. Latterly, the boy asked the one inquisition that I never wanted him to inquire. Angel gave me the third degree on who his real father is. The subject just changed.

CHAPTER 14

LIFE IS GREAT
MIZERY

Fucking with those Asians proved to be lucrative. They were sliding me authenticated bricks for twenty-four stacks a pop. When I cheffed it up, one did not lose a gram. My team received raw Tony Montana as well, but at the same time, I was pricing grams as if big Mizery had been still paying thirty thousand dollars a K. Therefore, making profit greater. The brothers weren't complaining—how could they—niggaz were getting pure coke that you could do whatever to. Our nativeland turned up. ChelRok looked like night of the living dead with crackheads up and down like zombies. This is what you call hoodrich!

Gladiator had San Andreas well-organized. All of the brothers and sisters were required to pattern themselves upon their scheduled hours to act as security. There is without exception, four members at the bottom of San Andreas directing fiends to cop. This unit is steady armed, ready for any surprise attacks. Another crew bulwarked up top, ahead of the stairs. Gladiator once again reminded me that ever since Mission Takeover those Roach niggaz haven't been around. He also mentioned that Fat Cheese even scrammed out of Shurtleff Street.

Gambino's Hawthorne Street needs to be straightened out. It is sloppy out there, but the hard Scarface being dished out had Crack City's cap jumping. Gambino clued me in on how Ghost got locked up last night with fourteen grams of crack on Beacon Street for driving drunk after leaving King Author's. Ghost has been held without bail, because he violated his county probation as well. Ghost is an Italian brother that used to be a member of a local clique termed *Ghost.* I was familiarized on how Loski backed him to be G-Fived. Ghost looks like an innocent white boy attending college. He's 5'7", average-sized, sports short cornrows, a chinstrap, and carries a good sense of humor. Many bros vouch that the homey is a dog. I arranged a rendezvous with Gambino for taking kindly to soldiers operating lackadaisical. Manito understood my concerns and put it on our flag to tighten up the Hawthorne circle. During this sit-down, I made a decision to switch Gambino and Gladiator's hoods, so Gladiator could whip into shape Hawthorne Street, while Gambino upholds the already systematized San Andreas.

Wolf is holding down Chestnut Street. He put me on with some white boy named Ricky from Charlestown that was paying thirty-two thousand dollars a kilo once a week. It was easy to trust him, because when Wolf introduced us, we instantly knew each other from South Bay. I have dealt with him in the past. He stays coming through on a straight paper wave. I know that you have heard about those screwball white boys from Charlestown that idolize robbing banks and armored trucks.

Dready had Cottage Street flaming hot. Every day, Bling Street, named after RIP Bling, flared up like Revere Beach in the summertime. For some reason, bitches were enthralled with Bling Street. Dready ministered two crackhouses, the Green Monster and Mona's. He is smart for that, because not only did Bling Street have that bomb piedra, but also it provided two places for fiends to get high in.

Projekt is going crazy in Boston. He is doing things a little different by cheffing up the entire product and stretching it. The crack was still potent. It is thirty and three zeros for UK representatives, but for outsiders, thirty-five thousand dollars a brick. Do the math, homey? Cathedral Projects is on a prosperous journey. You got all of the crackheads from Downtown Boston, Castle Square Projects, Villa Victoria Projects, Lenox Street, Shawmut Street, and the rest of the South End chasing that get-high. This nigga Projekt is cooked, no matter how much bread comes his way; the brother refuses to get low and out of the projects—now that's a true project baby.

Now that everything is good in both cities and our empire wealth started piling, concentration fell on the three businesses. The check from Big Fu finally cleared. Projekt and I signed contracts stating a 50/50 partnership for all three concerns. If anything should happen to either one of us, the other would receive full ownership of all three livelihoods. We amended a special condition in the partnership contract, which deposes that neither party could withdraw funds without the other person being present. Not that me and my nigga distrust each other, but this protects investments in case of a disagreement gone wrong. Ya-dig? Checks were sent to Mr. Serrano, Bolo, and a Massachusetts Cadillac dealership. After footing the bills, all of the accounts were on their last breath. Projekt and I planned to go back to the drawing board with Big Fu for one more vested interest. The two-man crew needed more legal tender to invest in the following materials:

BUSINESS LIST

(3) Business office phones

(2) Black office desks

(3) Fatboy leather chairs on wheels

(2) Ledgers

(3) Tom Tom GPS

(1) Computer w/ programs

(1) Photo/video recorder (must be computer applicable)

(3) 32'inch flat screens

(1) Play Station 3 (4) Remote controls (10) Sports games

(1) Pioneer surround sound

(1) Waiting room leather couch

(1) DVD player

(1) Big wall map of Massachusetts

(50) DVD music videos

(1) Full-wall barber mirror

(8) Sets of barber equipment

(2) Sets of braiding cosmetics

(1) Custom business sign

(2) Front glass windows

Projekt and I sat down and elected those who were going to be hired to run our businesses. Launching off with Royal Rydes, two managers got duty-bounded to add to the payroll three dispatchers and three drivers. I brought on board Titi Maggie. Projekt selected his mother. Both of these righteous women are dependable. I am sure that they will make a perfect team.

Off the rip, this guy named Fats had been appointed to hold down Diamond Kutz. Fats is Puerto Rican, white-skinned, average-height, butterball, has a curly afro, and for the most part is an old head from Bridgeport, Connecticut. The convict was locked up with us in Wyatt too. He ended up moving to Cambridge and falling back. I bumped into him one night at the Revere Showcase Cinema, while we were hugged up on our girls about to watch the new movie *Hunger Games.* Fats is a monster with the clippers. Old school did twenty-five years for a body and automatically ends up as the head barber in whatever joint the veteran lands in. So you tell me if old boy is nice? An assent underlining a wage of fifteen hundred dollars for the week legitimately validated itself. I deciphered the hustle spontaneously. By taxing three hundred dollars a chair every seven days; the vet stands in good stead with twelve hundred dollars. Not to mention whatever the old hand makes off his heads.

For Magik Entertainment, Tio Felix and Projekt's brother Stevo, who is from Columbia Point Projects in Dorchester, both filled the supervisory positions. When it came to our ho'z, I had three on deck: Nessy, Cindy, and Tiesha. All of these sluts would fuck for a buck. Nessy is Lady Roam's younger sister. She's a light-brown, petite, Puerto Rican shorty with long dark hair. Word has it that this stunt's brain game is decent. I ain't never fucked Nessy or even tried, but the first night that this pro puts in my pocket (P.I.M.P.), swallowing for respect follows suit. Cindy is average-height, thick, has coffee skin color, mixed Spanish nationalities, and short brown hair. I intended to sidechick that fatty till niggaz put me on how bands will make her dance. Yeah, I'm not going to lie, the jumpoff domed your boy off. Now Tiesha's main enthrallment is either that hoodrat's perfect ridiculous ass or those Angelina Jolie sexy lips that work magic. This lady of easy virtue swags different wigs every day to match various outfits. This mud is short, African-American, and shapely. I aired it out a few years back; it was on the first night home from South Bay, after wrapping up a two-year sentence. I smoked some loud, popped two G'z Up Ho'z Down ecstasy pills, drank two fifths of Hennessy, and had been Raekwoned the fuck out! A nigga's dick malfunctioned. Real talk—it would go hard, then soft, hard, then soft again. I just said, "Fuck it." peeled off the condom and quit. This scarlet woman ran all over the hood clowning big Mizery by telling everybody that I had a small penis. Fucking bitch! Now I am going to have those overlaps suck a hundred stiff ones.

Projekt came through with two Asian ho'z, May and Tya, who looked like innocent college bitches. May is short and thick, white-skinned, and packs some Dolly Parton titties. A flat stomach and shoulder-length pink hair only tacks on to the already chintzy doll. The shy one, Tya, has a delicate face, but suffered from noassatall. She totes a light-colored, tall and skinny body with longish light-purple hair. Nonetheless, they were definitely money-getters.

We convoked a party of call girls. Next, comes along transitioning these streetwalkers into evening ladies by their configuration and mannerisms. On the other hand, our sixty-four-thousand-dollar question is where do we find dainty homosexuals—"No homo!"— who are drawn to whatever? Guess it's best to bide one's time until advertising brings them to us.

I'm always thinking of Amandria and Angel. I miss them both. If only junior wifey would have addressed her lasciviousness for a commitment in an adult manner, then maybe our relationship would have come of something. But not after that stunt that she pulled. How can one trust a person that is easily manipulated by their emotions?

Baby boy ended up renting an apartment in Revere. My penthouse swanked presidents—an average-sized living room feathered a nest for a wooden entertainment center, which equipped an au courant sixty-two-inch plasma flat screen that was similar to Amandria's. It also included a Sony surround sound. BJ's package deal. You know that I had to snatch up an X-box 360 appending nothing but sports games. Embellishing one's prodigious living room splashed two black leather couches, one three-seater, and the other a two-seater. Additionalizing to the set constituted two black end tables, plus a good-sized coffee plateau. On the wall, I fitly clinged up light-brownish curtains, a large-sized wood-color stitched clock, and as well as two mediumistic rectangle mirrors that were surrounded by leather in a stylish form. On top of the entertainment center based a humungous fish tank indwelling an iguana that I named Special.

What a dinky kitchen. It was a hop and a skip away from the living room vamping wooden cabinets, white countertops, and those aforementioned curtains. The bathroom looked fresh with its black shower curtains, black towels, black toilet seat cover, black rug, black toothbrush, and black bath sponges that were all made by Playboy. The kingdom's king-sized bed, on sight, would get a bitch wet. What jumpoff could resist being fucked on a white and gold Christian Dior bed set? A fifty-two-inch Panasonic flat screen had been mounted on the wall, along with speakers in every corner. I even perforated in two bass woofers underneath my bed, which vibrated every little thing anytime that I jammed out, watched a movie, or played video games on the Xbox 360. On top of all this, a yellow dim light and full-ceiling mirror striped the penthouse complete.

I came-off on two male one-month-old Rednose pitbulls. Rocky is reddish-brown, pizzazzing a white stripe running down a short nose. He also has white splashes on all four of his paws and stomach. I christened the other one Terror, who is white with brown spots on its face and tail. But those glitzy blue eyes give him a manic visage. The kid bought these puppies from Lil' Javie, some little green-eyed Puerto Rican nigga from Dorchester that be fighting pits. The youngling trained an all-black Cobey pitbull denominated Onyx that was bred in Concord, North Carolina. Onyx is 7-0, Boston's finest. Lil' Javie put up twenty stacks and two Suzuki RM125 dirt bikes against an American pitbull addressed as Rush from Brooklyn, New York. I watched the fight on video, which lasted about four minutes, before Rush's owner waved a red bandanna, indicating that it was time to separate them by applying breaking sticks. Onyx forced Rush on a defeated back, while locked on the throat area, shaking and tearing hide bloodthirstily. You could see that in a couple of more minutes, Rush would have died.

Watching this fight inspired this dog lover to obtain two puppies. All of my life, I have been fond of pitbulls. Now I have the suitable circumstance to own one. Lil' Javie charged me one thousand dollars for each puppy involving official papers. Over and above, I saw pictures of their parents appearing vicious.

Me and Mizhai's relationship is faultlessly like how it's supposed to be. You know that I stay spoiling my little man. Mizhai clearly calls his father Papi now and flips out when I leave. Maliya is on some cool shit and grants baby-daddy permission at any moment to pick up minime. Bitch stays flirting, pussy begging for this curving mini bat. She be talking about the problems with her fiancé as if a nigga gives a fuck. I listen and give advice for us to be on relaxed terms, but really, one couldn't care less if Don Cuba punished that unmoralistic parasite, as long as he didn't touch Mizhai. I was thinking about all of this while lying in bed.

Damn! I fell asleep. I have to go pick up Laya from work. We are going to Foxwoods Casino this weekend. I withdrew twelve thousand dollars from the safe and got dressed. Even the Verizon cell phone got flatlined and thrown somewhere. This weekend is going to be special for Laya and me. While double-checking overall, my two little monsters were remembered. A scurrying man tore open four bags of Eukanuba. Therefore, expelling dog food onto the kitchen floor. Lastly, before breezing, I poured water into four rice pots, in order to make sure that Rocky and Terror were good.

I had been cruising on Revere Beach Parkway blowing on a half-blunt of Columbian Gold. In the mix of taking a left at the Chelsea High School, an all-black truck cuts me off, and then another same-color truck approached unnoticed from behind with four to six men jumping out of both vehicles aiming their guns in all directions shouting, "FBI! Put your hands where I can see them! UP! UP! UP!" Immediately, a nigga was snatched out of the truck and slammed onto the concrete.

"Where are the guns and drugs at, Mizery?" it was Agent Deraney speaking. The cracker used to be a Chelsea Police detective before becoming an official federal agent. Fuck that pig! Pistol popped his bitch-ass in the stomach.

"What are you talking about? There aren't any guns or drugs in this car. I'm not involved in that type of lifestyle anymore. I own legal businesses now," no matter how much positive debating was uttered on my behalf, it didn't convince them.

"Okay, ask me if we believe your bullshit. Do you think that investigators are not aware about the murders on Grove Street? Or should I say San Andreas? Understand that it is known that you are the man out here. How is Projekt doing in Boston?" Agent Deraney pointed out.

"Deraney? Come take a look at this," another federal agent announced. While still being facedown, all one could hear were chuckling sounds. "Today is your lucky day, guy. Now get the fuck out of here!" Agent Deraney dictated, once he returned.

A million things crashed into my medulla oblongata. Those alphabet boyz were acting crazy. They knew way too much. That only meant an investigation was underway.

Upon arriving at Laya's store, realization hit about her Coach bag being missing. Hilarity could not be kept a lid on. Big Mizery had been robbed by the feds. Laya climbed inside of my truck and catechized me on why I was so late. A brief rundown got expounded on the ride to Everett. This incident raised many flags as a warning sign. From this day on, I am really going to start planning to get out of the game.

After a couple of hours of Laya getting dressed, and as well as swinging back to my apartment to nab up some more dollars, we finally jumped on the highway. On our drive to Foxwoods Casino, I swayed Ms. Professional to smoke a Hydro-Blunt. She even swallowed a triple-stack Dolphin ecstasy pill.

It had to be around one or two a.m. by the time a hotel key was handed over. As soon as the both of us extended over the doorway, Laya came from behind and pushed me on a comfy bed. I had been given a strip show to some slow jams, and at once, admiring her sexy body and erotic faces being expressed. After unbuttoning a brand-new pair of Dior Homme jeans, Laya tugged them off, including the LV boxers. She meekly handclasped an inflexible boner as a salacious tongue began tracing swirls around a pulsing mushroom. Succeeding that, it hardened even more doused in saliva. I don't know how or where such a professional-type woman learned to dome a nigga off, but either way, your boy loved it. Surely, things did not freeze there; Laya massaged twinging balls, while glissading on one's manhood with no hands. In addition, when that extra-tight pussy slowly slid down on a seven-inch penis, I almost lost control. It had been a long wait for this, so everything felt extra special right about now. A loving couple made sweet love for thirty minutes before cumming together.

"I love you, Mizery. I haven't had sex in four years," she fessed up, explaining the tightness.

"I love you more, babygirl. And I better be the last to hit that. Today was a wakeup call with the feds. It is only a matter of time before reversing to jail. I may be Loyal 2 Da Hood, but the hood is never loyal," I meant what I had just said.

"Thank you for bringing us to Foxwoods this weekend. I know that you're going to miss Dready's birthday party, but we needed some alone time," Laya gave me a sexy wet kiss, after expressing her gratitude.

"I know, baby ..." were my last-minute words before drifting off to sleep.

CHAPTER 15

I'M THE BOSS
DON CUBA

My money has been hurting for a month now. Noise concerning Mizery and Projekt moving coke like hot potatoes has landed on one's lap. *Why the fuck hasn't Hitman taken care of this situation? Wasn't he given an order to handle?* After I talk to Maliya, I am going to hit him up.

I walked into a high-sounding parlor to witness Maliya and Mizhai playing Play Station 3. "Maliya, let me holla at you in our bedroom?" I requested in a normal tone, not wanting to alarm Mizhai. As soon as she skipped over, a nigga started rashing, "Didn't we come to an understanding on how you were going to be truth-telling whenever contact is made involving Mizhai's father?"

"Yeah, baby," she mewled in a low voice.

"Then bitch, why don't I know? Guess who said so? Mizhai! He shows me each and everything that his Papi buys for him!" I exclaimed.

"Baby, I'm—" she did not even get a fair shake to finish. I smacked the dog shit out of that snaky ho. I had never laid hands on her previous to now, but enough was enough.

"Ba-ba-baby," she sobbed. "What is the problem? Are you jealous of Mizhai and Mizery's relationship? Or does it look bad? Because I put it on Mizhai's life that your fiancée is true-blue."

For some reason, my heart felt bad, so an apology was called for. To make it up to Maliya, we went out to eat at a friendly cheesecake factory at the Galleria Mall located in the city of Cambridge. While waiting for our food, I phoned Hitman and directed him to be at our house in two hours. Maliya and I actually had a supereminent time. The two of us should go out more often.

Hitman was already out front of our spot in his blue Ford Explorer bumping some Rick Ross, not even detecting us coasting up the street. *What a dummy!* In the basement of one's three-floor condo is where the argumentation activated. "What happened to your order to take back San Andreas? Money isn't right! This is the final warning!" I wasn't playing anymore games, so he is either going to take the admonition serious or pay the consequences.

"Calm down, Don Cuba. A course of action is in progress. I am just pausing for the perfect day to come. Why am I being questioned? Do you know that Mizery is entangled with the Asian Mafia? I have been doing my homework. So be easy," it's apparent that Hitman is feeling a certain way due to his reply.

"All right. Then get it done. How about Projekt?" I casted doubt upon.

"Mizery's partner? He is from the Cathedral Projects in Boston. Dude is second on my hitlist. So relax, boss man. They are going to get hit hard," Hitman sounded confident.

"Relax? You fucking limping monkey! If this problem does not get fixed in a few days, I promise that you will be dumped in the swampy-ass Chelsea Creek! Now get the fuck out of my face!" I had enough of this back and forth bullshit. I said what I had to say. "Where's the house phone?"

"Mi amor?" Diamond answered almost instantaneously.

"What's up, Diamond?" I put into words in an aggravated temperament.

"Damn bro, you sound like shit. What's up?" Diamond urged.

"Actually, I need the girls to come assist me with a few headaches," I annotated, although glued on Hitman jumping into his Ford Explorer.

"Cuba, we are heading out there next weekend. It was going to be a surprise," Diamond unfolded.

CHAPTER 16

DEATH WISH
HITMAN

One of these days, I'm going to shoot Don Cuba in his face! His soft-ass thinks that he is mad tough. When it's me who pops that metal and pumps all of the merchandise. That bitch-ass nigga just sits at home catering to a venomous pigeon that should not be taken at face value. But I ain't playing Russian roulette with the Angels. Don Cuba's team are real-deal assassins straight from Cuba. Reports off the grapevine believe that they have executed politicians for Fidel Castro. On my way out, Don Cuba was heard speaking to Diamond. I need to get this done as soon as possible.

One's cell phone started vibrating in my jean pocket, which I pulled out and then answered, "What's up?" nothing but music, before a cutoff. Almost sliding back into the Truey's, it trembled once more. "Yo!" I hollered, while in the process of bouncing out of Don Cuba's white neighborhood in Prattville.

"Hey boo, why haven't you called or texted?" Fatima innocently asked.

"I've been busy doing mad shit. What are you doing tonight?" I hit, getting on my pimp talk.

"Nothing really. I'm hoping that your fine self comes to pick me up. No work today. But tomorrow is going to be off-the-chain. Those comma-throwing Unknowns are celebrating a birthday, so it's big spending at KA's!" she sounded excited.

"Oh, yeah! I'm coming through! We have to talk!" I spoke sharply, and then floored it to Fatima's. She did not know it yet, but a bloodbath was sure to be in her hands.

I met Fatima a while back at the Sprint store located in Downtown Boston. Shorty was three-deep with Stephanie and Nicole, two pretty white girls that are also strippers. Fatima is like 5'4", thick, has caramel skin color, long dark hair, and demands attention with such captivating beauty. She had been waiting in line to pay her cell phone bill when I strutted over talking on my horn. I know that money-hungry ho smelled cheddar, because the broad jumped on it.

That night, I had all three of those bitches smutting it out in a Marriot hotel room. It didn't take nothing but twenty-eight grams of snow, a few bottles of Dom P, and that official magic to get my big black dick some special treatment. Since then, Fatima has been stuck to me like glue.

A couple of hours later, plan B was activated. "What's Rebellating, Hitman?" Fat Cheese acknowledged me in an alerted nature.

"Don Cuba wants to know where that gwuap is for those five hundred grams of hard that big homey gave you a while back?" I asked, knowing it was absolute that he didn't have anything at all.

"Cuz, how do you expect me to pay, when those UK niggaz robbed us and took over our hood? I even had to move out of Chelsea," he spoke nervously into his cell phone.

"Doggy, that is not our problem. We want those big faces tonight or you and your family will be dead by tomorrow! Or your bitch-ass can repay us with a favor and at the same time a true friend can revenge Problem and Ugly's deaths?" I put forth an ultimatum.

Fat Cheese paused before reverberating. "Cool. Come get a nigga, cuz," he agreed. I thought that the clown would see it my way.

Okay, it's showtime! While I'm gunning down Projekt, Fat Cheese is hitting up Mizery. Chrisrock, a wanted man, and I walked into the Cathedral Projects. "What the fuck!" I exclaimed, as three UK soldiers ran in our direction gripping choppers. A tall and slender, whitish dude with a low haircut, looking like a Puerto Rican Shaggy from Scooby Doo, whisked right upon us.

"Who the fuck are y'all?" Shaggy investigated.

"Ain't no drama, dog. It's Hitman, reppin' Lucerne Street. Take the hammer," I uncovered it as I put my hands up. "I'm trying to talk to Projekt in regards to the reward for this rat-ass nigga," I brought forth, as I pointed to the wanted man.

Shaggy monitored me as if I was crazy and then put out a feeler, "Then why is he here so willingly?"

"What's your name?" I tested the waters with an extraordinary question under the circumstances.

"Pito," he gave a snappy comeback.

"Good question, Pito. I can see that you are very observant. Well Pito, as we speak, two of my gunners have his mother tied up with a shotty to her face. So be a nice little soldier and go get your boss," I directed. Pito hopped on a cell phone and then schooched away as numerous nozzles remained zoomed in on us.

"Follow us," Pito instructed.

Pito led us into a basement, where Projekt was standing by. "Hitman, huh?" Projekt remarked, all along grilling Teddy Bear. "Pito, tie this rat nigga up! Hitman, this is yours. Ten stacks," Projekt delivered, and then chucked an Adidas sneaker box at me.

As Pito duct-taped Teddy Bear's wrists together behind a chair, Chrisrock slid out a long chrome .357 Magnum, speedily pointing it to Projekt's chest and then threatened, "Try me and I'll blow your fucking brains out!" Chrisrock is one of those short and fat, longhaired crazy white bikers that represent the Hell's Angels. Visibly he's a hired gunman.

I shot Pito three times in the back, and as he fell, a hollow tip bullet went in and out of his skull. Rocking these clowns to sleep wasn't about nothing. I sized up Projekt with a vainglorious look. "You know why I'm here, right?" I brashly asked, as I waved my .45 caliber handgun around the basement. "When your UK niggaz plundered San Andreas it fucked up our money. From then on, you pledged war against the Don Cuba Family!"

"What the fuck is a Don Cuba Family? Fuck you and Don Cuba!" Projekt flipped, as Chrisrock zigzagged his gun on me. Projekt electrifyingly smacked the heater out of my hand. I panicked, until Chrisrock brought down the pistol on the bridge of a startled nose, cracking it instantly. Thereupon, I got bonded next to ten-thousand-dollar snitch. Life is over!

"You're probably wondering what went wrong," Projekt related, while laughing. "One should be more careful by hiring work. Chrisrock is a good friend of ours, you stupid motherfucker! When ratboy over here"—Projekt smacked Teddy Bear across his mouth—"had me and my niggaz fighting federal charges, Chrisrock had been caged up at Wyatt too."

Then and there, I seen Projekt and Chrisrock shake hands. "I know that it's about loyalty, but take this as a gift, my friend," Projekt insisted, and then much-admired Chrisrock before he accepted the sneaker box and split.

"Just me, you, and ratboy now," Projekt orated, as he positioned a pillowcase over Teddy Bear's head.

In the mix of piping Projekt approaching me, while holding another pillowcase in his hands, I started pleading, "Projekt! Don Cuba made us do this! He hates on y'all because the greedy nigga's money is fucked up in Chelsea and Boston! The faggot even has those UNLV kids trying to kill Mizery tonight!"

"Keep talking, nigga!" Projekt got amped, as if he was about to shoot me right there.

"Don Cuba has some UNLV Rebels ready to shoot up Dready's birthday party at King Author's," I revealed, trying to live by any means necessary.

"All right, pussy. I'll see you later," Projekt articulated, ahead of covering my head and walking out.

CHAPTER 17

SURPRISE
FAT CHEESE

"This is for our niggaz resting in peace," I amped myself up, as shells clacked inside of a banana clip that belonged to a SKS assault rifle. Blacked out, grey bandanna pressed against my face, murder is the case. Homey Ice was Rebel'd out in a grey army fatigue outfit. He hipped two .40 cals and then threw on his ninja mask. We laid-low out of view in the DJ booth. It's a foolproof setup. The two of us were spying through the surveillance cameras waiting for Mizery to blow in.

Ice is a pale-skinned Bosnian cat with a short haircut. My mutineer is from Somerville. He's about 5'8", 220 pounds, and is one of our infallible shooters. *UK KILLER* in sizable Old English letters can be espied tatted across the neck area. The nigga has been battling with the Unknowns for years because of his little brother Havoc's death.

A whole bunch of UK niggaz were already inside of the club. I seen one of the dudes that had my mother and sister hostage. That Twinkie is definitely going to catch a hot one. They caught me slipping that night; as a consequence, I was robbed for all of the crack that I got from Don Cuba. One's entire family is still traumatized. I am watching the birthday boy get lap dance after lap dance. Fatima finally straddled homeboy and commenced rubbing his dick with one hand; while all along stroking the nigga's long-ass dreads with the other; furthermore, she kept whispering some shit in the Twinkie's ear. She's fly, but strikes as a straight jumpoff, a walking disease. It's one twenty-two a.m. and still no sign of Mizery. The club closes at two a.m.... If Mizery does not show up in the next twenty minutes it's time for some action.

About ten minutes later, two girls came en route to hug Dready. Afterwards, they bought him drinks. Unexpectedly, all of those Twinkies surrounded a rectangle bar while taking shot after shot toasting to the birthday boy.

"Fuck this! Let's ryde!" I rapped out, rousing up Ice.

We came out of the DJ booth firing shots; as everyone started running; I caught birthday boy with rapid bullets to his chest. He died instantly. Ice jumped over a dead Dready, while flaming at that kid disporting two braids, the one that had my mother and sister hostage at gunpoint. Out of nowhere, a chubby girl blew Ice's top off. Ice fell out on a one-way ticket to be judged. Her accomplice tookoff by dumping a .380 caliber handgun at me, but when the SKS spat, I seen that bitch do a back flip over the bar.

"Oh shit!" I yipped in pain, as two bullets hit my right shoulder.

As I tried to run out of the side door, another piece of metal entered a nigga's calf. "Freeze! Don't fucking move! FBI!" numerous federal agents shouted, in the act of raiding the strip club.

Around six-in-the-morning, I found myself in a hospital room at Boston Medical Center with both of my ankles cuffed to a hospital bed. Two federal agents were sitting in small chairs guarding an entrance. Meanwhile, I was listening to a doctor explain how both of the gunshot wounds to a bandaged shoulder being suspended by a sling went in and out, causing no serious damage. He continued to translate that the single gunshot injury to one's calf is weighty because it exited out of a knee. It did not break any bones though, but it will take six months to a year before walking on it is a possibility. The doctor prescribed me pain medication and antibiotics, now leaving his patient open to the federal agents.

"I am Agent Conney and this is my partner Agent Deraney. You will be getting federally charged on two counts of first-degree murder. A video has been secured as evidence showing what eventualized last night. You're up against the death penalty if you are convicted. Do you understand that?" the agent raised in a serious manner.

"Yes I do, officer," was my petrified response.

"Okay, the government is in position to offer you a deal, which may help you for your cooperation in proffering evidence. If so, an indictment will be assigned onward to the Suffolk Superior Court shadowing a fifteen to life recommendation to the prosecutor. This shall provide an eligibility date for parole in fifteen years. Or you can roll the dice and knock on wood not to be sentenced to lethal injection at the hands of the United States Government," Agent Deraney tendered.

"No officer, I don't want to die in jail. How do you want me to cooperate?" the words just came out of my mouth.

"You must inform us on Don Cuba and Mizery's criminal enterprises, corroborate how Don Cuba contracted to kill UK members last night, and also complete the facts surrounding the murders on Grove Street. If you are not sure of something, make something up and fill in the blanks. When it's time to testify in front of the Grand Jury, a solid story is exigent," Agent Deraney construed.

What a fucked up situation! "I'm willing to do whatever it takes to be able to see the world again," my decidedness was final.

"Good decision, young man. We are going to begin this process by recording your statements. But be careful answering them, because if Assistant United States Attorney Robyn Blatt can prove perjury, any agreement could be withdrawn," Agent Conney broached this with a grin, as if he had a trick up his sleeve.

I was sitting there answering questions for what seemed to be like forever. I do not want to die in prison. Fuck it. I'm a rat, and when I finished snitching, I signed my statements.

CHAPTER 18

REDRUM
MIZERY

Sitting back eating brunch on a Sunday afternoon is how our last day at Foxwoods Casino played out. I ordered a plate of baked ziti with chicken and broccoli. Moreover, my hunger didn't stop there. I forced it with strawberry pancakes on the side. Laya had a ham and cheese omelet, home fries, light toast, and a small order of chicken tenders. The night previous, we were in the casino gambling until five a.m... Being tipsy from the liquor and rolling off ecstasy pills hoodwinked us into spending thousands.

"Baby, thank you for a beautiful weekend," Laya sounded and looked delighted.

"I had fun too," was my reply.

"Mizery, it's time to relinquish the drug game. Have you even thought about this?" Laya seemed distraught, in her worriedsome inquiry.

"I agree. Give me a few more weeks to patch some things up, thus I am going to counsel JB into moving ahead to Projekt's bloodline. Now my question to you—when I do, are you willing to jointly move in? We'll go pick out a house together?" were one's heartfelt words to someone that I wanted to wife up.

"I have been waiting for this invitation. I am in love with you. I certainly can see myself being up under you. My life feels organic. However, this means a ready commitment, Mizery?" she accepted, but seeked faithfulness.

"I'm ready now, in that bed, with you being naked and making sexy faces," I teased her.

"I'm serious, baby," Laya enounced, while trying hard to hold in a smile.

"It's only you, nobody else," I asserted, hoping to convince her by tonguing my sexy Laya down.

On our way home, notions came to mind regarding issues that I had to alleviate before I kissed the game goodbye. Laya injected an old school Boyz II Men CD, in front of sliding her seat backwards. "Concentrate on driving," Laya dictated, in the meantime, tiny fingers zipped down my zipper. *SPRING!* A snake jumped out of a hole striking its victim. Laya stroked it exceptionally slow, while all along soothing atingled balls. She started kissing me on the neck. I wanted to pull over right then and there to smash, but a nigga sat back to enjoy being dogged-off. Laya's slurping sounds could be heard over the slow music. It didn't take long before splashing.

As soon as I entered my apartment, all a nigga smelled was dog shit. This is why those pups were closed off in the kitchen. They don't know any better. Rocky and Terror were lobbed into the bathtub to be washed down. In addition, the kitchen floor got scrubbed with Pine Sol. After showering and dressing, I powered a lonely cell phone:

Incoming Text: Projektgunner

Where da fuk are u at!?!? Shit popped off!!
RIP
PITO

Incoming Text: Alizé

I miss u

Incoming Text: Lady Roam

LOYALTY MANITO!

Incoming Text: Gambino

WAR!!!!!!!!!!!!!!!!!!!!!

Incoming Text: Firu

RIP DREADY!!
RIP KAOS!!

Incoming Text: Gladiator

I need to c u

Incoming Text: Abuela

Te Amo...

Incoming Text: Titi Maggie

Are you coming to Steven's birthday party next week?

Incoming Text: Tio Felix

My brother Eli called. He said for you to send him a few hundred?

Incoming Text: Eks

I'll be back from NY in a few weeks.

Incoming Text: Tiesha

When can I get that donkey again? ☺

Incoming Text: Fats

I need a week off to go visit Mami in CT?

What the fuck is going on? I hit up Projekt quick. "Where have you been at? Mad shit popped off! Come to the projects!" Projekt roared all of this, as soon as he picked up.

"I'm on my way!" I voiced back, before heading out of the front door and onto 93 South.

I was stuck in traffic on the Tobin Bridge so I decided to call Firu. Voicemail—let me try again.

"Estas perdió, cabrón?" Firu asked loudly into his receiver.

"I was vacationing with my Asian shorty on some alone time. Put me on?" I demanded answers.

"Those Roach niggaz hit up Dready's birthday party at King Author's. They killed Dready and Kaos. Maniak got shot in the back but it missed his spine by centimeters. He's recovering though. Lucky's legs caught nine shots by a SKS. I don't know if he will ever walk again. Chino★Scarface's rib wounds are from a .40 caliber. Lady Roam is on the run eating. She off'd one. FBI agents are kicking down every location known for her. Fat Cheese was snatched up for the murders," Firu gave me the 411 without stopping.

"Firu, at ten p.m, I want everybody at the Holiday Inn in Somerville. Strip-search everyone! Understand?" I set forth injunctions. Firu is a militant brother that carries out orders without excuses.

"Say no more, manito," Firu insured me, and then hung up.

I was still stuck in traffic under the Callahan Tunnel when I rang up Lady Roam, only to reach a disconnected cell phone. *Smart move, sis. Because if those alphabet boyz are raiding shit, nothing is safe.* Finally, out of flux, I dipped off the Mass Ave exit, and in less than five minutes, I winded up inside of the Cathedral Projects. Projekt and as well as his ruffians had been expecting me out front. I fleetly popped Fives with everyone, before turning toward Projekt and saying, "Peep game, my nigga." I then broke down everything that Firu disclosed.

"All of that is already known. Niggaz tried to finish your dog off too. Don Cuba's right-hand man Hitman came over here trying to cash in on a reward, but Porkchop was one-step ahead. I know that I'm speaking in riddles, so just follow me," Projekt stated. We thereafter headed via a project building.

In silence, steps were taken alongside of Shizauto, a towering and heavyset lightskinned black nigga trending a low cut with waves. He's one of Projekt's gunners. Manito just came home from Walpole State Prison for shooting a couple of niggaz in consequence of being disloyal. We went down a flight of basement stairs with soldiers shielding us. On went a dim light, exhibiting two masqueraded people tied up in chairs.

"Okay twin, behind door number one we have Hitman, Don Cuba's right-hand man. This bitch-ass nigga told me that Don Cuba sent him and Fat Cheese to murder us both. Since you never showed up at King Author's, their hitsquad wild out!" Projekt blasted, and then began laughing, as he took off the pillowcase.

"Oh yeah, nigga!" I whipped out my black .357 snub-nose that I named Rhino and then shot Hitman in his face three times. Pieces of beef flew out an empty pate. "Now who's this?" I asked.

"Remember when your brother told you that closure to a book was nearing? Well, I set a ten-thousand-dollar reward all over Boston for UK's most wanted. Dead man over here tried to use ratboy to do us in," Projekt asseverated, as he exposed Teddy Bear.

Teddy Bear's disconcerting eyes called for a Kodak moment. I bet his short and roly-poly, whitish Ecuadorian ass never seen this coming.

The man's baby afro had been drenched in sweat. This Mickey Mouse nigga had to be shitting on himself. Death was certain and he knew it.

Rhino dropped into a deep pocket as out came a hunting knife. While fitting on a pair of black leather gloves, Teddy Bear heard the order to stick out his tongue. Ratboy refused, so Projekt then shot him in each leg. "Fuck! Fuck!" Teddy Bear squalled in pain. "I wasn't going to testify at trial! I had to do it! I got caught in Springfield transporting two birds! They forced it through prosecution to wear a wire! You see how the government continued your trial date three times because I rejected to testify! Don't kill me! Hitman's people have my mother at gunpoint! They're going to assassinate her!" Teddy Bear was codging and crying to be spared like a little bitch.

"Shut the fuck up, nigga!" Shizauto loudly said, ahead of punching him in the face two times.

"Fuck your mother! Give me that shit, before your face ends up on the wall too! Now!" I commanded, having the urge to torture him.

"Okay, okay," he gave in. Gripping it, as sharp teeth amputated a gooey tongue had been revengeful.

I turned to Projekt, who was laughing as always, and enjoined, "Set these bitch niggaz on fire!"

Projekt took hold of a lighter fluid can and began soaking Hitman and Teddy Bear till no more came spattering out. A Bic lighter flicked and *POOF!* We stalled, watching them burn. That's when I seen Pito laid out on his face in a pool of blood. What's known needs not to be discussed. Exchanges carried over to our next move—Don Cuba and the UNLV Rebels. Once an agreement had been reached, I made plain apropos to falling back and my intensions to plug Projekt in with the Asians.

"Damn bro, that Asian pussy is good, huh?" Projekt clowned, as the brothers exploded into laughter. "But it's all love, you're my dog. So whatever is fixed upon is respected," Projekt said some real shit.

"I'll still be around. Big Mizery isn't going anywhere. I'm just going to be on my legal shit now. Ya-dig?" I shot back, all the while smelling the strong odor of crackling, burning skin. "Let's be out, these niggaz are literally cooked food," were one's last words, before exiting the basement.

At ten p.m. on the dot, Boss One walked into a grieving hotel room. I broke the silence by setting forth direct orders, "From today on, all Roaches are to die on sight! I do not care if you see one of them with their mothers or kids! They must stop living! If it comes to light otherwise, one might as well pick out your own casket!" That is all that I invoked and left.

That same night, war with our nemesis surceased. Blackrob, Mexicano, and K-Rock went to flame up a Roach block in East Boston. Hammered-up behind tints is how they crept down Lexington Street in Mexicano's red Escalade truck. Grey bandannas rested on different body parts of nine individuals standing in front of a pink house. Bloodychino's black Blazer truck moved stealthily up Lexington Street conveying four-Five-six, Shine, Rizzo, Klover, and Dago. All at once, the brothers hopped out of their vehicles slaughterously.

four-Five-six shot Trigger, a short Cambodian kid, leaving a 10-gauge hole right through his stomach that splattered the unlucky individual's insides against a car door. Dago caught Gio, a slim El Salvadorian nigga trying to hop a fence, by ringing four .25 caliber bullets into an assailable back. As he was falling, Mexicano hit'em up with three rapid shots from a Keltic nine millimeter pistol. Blackrob squeezed off an Uzi, riddling two ill-fated Vietnamese motherfuckers. When said gunfire cutoff, both dead bodies continued shaking from the impact. Klover ran up on Eko, a slender white boy and aired him out with a five-shot nine revolver. The back of Eko's head exploded as the short dude dropped. A stocky Cambodian guy shot Mexicano's thigh, but K-Rock sent seven whizzing bullets from a .22 Ruger, which touched an ear, hand, and temple. Shine ran inside of the pink house, while racking-back a 12-gauge, as Rizzo trailed pumping the same type of shotty. *KLABOOM! KLABOOM! KLABOOM! KLABOOM! KLABOOM! KLABOOM! KLABOOM! KLABOOM!* Bloodychino gunned at three UNLV Rebels with a .380 automatic handgun. Luckily, they made it over a fence. I think that one of them got hit, but the chink just kept it moving. It didn't matter anyways, because today was the end of their existence.

CHAPTER 19

MY ANGELS
DON CUBA

For the past five months, ever since Mizery has been home, business has gotten slow. My right-hand man Hitman is still missing. A strong intuition says that Mizery is to blame. He must die painfully. It is thought after thought lately on how to stop this man. Even now, while lying in wait for a plane to land at Logan Airport in East Boston. I am anticipating the Angels' spirits, five female assassins: Diamond, Remy, Sulie, Negra, and Booty. All Cuban dimes.

Diamond is 5'8", has long brown hair, caramel complexion, green eyes, and always nurturing a healthy body. She is the queen lioness, which an old man chose to be the organizer and contact for the Angels before he dropped dead. Diamond was his favorite, because of her abilities to unfailingly be the first Angel to master each skill that made an assassin. A sister worthy of giving one's life for.

Remy's light skin color gives off a white girl appearance. She is 5'10", thickboned, has green eyes, and long blonde hair. An innocent-looking manipulator people easily trust. The girl can sell water to a whale, someone you would not suspect as being a triggerperson, until staring death in its face.

Negra is rapper-Lil' Kim's spitting image. She frames at 5'6" with thick-grooving long blonde hair. La mujer officially stands in as a human chameleon that could turn into whoever in less than twenty-four hours.

For instance, one time, Negra became a nun at a Catholic church with intensions to terminate their target, a priest accused of molesting Fidel Castro's nephew. It took fourteen days to poison this scumbag by means of some magic potion. Then the lady had to stick around for a few more weeks, in order not to bring attention to the well-formed, dark-skinned nun disappearing.

Loud mouth Sulie is the baby, one of Satan's worshippers, a girl infatuated with death and chopping people up. She says that it disrespects their souls, plus it shows ruthlessness, which makes people fear them. This little cutie stands at 5'5", is petite, has short dark hair, Egyptian skin color, and hazel eyes. The live wire!

Booty has the illest ass out of all of them. Mami's height is maybe 5'6", has a shapely figure, full lips, long dark hair, mocha skin color, slanted eyes, and allegorizes an inviting mental outlook. I forever wanted to fuck that beauteous woman and still do. Booty is smart and quiet, in addition to being very detecting. When something does not feel right, her opinion holds as a final ruling. Time after time the accuracy has proven itself, giving it an undefeated record.

The Angels harmonized in our world at a very young age, actually, between the ages of thirteen and sixteen-years-old. In fact, we were all teenagers. I am only two years older than Diamond, a middle child. Born in Santiago, Cuba is proudly stamped on my neck in a tatted flag. One day, our neighbor Viejo offered the girls a great deal of money to clean up an extensive house. As these young females performed their duties, Viejo took a liking to them. Then he felt comfortable enough to open up regarding the life as an assassin. They were immediately intrigued. Viejo was too old to be active as a hired gunman, but that didn't stop him from training five youngsters that got named the Angels.

"That's how people get killed, sleeping," Diamond's Cuban accent could be heard approaching from the rear. I gave all a hug and a kiss on their cheeks, but when it came to Booty, I kissed her on the lips.

"When are you going to be my wifey?" I proposed to Booty.

"Whenever you get rid of that bum-ass Dominican bitch," Booty replied.

"I'm looking for a reason to kill that bitch!" Sulie cut in.

On the joyride to my house, they were put on to all of what had happened in the last five months. I haven't told Maliya about the Angels coming to visit for a few weeks, because she is terror-stricken of them and knows that the girls are assassins who have no problem stretching someone inside of a wooden box. I'm expecting Maliya to wild out. I can hear her now. But to be honest, I can give two fucks on how Maliya feels. The bitch is probably sucking Mizery's dick, together with telling him many things in significance to me.

"So Maliya is Mizery's baby-momma?" Remy roasted me.

"Cuba? Get your mind right. How can you trust her?" Negra advocated.

I had to shut this down. "Listen, Maliya is not the target! Mizery is!" I raised my voice, unnerving them into muteness. One thing that is for sure; the Angels glorify and obey me.

CHAPTER 20

STILL LOYAL
MALIYA

What the fuck are these Angel whores doing here! I screamed in one's mind. I know that their Don Cuba's assassins. He's up to something, as things go every time that they come around to murder people. My fiancé is feeling a certain way toward Mizery over money, but the seriousness of it remains obscure. Don Cuba never talks to me relative to his business.

Lately, Mizery has been spending a lot of time with Mizhai. It is indisputable concerning their love for one another. I regret turning my back on him. Mizery had been good to me. We went through ups and downs like any other relationship. The two of us never allowed anything to come between an authentic love affair. However, when the feds destroyed our world, I thought for sure that he would get smoked. Attorney Joseph Machera provided the Discovery package, which included a Pre-Plea Presentence Report that got prepared by a United States probation officer. These documents stated that Miguel Angel Rodriguez, Jr. was charged in a five-count indictment. His offense level displayed at thirty-four, carrying a guideline imprisonment range of 188 to 234 months. The government also threatened to file a 851 notice and to supercede the RICO Act under conspiracy to commit murder. Therefore, when Mizery used to send tons of letters, or talk on the phone or at visits about the chances of beating the case because of governmental misconduct and entrapment, I didn't believe him. I just thought that the man's positive outlooks were that of being hopeful.

I know that it's fucked up that I sold his house, motorcycle, and vehicles, but a bitch got to live! I love Mizery. I wish it were possible to turn back time, because I wouldn't even had thought about leaving him for dead. In fact, his much-loved girlfriend would have played the position of wifey. If Mizery even mentions that he wants one back, I'd pack up in a heartbeat. Picturing him eating another pussy drives me crazy. My sexy chubby nigga doesn't love this Dominican princess anymore, it's seeable. He's all about Mizhai. Mizery hates the fact that Mizhai calls Don Cuba Daddy. I fucked up—it's wrong. Nonetheless, the truth is that Don Cuba has been there for us ever since that Mizery had gotten locked up. There's admiration for Don Cuba, but I am not in love.

While pussyfooting past Don Cuba's astronomic home office, I heard Diamond grilling Don Cuba, asking if he knew where Mizhai's father lived, in the interest of wiping Mizery out at his apartment. In addition, one gleaned Booty saying how one of them could act as if they wanted to fuck Mizery, in order to rock him to sleep. I could not believe what I was hearing. The Angels were planning to knock off Mizery. This isn't what goes. My loyalty is to Mizery. Point blank! As I snuck away, silence fell. *Did I get caught eavesdropping?* Damn, I have to call Mizery.

"Yo? What's up, Maliya?" Mizery sounded high as he acknowledged me.

"Miz! Mizery! Don Cuba is planning to murder you! I just heard him—"

I opened uneasy eyes to feel pain fluttering in the back of my head. I also found myself facedown, hog-tied on Mizhai's bed. "Oh, shit! What the fuck is going on?" I started yelling. "Baby, baby, where are you?"

"Shut the fuck up, bitch!" Sulie tongued. "I have been dying for a reason to put your life to an end."

"Baby, baby, are you going to let me die?" I raised, while all along praying that Mizery would come and save us.

"You fucked up, my love," Don Cuba muttered. "I cannot forgive disloyalty. Vaya con Dios!"

That's when I felt Diamond cutting the ropes. When I turned around, Booty and Negra were pointing two handguns at me. Don Cuba shook his head in abomination, as he ambled out of the room.

"My son! Mizhai! Where is he?" I burst into tears, after screaking out.

Remy grabbed a fistful of hair, and under protest, thrusted me Indian style—knees bent, hands together. "Don't worry, bitch. Both of you will be buried as a pair!" Diamond gave her word of honor, as she jabbed a knife to the side of one's face. It sliced down; ripping skin. Negra bashed an absented-minded mouth with a hammer, instantaneously breaking off a few teeth from bloody gums. By then, a dizzy feeling took over, until a bullet sent at the hands of Negra crashed through my skin, bones, and a lung. And subsequently, another one entered a vincible stomach area.

As my life faded away, Booty bellowed, "Stop fucking around and get the little rug rat!" Through one's blurry vision, I witnessed Remy slam Mizhai's babyish body on top of the dresser. Thereafter, Sulie went ahead with chopping up itty-bitty mortal parts by means of an axe. Mizhai was decollated and his head rolled off the dresser. He never cried!

CHAPTER 21

I LOVE YOU, MIZHAI
MIZERY

"**H**ere, my nigga," I verbalized, while holding in the marijuana smoke. I then passed Projekt a blunt of AK-47. "Maliya just called, talking about Don Cuba is planning on murdering me. Then the call disconnected," was this villain's unruffled voicing, in back of exhaling that fire.

"Fuck that bitch. She's sleeping with the enemy," Projekt said. My nigga was right, fuck that bitch. I'll be damn if I let a ho get me killed.

Then and there, my cell phone vibrated again. "What's good, Maliya? Why did you hang up?" I answered.

"Listen, you Twinkie-ass nigga! This is Don Cuba, you know, a dog ready for war! Go to the Admiral's Hill docks right now! And you might get your bitch and son back!" he yelled, in front of the call ending.

The Admiral's Hill marina harbors personal and business-owned boats. It also has a restaurant above a fishing store, an extravagant field with a kid's playground, picnic tables, and a gazebo with a few slabs of concrete used for resting. Anyone can walk over a short steel bridge connected to a wooden dock, which is located above river water, where many people visit at night in company of their significant other, in order to enjoy the illuminating fluorescent view coming from our nativeland's Tobin Bridge.

I grabbed Rhino; jumped inside of Projekt's GT Bentley; and burned rubber to ChelRok. Upon parking near said gazebo, with viperous intensions for a dead man walking, I vehemently sat in the car for like twenty minutes before Don Cuba called. "Walk to the wooden docks!" he exacted. I dogged it, burner and cell phone in hand. When I looked up at the Tobin Bridge, I heard, "You see this?" Don Cuba could be seen carrying an unclear object on his shoulder. "Kiss your bitch goodbye!" a piping utterance had been perceived, as a garbage bag came into view and got slung over the Tobin Bridge. When it slammed onto the water, Don Cuba's voice resurrected, "You see this?" Now I saw him with a smaller garbage bag. I knew that it couldn't be anyone but my son.

"Don't do it, nigga! I'll find you in hell!" I vociferated, not believing the situation.

"Don't worry, killer. He's already dead," were the last words that I heard. In slow motion, my son's being came to an end as he splashed back to his original mind—the Ruler of Heaven.

Five shots banged off in the direction of Don Cuba. When Rhino's hammer clicked on an empty cylinder, it was thrown out of anger, which landed in the water. I fell onto my knees and vowed to avenge his death. "I love you, Mizhai!" I roared.

It was three a.m. when I woke up dripping in sweat. I had been dreaming about Mizhai and Maliya, visualizing Mizhai and I playing catch with a tennis ball at Admiral's Hill, and as well as Maliya rocking on a swing smiling. Then my dream switched over to some porno shit with Maliya and I on the beautiful sands of Clearwater Beach in Florida. It felt real. I peeked over at Laya, who had been sleeping like baby, and that's when it mentally hit. I could get at Don Cuba through Laya. She told me how he be trying to spit game. So you already know, I texted this nigga acting like Laya.

Outgoing Text: 857-558-3090

I am having one of those nights.

It took ten minutes before Don Cuba responded. Stupid-ass nigga doesn't even know that I'm connected to Laya, so he isn't going to be leery:

Incoming Text: 857-558-3090

Do you need some company? I would love to join u.

I quickly texted back while laughing to myself. This clown does not even know that his life is about to end:

Outgoing Text: 857-558-3090

I live on Franklin Ave at the Soldier's Home Apartments in Chelsea. Make sure that you park in the small parking lot. I will see you through my window.

I erased all of the incoming and outgoing text messages from Laya's cell phone. That shit was gay kicking game to another nigga. But the plan worked. This UK Gangsta is about to blow holes through him. All I've been thinking of is Mizhai. I am not going to lie; I'm going to body this faggot for Maliya too. I got blacked out, handgripping my twin .45 calibers that I just copped from Han. Thenafter, I crept out of Laya's apartment, so Sleeping Beauty wouldn't hear me. She can serve as an official alibi if needed.

I parked Laya's Nissan Maxima down on Orange Street, a few blocks from the address that I gave Don Cuba. Champion hoodie coned up, black flag raised over my face, cannons locked and loaded—I'm off. Don Cuba sat in a silver Jaguar with pussy on the sucker's mind. I went straight to the driver's side. *BOOM! BOOM! BOOM!* Three rapid shots left the Jaguar's windshield and steering wheel bloody. Glass shattered everywhere. I opened the car door and put three more bullets into an attackable body. I thenceforward dragged him into the middle of the street in order to blow holes in his face as promised. I thereafter walked away without a care in the world.

In a black Armani suit, styling a gold tie, surrounded by loved ones, is how Maliya and Mizhai's funeral took place. It ended up to be the saddest day of my life. We did not have a wake; moreover, a closed-casket funeral was the only option, seeing that both Maliya and Mizhai were hacked to pieces. One's eyes had been bloodshot-red all day. Maliya's family appeared—her mother, grandmother, sisters, brothers, and cool-ass stepfather. The feds also showed up, disrespecting outside of the cemetery by taking pictures. Some of the manitos and manitas dropped in out of respect. Projekt made the scene being escorted by newfound Magik Entertainment ho'z. Even JB and Han's presence were felt.

Amandria and Angel even turned up. Amandria pulled me to the side to say, "We need to speak. Not about us, genuinely it is more important. But right now isn't a proper time. I want you to know that I am here for you no matter what. Remember, I am your best friend for life." Amandria set right sincerely.

"I miss you, Mizery," Angel denoted sadly.

An assurance to visit soon came along with hugs and kisses. I miss Amandria, having feelings for two different women are confusing. *Was that Lady Roam that just passed me in concealment by way of a blond wig and glasses?* Lady Roam and Maliya were close so I wouldn't doubt it. She is Mizhai's godmother. Abuela and Titi Maggie surfaced. They couldn't believe what had happened. Laya stayed supportive, as both caskets were lowered into the ground.

Three months later, and Laya still hasn't mentioned anything concerning our plans, maybe not wanting to put pressure on me. Drama had ceased, those Roaches were exterminated and Don Cuba is a ghost. The businesses are up and running as projected. Actually, Diamond Kutz tookoff buzzing through the 617 area. Fats did some broadminded shit by traveling around Dorchester, Charlestown, Roxbury, East Boston, Revere, Jamaica Plain, Hyde Park, Everett, South End, Somerville,

Mattapan, and a few other cities to hire sought-after barbers that strung along their clients. Magik Entertainment hasn't reached the fifty-call-a-day purpose of action, but certainly on its way at thirty. Royal Rydes is a dud so far. We are losing money, rather than profiting.

Tsunami Rekordz is a billion-dollar record label in the making. I handpicked Raffito, a tall and slender, white-colored Boricua to produce quality music. Dude is a beast creating beats, engineering, and promoting. Plus him and Joshua, another tall and slender, white-colored Boricua have their own reggaeton squad called *Lyrikote*. Gambino's face reps Tsunami Rekordz on a hip-hop level. Moreover, this dog, you already know, CEO status. I contacted Mr. Serrano and asked him to find me another abandoned building to reconstruct. He tracked down a three-family house on Revere Beach Parkway in Chelsea, which looked as if got hit in 911. Mr. Serrano angled for seventy thousand dollars. The eager beaver must be insane. That shit was probably a giveaway to anyone stupid enough to own it. I worked his hustling-ass down to thirty thousand dollars. Projekt did not want any parts. This only meant that it would take your boy a little longer to accomplish.

Bolo charged me sixty thousand dollars on paper and sixty more in cash. He explained how this job may take anywhere between four to six months, maybe even longer, depending if his crew came across unplanned situations. All three decks will serve a purpose. The company's black marble floor shall consist of our TR logos throughout. The recording studio shall be divided in half, separated by a soundproof window. An engineering room containing ultramodern equipment stands tough just like Def Jam, Shady Records, Young Money, Diplomats, and other professional record labels. We will be contenders, and we'll also be dropping multimillion-dollar hits. Directly across, a heavyweight booth awaits lyrical punishment. Above the studio, a promotional department has been mentally established to print official CDs, CD covers, promotional posters, business cards, flyers, order forms, plus anything else thought-of. Not just for our artists either, for any record label willing to pay. I see dollar signs written all over that. On the top floor, ideas for producing music videos are being considered.

Projekt and I doubled up on bricks. We were now grabbing twelve kilos a week, six apiece. Our UK family has been growing in numbers and now spreading into other cities. Life seemed perfect, too perfect. Projekt got this Cuban girl named Diamond by his side at all times. Let me find out that shorty is licking that nigga's ass. She a bad bitch. I remember taking notice of her at Maliya and Mizhai's funeral and thinking, *Yup, another new recruit for Magik Entertainment.* Diamond is cool though. I'm crushing mami's girl Remy, but really fiend for Sulie.

I was at Abuela's house enjoying a family day with Titi Maggie, Tio Felix, and Cousins Daniel and Steven. Daniel and Steven are Puerto Rican and Cuban, have white skin color, stand at about 5'7", rock short hairdos, and are chunky and complete opposites. Daniel is the older of the two. He is street-orientated. My primo turned an ensured football career into an unpromising life. While Steven on the other hand is a conservative type of person. He's a bit skittish, but has his mind set on becoming a movie director.

Cousins Christina, Patrisha, Alexander, Adriana, Xavier, Victor, Joel, BD, Fat Joshua, Boo Boo, and Nelly have not showed up yet. Christina and Patrisha are short and squat, longhaired, light-colored, and are exceptionally nice-looking young ladies. Their father Uncle Eli will not be coming through today because he's doing a fed bid for money fraud. Though he used to be an East Boston Police detective, I've always respected the man. Tio Eli is 5'6", husky, has a baldhead, and a tan complexion.

Alexander, Adriana, and Xavier are brothers and sister. Alexander is light-brown-skinned, skinny, average-height, and sports a low haircut. He is a music producer. Adriana turned out to be a graceful young woman with lengthy dark hair accompanying a healthy body. She stands at 5'6", is whitish, and looks like her mother. She's an intellectual college undergraduate, who is determined to succeed in life. Xavier is 5'7", white-colored, hulking, and has short dark hair. Xavier is attending medical school to become a doctor.

Victor and Joel are two white-skinned brothers with short haircuts. I used to look up to them when I was between ten-and-eleven-years-old. They showed me how to dress and get fresh for the girls at school. Victor is a health freak that lives at the Chelsea YMCA. He's about 5'7", is firm and stable in shape, and loves to party like a rock star. Joel is completely different. He's 5'7", round and plump, and chose the family life.

Fat Joshua and BD are brothers that are UK Gangstaz as well. However, the two are doing the family thing. They have decided to fall back and enjoy a righteous living. But don't get it twisted, if needed, my cousins have no problem turning up. Fat Joshua has to be six feet tall, is light-skinned, three hundred pounds, rocks a bald fade, and works as a cable man for Comcast. BD is about six feet tall, light-skinned, lean, maintains a clean cut, and is also a cable man for Comcast.

Boo Boo is not really a blood cousin, but is treated and loved as one. Titi Maggie adopted the little nigga, because his mother, Serayda, Titi Maggie's friend, got addicted to crack cocaine by getting mixed up in the wrong crowd. Boo Boo is a handsome young high school kid, who is around 5'6", Puerto Rican, yellow-skinned, slinky, has short dark hair, and exploits a mature outlook.

Nelly has always been my favorite cousin. She used to hook me up with older women when I was barely a teen. In fact, cuzzo showed me how to drive a standard car. But when I got locked up in DYS, her and her son Angel moved away to Virginia. I guess Down South did not work out, because the apple in one's eye returned. Nelly is medium-height, light-skinned, has short dark hair, and vaunts a thick body.

My brother Danny and sister Priscilla will not be attending either. They're still in the marines doing their military thing. I really miss them. Danny is the middle child. The both of us grew up as close brothers, although we stayed fighting like two pitbulls over a piece of steak. Danny will perpetually be a UK Gangsta, in spite of the fact that he had to change course for reasons only his big bro knows. He's at least 5'8", is slightly built, white-skinned, and now rocking a marine buzz cut.

Priscilla is the baby. I missed out on her upbringing due to me constantly being incarcerated. When Mami passed away, Danny and her moved in with Titi Maggie. Priscilla was a studious student that earned excellent grades. She focused on a positive future and never allowed herself to fall victim to the streets. Moreover, little sis decided to join the Unites States Marine Corps. Priscilla is 5'6", white-skinned, in shape, and has a buzz cut as well that gives off a boyish appearance.

Abuela also had some church friends over. Grandma cooked arroz con gandules, pernil de cerdo, y pasteles. On top of all this, she hooked up some bangin'-ass potato salad. Lastly, for desert came arroz con dulce. I ate two pieces, and as a matter-of-fact, I was thinking about a third one when Abuela handed over four missives from Bless at Wyatt Detention Facility in Rhode Island, Baby Wise at Walpole State Prison in Massachusetts, Hyper at Shirley Max in Massachusetts, and Pistol at USP McCreary in Kentucky. I decided to read them:

Lu$ipher,   All Dogz Ryde

What's da deal, bro? I go to trial in 90 days and my lawyer is asking for more money. Can you holla at the nigga? I been hearing krazy shit!! Yall need to be eazy. These fuzz niggaz offered to dismiss the whole indictment if I cooperate. Niggaz is krazy!! They wanna bring down the UK Hitsquad. Especially you-n-Projekt. Do the math, manito. Somebody is gonna get wired up. Krack, Rattle, Ace, JK, and the rest of the Blood homeys send their People Love. Get at me!

"Bless"
Take★One

For a while, I was upset with Bless for introducing me to Teddy Bear. Obviously, he didn't know that ratboy had the team under the FBI's scope. Actually, manito warned us all of his gut feeling that Teddy Bear's movements were shaky. But the brother is good now, the government no longer has a star witness. So eventually, we'll be popping bottles together. My dog Bless is an official gunclapper. He's Puerto Rican and Jamaican, slim, baldheaded, is 6'1", has whitish skin color, and befits loyalty. I met the nigga years back while serving a twelve-month sentence at South Bay. Right now though, during the bro's little stay at Wyatt, homey pulled a Caucasian nurse and a Dominican CO. I get up with both of those broads once every other week in order to swing manito whatever hankered for.

What's Good, Big Homey,   Loyalty

One... I got word that one of those insects that got at Dready is on the way up here. You already know that we are on that. Shit up here is all love-love. That nigga Pretty Tony is stuck in 10-Block on PC status. He's a coward! Send my love to Projekt. Tell him that the fam appreciates the $5,000 that was spread around. Squeeze and Heavy want to talk to you about opening up a youth center. The two of them said that they're going to call you next week. Until yours.

BANG☆BANG
Baby Wise

As for Baby Wise, we encountered each other in the hole at Norfolk State Prison in 2006, during a short-lived stopover on 52a status, before I got sentenced to a six-month probation violation to be served at Billerica House of Corrections. I fuck with the nigga because he's a goony. Manito is my height or maybe a bit taller. He is Puerto Rican, tanskinned, fit, and keeps a clean cut and a taper with a hairless face.

My Beloved Brother,   1/10/13

Good look on the three stacks that you put in everybody's account up here. We all send our gratitude to an official bro. I'm sending you a kite, so you can three-way it to Baby Wise. Do me a favor and try to bring my sister up next week for a visit? Her car got fucked up. As always......

A TRUE LION
Hyper

My dude Hyper got G-Fived at Cambridge Jail by Bling and I, ahead of the deadly shooting that ended Bling's life on Cottage Street. Hyper's life sentence came about from a shootout with some Dominican cats inside of a smallish club in Lynn called *Casa De Sol*. A mistaken bump led to shots being fired in both directions, which resulted in two men dead from gunshot wounds to the skull. Hyper's bulky-ass flosses a low haircut with a bald fade. He is 5'8", white-skinned, and one hundred percent Puerto Rican.

Mizery,   !!2 Gunz Up!!

Okay!! That's what I like to hear!! Bloodshed nigga! Fuck those bitch made Roach niggaz! What's the word, big homey? I'm up here getting swollen. I am waiting on my appeal, in order to hopefully get this 25 down to 15. Shit is looking good. Villain sends his love. That little nigga is big as shit. We're on some militant shit up here. Here is a picture of all of the brothers in the yard. What's up with Lady Roam? I heard! Send pics? Send me your new number too. You be changing numbers like every week. Good look on the $$$$$. Holla back at your boy.

PISTOL
a.k.a.
FBI KILLA

Crazy-ass Pistol is cut from the same cloth as me. I was ninety days to the door from executing another South Bay bid, when I received a kite from Chi-Chi about Pistol clapping up Agent Deraney at the Puerto Rican Festival in Crack City. This nigga went to trial, as if a jury would actually disregard testimony from over ten police officers that witnessed the shooting. But he's a dog for that. One can only respect a convict who brings the oppressors to war. Nevertheless, he got smoked. My twin is nearly 6'3", big-boned, light-brown-skinned, Puerto Rican, has long-ass braids, and is def about that life.

After reading these scribes, I unhesitantly responded. I dropped a few lines keeping them in the loop and enclosed some photos. A nigga knows how it feels to be locked up. The littlest things mean everything. Projekt and I are going to put up the bread for Bless' attorney. We are also going to purchase a vehicle for Hyper's sister.

Tio Felix signaled me over toward the backyard. "Son, you guys are flaming! Don't think that the feds ain't building another case or surely I have raised a dummy. Those motherfuckers hate to lose. Why are you still playing with fire? You have legal businesses, a beautiful girlfriend that is wifey material, and a great deal of money put away. What else do you want? Facing another life bid would be mania," he spoke in an ail manner.

"I'm hip, Tio. The wheel is already in motion," I simply responded.

"I hope so, son. Well, send my undying love and loyalty to our family," he said, and then popped the Fives with me.

CHAPTER 22

OPERATION ROYAL RUIN II
AGENT MICHAEL SIELANDER

"**G**ood afternoon, gentlemen. Today is formally the opening of Operation Royal Ruin II. Keep in mind that things turned out badly on our first attempt. This investigation will once again target the Unknowns. Two cooperating witnesses referred to as Eko and Bravo are under government agreements, in order to escape prosecution for drug-related charges stemming from two separate police stings. For their assistance, complaints have not been filed. The paid informants came to be as follows.

"Massachusetts State Police pulled over Eko in East Boston, after executing a control buy through an undercover state trooper that purchased three twenty-dollar crack rocks from him. Trooper Mgeary telephoned Eko pretending to be a friend to a Lisa, a known drug addict and customer of Eko. Directly after their momentary debate, Trooper Mgeary convinced Eko that he was not law enforcement. They agreed to meet at a Mobil gas station on Meridian Street. During a search of Eko's motor vehicle, a 12-gauge sawed-off shotgun, together with thirty-eight packaged bags of crack cocaine, ready for distribution, were seized by the troopers. At the interrogation, which was conducted at the Massachusetts State Police Barracks on Revere Beach, Eko volunteered to become an informant," I reported all of this, while shuffling through some paperwork.

"Bravo had been caught in the net by a known drug abuser and prostitute. A Boston Police detective was approached by a Krissy Harris flagging down his unmarked Crown Vic in an attempt to entice the detective into paying a fee for a blowjob. Detective Sanchez identified himself as a Boston Police detective, and in a jiffy, Krissy Harris begged Detective Sanchez not to arrest her. She suggested informing on a well-known drug supplier for crack, which ended up to be Bravo. Detective Sanchez showed a photo array to Krissy Harris, who pinpointed Bravo without hesitation as the source. Because Bravo popped up in our computer system as a person of interest to the FBI, Detective Sanchez contacted Agents Slater and Lazar.

"Krissy Harris, on a consensual recorded phone call, arranged to make a controlled buy, in exchange of eight twenty-dollar crack rocks for one hundred and sixty dollars in US currency. The aforementioned drug transaction took place at the New York Pizza shop on the corner of Mass Avenue and Tremont Street in the South End. Once the drug transaction got executed, agents rushed inside of the pizza shop to arrest Bravo. On Bravo's person, a loaded black .32 revolver and as well as forty-four grams of heroin were recovered. At the Boston Police Headquarters in Roxbury, upstairs in the FBI division, Bravo waived his rights and requested to speak with agents," I took a breather and then passed around the two reports.

"Fat Cheese is a witness that will be testifying regarding several murders to an ongoing feud between the UNLV Rebels and the Unknowns. His proffers implicate Intel relative to our two targets referred to as Boss One, a leadership role for their respective groups. Mizery and Projekt are alleged to be provided with twenty to thirty kilos on a weekly basis. Their source of supply is unidentified at this time. Because of Fat Cheese's credible mutual effort, he has been sentenced to fifteen to life in the Massachusetts Department of Corrections," I finally finished debriefing Special Agents Lazar, Deraney, Conney, and Slater.

Agent Deraney is a tall and flabby white American man with short black hair. He got promoted from a Chelsea Police detective to a federal agent for his victories against gang violence. He's been the leading detective in several operations, which has lowered the crime rate in Chelsea since the late 90's. Agent Deraney received a heroism award for surviving the catastrophe with the notorious gang member Pistol.

Agent Deraney's best friend and partner Agent Conney did not lag far behind. He was also upgraded from a Chelsea Police detective to a federal agent, due to remarkable undercover drug stings that wreaked havoc on the Columbian cartels in the Suffolk County. Agent Conney is a tall and well-built white American man with short blonde hair that always seems to have a chip on his shoulder.

Agent Lazar came from the Alexandria, Louisiana FBI division as someone who specializes in communication. It is said that his interrogation skills is rated above excellence. The man is a tall and slinky white American man with an untanned baby face and black hair.

The guy's partner Agent Slater tagged along in hopes to assist us in our investigation with his stalwart ways to fight the world's war on drugs. Despite that, one would underestimate the agent's toughness, because of his small thin frame, baldhead, and white American innocuous-looking mug. Even so, we were warned to keep him on a short leash.

"Do the two cooperating witnesses know of each other's position in this investigation?" Agent Slater questioned.

"Good question. No. This way it prevents any type of leakage between these informants," I answered.

"Do you think that Eko and Bravo are in a position where they can buy a large quantity of drugs directly from our targets without raising any suspicion?" Agent Deraney inquired.

"Eko and Bravo are members from certain neighborhoods in Chelsea and Boston. The Unknowns have a pecking order for their drug trafficking. In Chelsea, Mizery has four drug suppliers acknowledged as the Four Horsemen. Gladiator is in control of Hawthorne Street. He originally organized Grove Street for Gambino. I suspect him as a shooter, if not an organizer to all of these unsolved shootings and murders. According to Eko, Gladiator is purchasing seven hundred and fifty grams of cocaine directly from Mizery every few days.

"Wolf runs a tight ship on Chestnut Street. He is another noted triggerman. Recently, this man completed a ten-year state sentence for a masked armed robbery conviction. He's skating on thin ice, trying to avoid violating a probation matter that is dangling a ten-year suspended state sentence. Eko has informed us that Wolf purchases two hundred and fifty grams of cocaine on a weekly basis.

"Following Dready's murder at King Author's, Mizery selected Chino★Scarface as Cottage Street's Horseman, who sharp-wittedly minimized unnecessary traffic. Two crackhouses generating thousands of dollars daily have been under surveillance for quite some time now. Eko is not sure how much cocaine Chino★Scarface is buying, but in his opined statement, he believes it to be a kilo once a week. Take a long look at a recent photo of this guy that we just added to the file. He's the slim and white-skinned, Puerto Rican punk with braids. The one standing in front of Grove Park, baring a scar on his face. My guess says that the man is about 5'8".

"Gambino is a cub that is still learning how to walk. At eighteen-years-old, he is leading his own pack on Grove Street. Eko is certain that the young fellow markets five hundred grams of cocaine weekly. Gambino actually resides on Thorndike Street in Revere with the adolescent's girlfriend and son.

"Projekt's Lynchmen are 357 and JP, two young Dominican kids with a history of firearm charges. 357 is originally from Mozart Park in Jamaica Plain and JP represents Morton Street Projects in Mattapan. Both men are given one kilo each to split every four days. JP and 357 have been mentioned as participants to a double homicide on Blue Hill Ave in Dorchester, where two members of the DDP gang, Dominicans Don't Play, were shot execution-style in broad daylight. Photographs of the two have been taken by our surveillance teams and have been added to the file. 357 is the skinny and short guy sitting on the motorcycle with the light-brown complexion. His braids are hidden in the hat. JP's height is figured to be 5'9". You cannot see the teen's shoulder-length braids due to the hooded sweatshirt, but he's the trim and tan-skinned kid holding the liquor bottle. Three eyewitnesses identified these individuals in a photo array as the shooters, but then refused to testify in front of a Grand Jury. The attestant's claimed that they were afraid of retaliation by this vicious gang and would not put their family in harm's way. These attesters were so scared, that the trio went ahead and hired private attorneys to present sworn affidavits to the Federal Bureau of Investigations stating that the pressure by authorities led them to identify the wrong suspects. Furthermore, the Cathedral Projects highly respect their hierarchy," I explained, knowing the next question that was coming.

"So how are we going to have our informants jump this criminal enterprise's chain of command?" challenged Agent Conney.

"Well, that's why you are a special agent and get paid the big bucks!" I barked.

"Do you think that we can get either Mizery or Projekt to inform on one another? If possible, that can bring down the whole organization," Agent Conney put forth.

Agent Lazar quickly jumped in, "You can forget about that idea. Mizery and Projekt are true convicts that would rather die before being labeled a snitch. What if our CWs retrieve confessions from UK members relevant to unsolved crimes while being wired up with audio and video equipment?"

Agent Lazar's viewpoint had everyone nodding in agreement. "That is unquestionably going to be one of our approaches," I commented, all along scribbling down notes on my notebook, whilst ignoring a ringing cell phone.

"One of Eko and Bravo's objectives should be to find out who is Mizery and Projekt's drug supplier. Then we can set up a sting to catch all three big fishes with one hook," Agent Deraney brought forth.

"Okay gentlemen, sorry to cut this short! We have to move out! I just received information on Lady Roam's whereabouts! Let's go get her!" I commanded.

We surrounded 207 Woodrow Ave in Dorchester, an apartment rented to a Nessy Vega, Lady Roam's sister. It's three twenty-seven a.m. and all of the lights were out. Tactical teams secured both entrances and were awaiting orders to move in. Federal agents maintained a boundary while aiming their weapons at the front and back windows. A helicopter encircled the premises with its spotlight illuminating the entire scene. There was no way out.

As team one headed up the stairs, all that I could hear was a loud barking dog. *KLOP! KLOP! KLOP! ... KLOP! KLOP!* "Open the fucking door! FBI!" I shouted, and then caught wind of some footsteps running past. "Team two, move in!" I ordered through my portable radio.

As we crashed through the front door; a white and brown husky pitbull attacked us. Foaming from its mouth is how it had leaped. Agent Conney blew that dog to chunks with a double-barrel shotgun. Thereupon, someone fired five shots from a bedroom around the corner. One of those bullets hit Agent Conney in his throat. Two louder shots echoed at the back door, backing up team two. I dragged Agent Conney's body halfway outside of the doorway. Blood squirted out of a hole where an Adam's apple used to be.

"Come out with your hands up!" I exclaimed, checking on Agent Conney's pulse as he took one last breath.

A female voice responded, "Get the fuck out! I am not turning myself in! The only way that you are getting me out of here is in a body bag!"

"Lady Roam? Is there anybody else in the apartment? Like any children? We don't want to hurt—" Three more shots were sent my way. I couldn't see her, but every chance that she got, shots erupted down the hallway. Both teams subsequently entered, stopping short sideways at a bedroom door. "Lady Roam! You are closed in! Agents are ready to shoot to kill if you fire again! Put down the gun and come out with your hands up!" Agent Slater warned.

BANG! BANG! ... BANG! BANG! BANG! BANG! ... BANG! Lady Roam's gun blasted off again, but got rashly interrupted by MP5 machine guns. Over one hundred rounds zipped through the bedroom door, which fragmentized into chips of wood. Lady Roam was flat-out dead, riddled with bullets. A P220 Sig Sauer .45 caliber steamed within hands' reach. What I saw next totally shocked me. Her twelve-year-old son Cartier laid lifeless with his eyes open. Somehow or another, he still gripped a .38 revolver.

CHAPTER 23

FEEL MY PAIN
DIAMOND

I have been fucking Projekt for four months now. I got him sleeping like a baby. Last night, on Valentine's Day, we ate some well-prepared seafood at a five-star restaurant somewhere in Boston. A lobster tail, rice pilaf, and asparagus are what my plate consisted of. Projekt ordered seasoned Alaskan crab legs, steamed blue oysters, and baked salmon. He topped it all off with a big bottle of vintage Chardonnay. Projekt looked real smooth in his blue pinstriped tailored Versace suit. He's like 6'2", Puerto Rican, on the chubby side, flaunts long braids, has coffee skin color, and presents a sexy demeanor. This pretty princess, the next American Top Model, was wearing a custom-made fire-red Vera Wang dress. Our chats eventually came to a commitment in this phony relationship of ours. Anything to kill this fool.

Thereafter, a chauffeur escorted us outside to an awaiting horse and carriage. For hours, this twosome strolled through the beautiful streets of Boston. Projekt even lit up a blunt of Granddaddy Purp during our romantic ride. And just when I thought that the night was over, we dismounted at a Marriot Hotel. Upon entrance to an ostentatious hotel room, Mr. Philanderer stuck his tongue down one's throat. At that moment, I felt togetherness between our inner beings. On the other hand, maybe my dripping wet pussy had been flummoxed.

"Papi, tu quieres esto?" I seductively offered, ahead of guiding his hand underneath my dress so that he could feel a drenched thong.

"Eso es mió," Projekt claimed, intrepidly sliding his pudgy fingers inside of my kitty cat.

"Si papi, esto es tuyo. Ensáñame lo que tu quieres?" I welcomed him with a sexy response.

Project rested a thirsting woman on an enormous bed; furthermore, he began removing my clothing. The man on the make got on the way by licking and fingering a sloppy vagina. I couldn't help but to cum on his face. Projekt's freaky-ass kept going faster and faster. I was craving for some hard dick. Nonetheless, even with that, someway or another, I ended up straddling a calling mouth. The pussy eating began where it let off, until wetness imbued a quivering asshole. I slid down a lengthy body to unbuckle a Versace belt.

"Yo te voy a romper ese bicho a besos limpio," I tantalized him, and then stroked Projekt's thick dick while sucking it, as if it were a lollipop.

Projekt commended, and afterward grabbed the back of my head and guided me up and down his pole. "Así me gusta, mami," he voiced.

The way he said that made me go wild like a porno star. I spit on a beating bicho and then deep throated as much as achievable. His butt cheeks tightened up, indicating an explosion building up. I swallowed every drip of cum shooting out, never ceasing sucking a dwindling dick. Even when fast hands tried to nudge my head away, they were swatted down.

"Give it to me!" I energetically said, while getting into a doggie-style position.

"Do you want this dick?" Projekt posed, before smacking my ass really hard and inserting a semi boner inside of me.

"Ay papi, asi! Fuck me! Papi! Harder! Smack that!" were my sex commands, as I felt him nut again.

That nigga fucked me good last night. I think that I even told Projekt that I loved him. It's going to be a shame when we crucify Projekt and Mizery. They will feel my pain. Word on Don Cuba's soul. *Where are these hitches?* I have been waiting for over twenty minutes for them.

A tall and skinny white boy with a baby face came over for a second time and inquired, "Are you ready to order?"

"No. I am dallying around for some friends that are running a little late. But I'll have another Sex On The Beach? Please?" I nicely asked for.

As soon as the waiter walked away; these bitches walked inside. "What's good, girl?" Negra was all smiles, as she greeted me.

"Where have y'all been at?" I raved.

"Damn Diamond, you're acting like Boston traffic isn't serious. Plus, we have been on a parking hunt for almost ten minutes," Booty retaliated with an attitude.

"Listen, it's almost time to annihilate these clowns. First, we take care of Pork Fried Rice. There are two more assignments lined up following this one: California and New Mexico. These two berths could perhaps be our retirement money. The target in California is a mobster by the name of Fat Tony. This rat is testifying against the Montemarano brothers, mafia bosses awaiting trial for big indictments, which include racketeering, murder, extortion, and the list goes on. The pay is two million dollars if we're successful. But it's easier said than done. Fat Tony is under twenty-four-hour surveillance at a federal witness protection building. Does anyone have any ideas?" my question lingered, as I received a fresh drink.

"Yo tengo hambre. Excuse me; can I please place an order?" Sulie addressed the waiter.

"What would you like?" the young white boy offered his assistance.

"I'll have a turkey club sandwich with a small order of French fries and an orange juice," Sulie desired.

"Is anyone else ready to order their lunch?" the waiter asked.

"Yo tengo hambre también," the waiter stared at Booty confused at her obfuscated language.

"I would like fried brown rice with some steak tips?" Booty requested with a flirtatious smile.

"And what would you like to drink, beautiful?" this young white boy found the courage to say.

Booty simpered and rejoined, "A Sprite, no ice."

"Can you please bring me another Sex On The Beach?" I seeked, being on my third one. "Booty, cut it out. You are going to make that little boy cum in his pants," everyone broke out whooping at what I just said. I could tell that the waiter got embarrassed.

"Leave him alone. He's a cutie. Can you please bring me a chicken salad, along with the same drink that this drunken bitch is downing?" Remy put before the blushing waiter.

"I just want a Sex On The Beach too," Negra seeked.

"Back to our analysis," Booty whispered, as soon as the white boy walked away. "I have a bad vibe on this California swindle. It's too complicated and risky. I'm also getting negative notions concerning the mark out here," Booty opined.

"Booty? I'm just giving you hamponas a brief summary of what's coming next. As for the current game, there isn't anything or anybody that is going to stop me. I am my brother's keeper. Now moving on. In regards to the prey in New Mexico, she is the daughter to Honesto, someone that chose to be greedy and cannot repay his debt to El Chapo. A four-hundred-thousand-dollar opening. Our new friend is demanding that her head be gift wrapped in a box, specifically delivered on April 11, 2013. He's insisting on making a statement at their family reunion," I explained the New Mexico stint.

"I like our new friend already!" Sulie's crazy-ass volcanically voiced absentmindedly.

"I expected your devious reaction. That's why this one has you and Remy's name written all over it. But before lining up the next pawns, let's terminate these easy ones," I changed up my chalk talk, as that teenage boy returned to serve us.

The waiter handed Sulie a turkey club sandwich surrounded by crispy French fries. He also gave the devil's advocate an orange juice. Booty's plate and drink was passed to her as well. The white boy sneered at Negra, while engrossed in placing a drink at hands' reach. Lastly, Remy accepted a chicken salad, together with the requested drink.

Then our nice waiter set down ten Sex On The Beach drinks on the table and said, "This is for you beautiful ladies from me." He surprised us all before stepping off.

"I'm going to feel bad murdering Mizery. He has a fat dick and eats pussy like a professional. I call him the pussy monster," Remy had us all in stitches at her funniness.

Negra gushed, "Damn, so I can't get any of that dick?" We continued in amusement till I brought us back to reality.

"Remember, Mizery killed my brother!" I outcried, in case these bitches forgot.

"We know, Diamond. Don Cuba was a brother to us all as well. These motherfuckers are going to suffer. I promise," Sulie surefired, expressing evilness.

I miss my brother so much. I remember one late scary night at a young age; my stepfather woke me up carrying a strong odor of alcohol. A cold metal blade threatened this little girl to be butchered if she made a sound. Pajamas and panties slid off an immature body; thenceforth, a grown penis circulated around her underaged vagina, groping for a way in. Tears poured down an angel's face that felt the pain of skin ripping from violent thrusts. The torment was unbearable, as it would be to any normal twelve-year-old virgin.

Big brother swerved into the room to catch my stepfather raping me. Don Cuba wasted no time cracking him with a wooden baseball bat. The rapist fell unconscious while Don Cuba kept bashing various parts of his body. One could hear the sounds of a bat breaking bones after each swing. I have never seen so much blood. I even yelled for Don Cuba to stop. Not that I didn't wish the rapist death, but for the sake of big bro. We stood up for two whole days grinding flesh in a meat grinder and scrubbing blood off the floor. Nobody knows that this situation ever took place. It was our little secret. Everybody thought that he just up and left.

"Excuse me; do you know where I can find the Tobin Bridge?" I blurted out, catching this female's attention that was legging it to her car.

"Sure. Go straight down Broadway and take a right before the pawnshop," the woman responded, but never noticed Negra on stealth mode.

"Wake up, stinky chinky!" Sulie yelled, behind slapping Laya across the face.

"Where am I? What is going on? Why am I handcuffed?" Laya went spasmodic with ongoing queries.

"You are going to die! But first feel my pain!" I ejaculated, while shaking in anticipation for Sulie to behead this bitch.

"Please, I don't want to—" she tried to protest, but was shortstopped.

"Shut the fuck up!" Sulie shouted, as she did a transmogrification into Lucifer, ragingly mangling humanity and cartilage.

CHAPTER 24

MY LAST BREATH
MIZERY

"**W**hat's good, Mizery? It's Spooky," I heard him say, as I answered my cell phone.

"Manito? It's four-in-the-morning. Why are you calling so early?" I remarked, ready to hang up on this stupid nigga if it wasn't important.

"My fault, bro. I need some coke. But nobody is around. Two cousins of mine traversed from New Hampshire to snatch up four kilos," he put forth, sounding wide-awake.

"Damn Spooky, you know the rules!" I got up from my bed and walked into the bathroom to take a piss, following the ill-tempered response.

"Mizery, they are willing to pay thirty-five thousand dollars a kilogram!" Spooky beefed it up, knowing that I was not going to resist.

"All right, but come to my spot by yourself," one capitulated to his offer. Paperboy is about to come up on one hundred and forty thousand dollars. Yeah, it's going against our family rules, but, dollar signs!

When I first met Spooky's tall and stubby ass at the meeting, I thought that he was a white boy with braids, because of the colorless skin color. When the brother revealed his Boricua heritage, it surprised me. I like the young buck. One can only respect a paperchasing nigga.

I checked my cell phone to see if Laya texted—nothing. That's weird, because usually she hits me up right after work. Trophy must have been burned out. I'll surprise her at the computer store tomorrow. The stash had exactly four birdies left. Two were already DMX and the other two were still on whitegirl status. I'm not hearing shit, Spooky is grabbing all four. Nigga is already heretofore in violation for breaking our family's chain of command. Shit, I am too.

It took about twenty minutes for my brother to arrive. Spooky came inside of the crib, popped the Fives with me, and then asserted, "Here, count it. It's all there."

"I trust you, bro," I mumbled to him, as I flipped through crispy hundreds and fifties. "What, y'all just came from a bank?"

Spooky snorted, before saying, "Nah, my cousins be into a lot of monetary scams. You know, like money laundering."

"I dig it. Check the move—I have four thangz, two are straight yayo and the others are cooked-up. But not no crackhead surprise or oil or blown-up, it's decent though. Your boy was going to swing these two bricks of powder to my Charlestown white boy tomorrow so appreciate the solid. Keep it between us, okay? For you, here's two Gs," I let him know, as Boss One tried to pass him the money.

"My cousins will take whatever is given right about now. They have been looking to re-up for a week already. Their connect is dry for another two weeks. Moneymaking Rich and Slime Ball be caking it out there in New Hampshire by charging one hundred dollars a gram.

Good look on the dough, but I'm good. I get mine off-top," he rejected a commission, after explaining about his cousins' neediness.

Spooky denied paper? What the fuck? That shit is funny-money because one cannot see how he would profit at thirty-five thousand dollars a brick. *Should my .44 Bulldog gun this nigga down right now? Am I getting set up?* I'm trippin'. It's Spooky, a certified shotta, who let an eight-shot pump bomb on a state police cruiser in Lawrence out of a stolen Mazda RX7 that Rizzo was acting nasty in.

I woke up to Rocky and Terror growling at each other over Laya's oversized monkey, a stuffed animal, that by now, I'm sure was shredded. Cotton hurricaned my apartment. Big Mizery got up and punched the shit out of both of them. Last time that they fought, Rocky ripped Terror's ear a little bit, this resulted in him being taken to a veterinarian to be stitched up. Both of those niggaz are getting bulky.

Rocky is crazier than Terror. He tries to take a chunk out of anyone that comes around. It might be the coke. I remember cheffing up a K and letting Rocky and Terror lick like three and a half grams off a plate. Those whacked-out pits stagecrafted viciously by carnaging Laya's cat and two loose parakeets. The next time that chefmatik baked cakes in the lab; Rocky guarded me, expecting to get his shit off-top with hungry eyes locked on every piece of coke being shifted. Two crushed up grams were fed to a beast. This became a routine between cokehead Rocky and I.

Outgoing Text: Sexy Laya

Good morning. Call me.

I shot Laya a text and started boiling six eggs. Two slices of bread slid down into a cheap toaster and thenceforward I grabbed deli products out of a brand-new refrigerator. "Who is it?" I yelled, when I heard someone knocking.

"UPS! I have a package for a Miguel Rodriguez," a girly voice announced.

Sniggering came double-time while looking at this gay-ass deliveryman wearing an extra-tight uniform. I signed for the package, all along forgetting about Rocky and Terror. Those bigheaded monsters came blitzing. "Oh my God!" the UPS dude screamed, as he took flight.

Before they got a chance to devour something, my door slammed shut. Stair tumbling noises were heard in a distance. After propping the gift on top of an actual crystal table, a curious man's absorption fell on an attached orange card:

GUESS WHO?

I opened the box to begin unraveling layers of black plastic. When Laya's head came into view, I blanked out. It had been cut clean from her chin up. My love's middle finger flapped out of an unshut mouth. This is beyond disrespect. Hatred represented a message.

I met up with JB and Han to explain what had happened. An awkward talk concluded when JB turned to me with death in his eyes and threatened, "Today we're in peace, but tomorrow we'll shed blood."

I knew that some serious drama could possibly pop off, so my gunners are ready to turn up. Images of Laya flashed nonstop through a nigga's mental. JB and Han should realize that I was not the one who killed Laya. I loved her too. We had every intention on marriage and living happily ever after. JB's grief is understandable. They were joined at the hip. I feel'em. Han related how Laya got cremated. There wasn't going to be a wake or a funeral. He also gave away that every day JB sprinkles a little bit of Laya's ashes in his Watermelon Kush. Homeboy truly believes that Laya's spirit will be within him. That shit bugged me out.

A grieving man has been driving around all day trying to figure out who would do this. It had to be done by some professionals. *A head sent UPS? Straight gangsta!* The situation got your boy paranoid. If Don Cuba wasn't dead, he'd be the number one suspect, because of how Maliya and Mizhai were mutilated. Nine months of craziness! Everyone close at hand is dying. Things are not supposed to be this way. I'm ballin'. *What the fuck am I doing wrong?* I was deep in thought when my cell phone rang.

"Yo?" I uttered, picking up on the second ring.

"It's Mexicano. Mizery, do you have two of those thangz on deck for my peoples in Springfield?" I almost pressed the End button at his unexpected query.

Mexicano is obviously Mexican. He is tall and twiggy, has light-brown skin color, and sports long cornrows. A spoiled brat that grew up with a wealthy family that owns the Cinco De Mayo restaurant in Chelsea. Nevertheless, gangbangin' in ChelRok turned a good-natured heart cold.

"Manito, right now my mind isn't right. Plus, you know the fucking rules!" I roared, and then deaded the phone call assertively.

Precipitously, my cell phone rang again. "Como estas, papi?" Remy asked, while giggling with somebody in the background.

"I'm stressing, ma. Someone took my wifey's life. I have been driving around in circles for hours trying to figure out who wants to put a nigga's lights out," was one's reply.

"Oh my God! Are you okay? Where are you? Sulie and I rented a room at the Town Line Inn in Malden. Come over?" she sounded worried.

"I'm on my way," had been my immediate response, as another cigarette got flamed up.

On the cruise to Malden, I became aware of someone following me from a distance in a tinted black car. It was probably those alphabet boyz. Even so, I paid it no mind when it eventually turned down another road.

I staggered inside of a dim hotel room, where Remy and Sulie were both barely dressed in Rolando Lavia bathing suits. Remy pantomimed this sexy chubby nigga over by using her index finger. Sulie aggressively pulled down my DKNY jeans to unleash a lion. The two females began licking and sucking various parts of my body. Sulie nibbled on a thrumming uncircumcised worm, making it swell.

Remy pushed this pussy-killer on a scrubby mattress as Sulie slid down on my dick backwards. Remy watched Sulie pop that bubble up and down. The harder that Sulie dropped, the wetter that pussy got. She had to have came, because it turned gushy. Sulie hopped off and Remy hopped on. A visualization of angel wings tatted on their lower backs alerted me.

Sulie trudged over to cuff one's right hand to the bedpost, but when she tried to lock my other hand, I jerked away. Fuck being trapped. Sulie made an aggravated expression and unearthed a black snub-nose nine revolver. "Cabrón! You are going to be buried with both of your bitches and kid!" Sulie screamed in a psychotic voice.

My loose hand finger-danced for the four-pound under a puffy pillow, while all along feasting one's eyes at Remy and then at Sulie. "What's this about?" I seeked, trying to stall the situation.

Remy dawdled in her response, "It's simple papi, you killed Diamond's brother Don Cuba and now you're going to die with a stiff dick!"

I threw myself to the right, in the mix of gripping a .45 cannon. Three shots entered Sulie's stomach. That bitch fell backwards, but not before firing back, which hit a clamped hand. Remy attempted to gain access to Sulie's gun that dropped as four bullets tore her face up. The handcuff got bucked off, ahead of warning Projekt.

Outgoing Text: Projektgunner

Diamond is Don Cuba's sister!
!!911!!

I scrambled over to both of those bitches that were stretched out on the hotel room's carpet floor and gave each one a head shot to make sure that they were dead. Not sure, what to do next, an aching and bleeding hand got attended to. On the way out, JB and Han bustled inside of the hotel room with murder in their eyes. And then darkness took over.

CHAPTER 25

I'M A PIMP
PROJEKT

I'm twisting two braids in my hair getting fresh for Diamond, Booty, and Negra. They were all talking some freaky shit over the phone. On went a new pair of black Sean John jeans that were stitched in red. All-black waterproof Timberland boots and a red, black, and green Gucci belt arraying 26's had been chosen. I kept it simple with a white tee and du-rag. Those ho'z rented a room at the Radisson Hotel in Nashua, New Hampshire. It is close to an hour's drive, which isn't that long. A speckless red Champion zipper hoodie attuned a black Chicago Bulls fitted hat with the red patent leather brim and button atop. A chrome .25 Colt was tucked inside of one's boots. Jesus piece swinging—I'm out!

The girls were before now drinking, smoking, and popping Bart Simpson ecstasy pills. Reggaeton bumped from a little Sony stereo that had them grinding on each other. They looked like sizzling-hot models in a music video. Diamond wore an emerald-green Roberto Cavalli cat suit harmonizing emerald-green Alexander McQueen boots. You could see the imprint of that camel toe. Negra donned a goldish-brown Louis Vuitton short set, which was teamed up with some goldish-brown

Louis Vuitton knee-high boots. Booty maintained her elegance dressed in a pair of red Dereon jeans, a white Prada blouse, and a pair of white red-bottom Giuseppe Zanotti stilettos. The air smelled of Dolce & Gabbana candles that were burning inside of gold containers.

Pimping like no other, I steered Diamond's head toward an erection. This Cuban dime downslid to do her thing. She gives the best spitburger ever! Negra and Booty French-kissed, sooner to stripping down and wangling into a sixty-nine position on a well-made bed. In midwaft, Diamond went to go help Negra eat Booty's running river by guiding Negra to scoot over a little. This gave me an opening in-between two fat butts and an upside-down face. I joined in by hovering big balls over Booty's naughty lips and fingering both Negra and Diamond at the same time. That is until Booty had enough of sucking balls and begged for some dick missionary-style. Thick legs lolled on my shoulders as a desperate bicho began beating that shit up. Knees touched ears while I hit nothing but pussy. Negra and Diamond were sixty-nining it now. It didn't take long to let off in a tight situation. Nut got everywhere. Negra was next after a brusque piss and a wash up.

I shot out of the Radisson Hotel bathroom and latched onto Booty's hair; thenceforward I shoved a .25 caliber into a shocked mouth. *BANG! BANG!* Negra made an attempt to gore me in the chest with a long sharp kitchen knife, but as I bumbled backwards escaping a stab wound, two wild shots found an exposed neck. That bitch dropped on the floor, while in the process of trying to cover a blood-oozing hole. Even though on my ass, Mr. Two-Five caught sight of Diamond aiming a .22 Ruger. We exchanged gunfire, which concluded with Diamond spread out on top of a collapsed table. Twitching hands were inelegantly positioned. She was gasping for air and drizzling blood down the sides of her mouth.

My elbow was grazed; withal another bullet had entered and exited an unlucky ankle. That shit hurt like a motherfucker! Those little injuries wring the most. Whatever possible had been wiped down in the hotel room before I flexed.

While shifting gears to the Cathedral Projects, Mizery's cell phone endlessly rang. *What's good with this nigga?* He gives me a heads-up in a text and then vanishes.

"Hello," a male voice was heard.

"Put Mizery on!" I snarled. Mizery should have been on standby to find out that I am not dead.

"I'm sorry sir; this is Doctor Strom at Boston Medical Center. Your friend is a victim to a violent shooting," at first, I took what he had said for a joke.

"Is he going to live?" was my concerned inquiry.

"I'm sorry sir; I cannot disclose such information over the phone. What I can tell you is that he is being treated by the best doctors that we have," the doctor explained calmly.

"I'm on my way!" I uttered sharply.

"Sir, only family members will be allowed to visit. The FBI, the Boston Police Department, and the Chelsea Police Department are conducting tight security because of the seriousness to this situation," Doctor Strom informed me.

"Thanks," I simply said.

Fuck! I don't have any of Mizery's people's phone numbers. The only one that I have is Amandria's. Fuck that, I am going to go get her. Nothing less than ninety miles per hour to Chelsea.

"Hello?" Amandria spoke into the speaker.

"This is Projekt. Get ready. I'm coming to pick you up in five minutes. Mizery got shot," I made plain, before tapping the End button.

Amandria and her son were now tarrying outside for me. I honked the horn and afterward waived them over to get in. "Projekt, what happened to my baby? Tell us that he is okay?" she asked, while being in a state of delirium.

"I don't know. The doctor sounded like it was serious. He's poised that Mizery is in superlative care," I put her on.

"Oh my God!" shorty went even crazier, hysterically expressing concernment. Angel started crying too. I have always wondered why Mizery never wifed up Amandria. It is obvious that she loves the nigga.

"Amandria? You have to roll me in a wheelchair when we get there. I got popped in my ankle and won't be able to put any pressure on it. It's not crucial though. The bullet went in and out. I am not trying to see a doctor. I don't want the police to get involved. I just have urgency for pain medication and as well as antibiotics. I'll hit up Preme to deliver it," I explained, without going into detail.

"I'm not even going to query about what happened. However, do not worry. I will push your big ass in a wheelchair. If anybody pries into your injury, merely just say that you twisted an ankle playing football with Angel," she put forth the perfect story.

At the emergency room, Amandria obtained a wheelchair for me, and afterward she moved into parkland. One was inhaling a Newport cigarette when I seen one of the FBI agents that arrested us on the Operation Royal Ruin indictment. The man has to be at least 6'4" and 250 pounds. His short blonde hair and blue eyes give him that Irish look. He is a big goofy-looking motherfucker. The only reason that my case got thrown out is because of his false testimony in front of the Grand Jury. That dumb-ass cracker claimed to be in possession of two consensual recorded phone conversations, where I supposedly priced a few guns. After continuously requesting this evidence to be produced, the government's remedy had been a dismissal, rather than to charge their precious leading agent with perjury. Agent Sielander's Big John Stud ass walked by ice-grilling. The copper then smirked, stopped, and was about to tread backwards but kept it moving upon witnessing Amandria, Angel, Felix, Maggie, and Mizery's grandmother coming toward our way.

"Why was he staring at you like that?" Maggie knocked.

"I don't know," I answered her.

Amandria pushed me along through the lobby doors until reaching a receptionist's desk. We were directed to security, who requested identification and inquested our relationship to Mizery. After a twenty-minute wait, a Doctor Strom met the family at the trauma center in order to enlighten us on Mizery's condition. Doctor Strom is a large, blue-eyed and blond-haired American man that seemed hackneyed from sleepless days. His worrywart visage told it all. He better not mark my nigga dead.

"Doctor Strom, can you please explain to us what is going on?" Maggie manifested worryingly.

"Mr. Rodriguez suffers from five gunshot wounds. One in his stomach, one in his chest, one in his buttocks, one in his back, and one in his right hand. Only one of five bullets has caused a fatal injury. X-rays confirm that bullet fragments are only centimeters away from a fainting heart, which has flatlined twice already. And to be honest, our expectations that Mr. Rodriguez will make it through the night are very slim," Doctor Strom gave details on Mizery's circumstances.

Whoa! They went bananas. Screaming; crying; and breaking shit; all until Mizery's grandmother passed out. Doctor Strom helped me calm everybody down. We laid Mizery's grandmother on a hospital bed that was up against the wall, where her eyes stared aimlessly. I ain't counting my nigga out just yet.

"Doctor Strom, did Rodriguez come in with anyone else?" I raised, trying to make sense of this mess.

"Actually, two women were pronounced dead on arrival from multiple gunshot wounds. Are they related to your family as well?" he replied with interestedness.

"No. I'm just a little taken aback. That's all," I minimally riposted, not wanting to sound suspicious.

"I understand. I am going to return to tending to Mr. Rodriguez now, but I will be coming out periodically with updates on his health," Doctor Strom stated, showing no facial expression.

"Thank you," I vocalized sincerely.

Gambino aggressed one-way into the emergency room's waiting room with at least twenty-five brothers and sisters, maybe even more. Looney, Young Gunna, Loski, Rizzo, Mexicano, Eks, Spooky, Eddito, Wolf, Koka, Preme, Chi-Chi, Gladiator, Blackrob, Pluto, Tizzy, Gato, 357, Kan-Kan, JP, Pro, Klover, Shizauto, four-Five-six, Dago, Freddie, and a few others rushed inside all rowdy. Federal agents and police officers came storming inside with their weapons drawn. On the contrary, when they peeped all of us poppin' Fives and the brothers and sisters showing respect to Mizery's family, law enforcement retreated.

"Here, Projekt," Preme gave tongue, before giving me twenty Percocets and a pill bottle of antibiotics.

Brother Preme has been around for a while. Manita Kaos is his niece. Since her death, we have had suspicions of him using heroin. And that's a no-no in our family. But to me, he appears healthy with that short and fat body, although homey's longhair was out of control. Nevertheless, today fatso's Puerto Rican tan skin looks ghostly, probably shocked at the circumstances.

"Good look, manito," I thanked my dude, and thenafter a hurting man popped six Percs and two antibiotics.

I explained what I knew, but everyone stood confused. Because if those ho'z are all dead, then who shot Mizery? Approximately at one thirty a.m., hospital security respectfully requested that we reduce our visitors to seven people. Everybody left, except for Amandria, Angel, Maggie, Abuela, Felix, Gambino, Preme, Wolf, and me. Well, nine is better than thirty plus.

CHAPTER 26

THIS CAN'T BE
AMANDRIA

It was five thirty-eight a.m. on the dot, when Doctor Strom exhaustedly loomed up to publish bad news, "Proficiently, our surgical team removed that life-threatening bullet. Unfortunately, Mr. Rodriguez has slipped into a coma. A life-support machine upholds his physical body. Now I come to you all with a tough decision to make. Do we pray for a miracle or let him rest in peace? Today, your answer is not necessitated. Any minute now, Mr. Rodriguez will be transferred into the intensive care unit, where visitations are allowed."

"Doctor Strom, what are the chances of him waking up from this blackout?" Preme needled.

"Doubtful. I'm sorry," Doctor Strom shot back.

Inconversable, lost in our own thoughts, is how the family sat. One cannot believe what is going on. *Do we pull the plug or hope on a supernatural occurrence?* What a choice.

Wolf had been the first to break the ice, "I think that the family should permit Mizery to meet his maker. He's unequivocally suffering."

"I agree. Even the doctor said that it is unlikely that Mizery will regain consciousness," Maggie opined, while sobbing in her seat.

"I have no input. Whatever resolution is reached can only be valued," Gambino put forth.

Felix attempted to shrug off the conversation by saying, "Let's discuss this another day, when we are all clear-minded."

"No! No! No! Nobody is going to play God to my grandson! If God wanted him dead, he would have done so. My grandson is still alive for a reason. We shall stand strong as a family and pray. Only God should make that determination," Mizery's grandmother put her foot down with authority.

Everyone looked at each other and adopted Mizery's grandmother's edict as final. It took a lot of pressure off us. I don't know what would have been my theorem. During our wait for Mizery to be reassigned to ICU, Angel fell asleep on that same hospital bed that was up against the wall. Preme's fat ass began snoring like a beast. He rumbled like a Harley-Davidson doing one hundred miles per hour in a tunnel. Mizery's grandmother and aunt were sound asleep, while drooped in their chairs. Felix eyeballed a television watching an episode of *Cheaters*. Projekt kept dosing into the arms of Morpheus. I caught him drooling on himself a few times. Gambino and Wolf were vigilant, as if they had been sniffing coke. They were in and out of the men's room having a talkfest. I felt wholehearted love in the hospital. Mizery has many people that cherish his heart of gold.

"Excuse me; you can now see Mr. Rodriguez. The intensive care unit is on the fifth floor. He is in room #7. You'll find the elevators down the hall and to the left," a young black nurse directed us.

"Thank you," I graciously said, as everyone followed me out of the emergency room.

Upon arriving at Mizery's hospital room, I was the first person to walk in. My baby laid in bed while hooked up to machines. I recognized a trachea in Mizery's throat area, IVs inoculated into his veins, and all along hearing the beeping sounds to a heartbeat. He appeared comfortable.

Mizery's grandmother staggered inside, quickly summoning everyone to stand around Mizery to hold hands in benediction. "Jesus Cristo, Papa Dios, as a family we beg you to give my grandson the strength to overcome this current situation. He deserves a second chance at life. Miguel is a great man who has made many mistakes. Please help his way of thinking. Amen," at that moment, after her short prayer, Mizery's grandmother made the sign of the cross.

Gambino and Wolf placed their black bandannas on the hospital bed's railing, said goodbye, and then departed. Felix, Maggie, and Mizery's grandmother also announced a parting. Angel, Projekt, Preme, and I stood there for almost two more hours, before heading out ourselves.

On the ride home, I overheard a conversation between Projekt and Preme. "So who is going to be Boss One of Chelsea now?" Preme inquired.

"For now, I'm going to hold down both cities. Everything goes through me, even in my hood, until we get things back in order," Projekt set forth.

Those were the last words that I heard of their confab, because we pulled up in front of one's condominiums. I said bye to both of them, woke Angel up, and then went inside. Angel straight away pancaked on his bed, giving me time to run over to Mizery's apartment in Revere. The hospital security gave up the keys, cell phone, wallet, and everything else that he had on him. I have to make sure that my baby's apartment isn't storing anything incriminating, ahead of the police conducting a search claiming that it's part of their investigation to catch whoever had been responsible for the shooting.

As soon as I skedaddled into Mizery's apartment, I heard puppies whimpering. In the kitchen there were two big mean pitbulls that began growling. Thank God, those animals had been chained up. Mizery told us about his six-month-old puppies. It's going to take some time for these dogs to get comfortable with Angel and I. "Rocky, Terror," I called them, and thereafter both dogs titled their sizable heads to one side. I risked moving closer, but the reddish one came forward snapping at me. If it weren't for a short chain tugging him back, teeth would have gnawed on a human body. Okay, that's enough of playing with those puppies.

The living room is beautiful. First thing that caught my attention had been a sixty-two-inch flat screen television. "Copycat," I said aloud. A lizard rested in a tank on top of an entertainment center, and right above it, framed-up was a blown-up picture of Mizhai. His leather couches smelled new. What an amazing bedroom. Imagining him having sex on that king-sized bed triggered anger. *Who wouldn't want to make love in a room like this?* I know that I would. Look at this ceiling. It's one big mirror.

Baby? Where is the stash? By the time mentioned, a second round got underway, by rummaging through nightstands, between mattresses, and the draws to the bureau and dresser. Under one of Mizery's Gucci pillows, I found a silver gun, which nosedived into my Coach bag. Back to the bathroom—nothing. I only had seen a pink thong that had been chucked into an undersized tub. *Damn, Mizery!* I was deep in thought, trying to figure out a location where Mizery is likely to tuck something away at and that's when keys were heard jingling. The dogs started barking, as one's scary-ass hem and hawed into Mizery's bedroom closet, in order to hide in-between two stacks of sneaker boxes that were stacked taller than me. It got so quiet that I heard the key enter the lock and then turn.

"Come inside, Preme. Stop being a pussy. Rocky! Terror! Shut the fuck up!" Projekt shouted at the dogs. They did not stop growling or pulling on their chains. "They're still puppies that don't even know how to bite yet," Projekt supposed, but it sounded as if he didn't even get close to the dogs.

"So why don't you go play with them, tough guy?" Preme taunted.

"I ain't fucking around," Projekt kept it real.

"Do you think that Mizery has twork and bread here?" Preme threw out there.

"I don't know, my nigga. But we are going to check, just in case," Projekt worded.

Ensuing an all-inclusive inspection, Projekt called it a day by saying, "Let's be out, Preme. My nigga doesn't have shit here. He probably has a brickhouse."

"All right, but what's up with those puppies?" Preme raised.

"Amandria is probably going to give them to Angel. Plus, you're too shook to even go into the kitchen, never mind anything else," Projekt capered.

"Fuck it," I heard Preme say, and then the front door opened and closed.

It took ten minutes of assurance to come out of hiding. While treading warily around piles of boxes, I felt the floor creak, as if it had moved. At once, I kneeled down to uncover a secret compartment that was secreting a bolted in digital safe. One, four, nine, three—Mizery's grandmother's last four numbers to her house phone. He's so predictable. There had to be at least two hundred thousand dollars and three kilos of cocaine sitting in this safe. I found another gun. This one black though. For the next couple of days, I am going to clean out Mizery's apartment to be assured that there isn't anything else hidden. At the same time, Angel and I can bond with Rocky and Terror. Because if not, we'll have no choice but to call animal control.

CHAPTER 27

CAN'T STOP, WON'T STOP
PROJEKT

I was smoked out in the whip thinking to myself. *How can I make contact to continue to do business? Will those Asian cats fuck with the second-string?* I got JB's number from Mizery's cell phone, when the hospital security gave Amandria all of his property. That is how I got hold of an extra key to Mizery's apartment; I slipped it off the key ring. One can't wait to go into my crib and knock out. Three more Percs should do it. At the hospital, Amandria cleaned both of the gunshot wounds and tightly wrapped a swollen ankle with an ace-bandage. She even stole a cane for the kid from someone else's hospital room. Shorty held a nigga down on some sister-in-law love. Let me call JB and see what it is.

"Dragon Kitchen!" an Asian man answered.

"My fault, wrong number," I put into words, after realizing that this was that Chinese restaurant on Everett Avenue in Chelsea.

"It's JB. I'm just fucking around. Who's this?" he asked, while chortling at the same time. I started laughing as well. Homey had me going.

"This is Projekt, Mizery's partner. Are you aware that Mizery got clapped up and stretched out in a coma? The doctors keep saying that he will never be wakeful. Your rules ain't disrespected, but continuation on our paperchase is a must," I put in for.

"Mizery spoke highly of you; furthermore, he construed his position to pass the torch to you when our friend retired. Let me know what hospital that he's in, so we can meet there tomorrow," JB planned.

That went smoother than expected. Mizery had already been in the process of plugging me in. Only seven birds and everybody is in requirement. Let's see, Spooky's cousins from Hew Hampshire want four birds at thirty-five thousand dollars a K. Now I know how Mizery was caking it. They are definitely going to get that. In addition, Gladiator, Wolf, and Gambino ordered a bird apiece. Loski needs one hundred and twenty-five grams. JP, 357, and Eddito requested a half-kilo each. Withal, eight bricks and six hundred and twenty-five grams, easy math.

There is not enough yayo to cover all of the arrangements, so you know what it is—whip it, whip it, real hard! No sleeping tonight. I had been zoned out in dollar signs until reality hit me that I was still sitting in the car high as fuck. As Cathedral's Boss One locked up the whip, my cell phone rang.

"You have a collect call from "Baby Wise" at Cedar Junction State Prison. To accept—" The number one got pressed to accept the call before the machine finished its stupid recording.

"What's good, Projekt?" Baby Wise broke through.

"Ain't shit, comrade. How are you maintaining?" I stated, showing personal interest.

"I'm good. We about to handle. He landed. Is Mizery fucked up?" one could hear the convicts in the background living that trap life, as Baby Wise spoke.

"Shit is sad. Mizery's grandmother doesn't want to pull the plug," I explicated, while finally walking through my front door.

We kicked it for like fifteen more minutes, previous to our phone call ending. It's kitchen time! Looney and Pro were mobilized to play as security.

Looney is a tall and flabby, white-skinned nigga straight from Puerto Rico. He stays rocking a du-rag and fitted hat, draping his cornrows. Manito doesn't speak too much English but he is trying to learn. His family moved to Boston in avoidance of Puerto Rico. The little nut almost died in a shootout from being struck five times by an AK-47. The war with a bichote sparked up because Looney robbed him for two kilos of heroin and thirty-seven thousand dollars.

Pro is another Puerto Rican young buck from the Cathedral Projects. He is 5'11", thin, white-skinned, has short braids, and full of energy. A good kid dedicated to school and playing sports. However, ever since that Looney and him linked up, he's been knee-deep in the hood. Just last week, drama popped off with some cat claiming those projects from down the street. That sparked the combat back up between our bricks, but fuck it, ain't nothing that we can't handle.

While waiting for my young gunners, I took out a Motorola digital scale, one rubber hammer, Prosec, baking soda, three spoons, ten big Ziploc freezer bags, and a big Corning Ware glass pot. Seven bricks were laid on the kitchen counter. One hundred and twenty-five grams of coke from each bird had been weighed, thereupon, transferred into a big Ziploc freezer bag. The rubber hammer broke down the hard coke to powder. Adding one hundred and twenty-five grams of Prosec to each package, magically puffed eight joints.

"Who is it?" I shouted, as someone was knocking on my front door.

"Looney nicka! Abre la puerta, cabron!" Looney's accent is crazy.

"Where is Pro?" I questioned.

"Viene pronto," Loony unzipped.

I headed back into my workshop and set down Boston Herald newspapers onto the floor. Five hundred grams of powdered cocaine and as well as two hundred and fifty grams of baking soda were all dumped into the glass pot. Slowly adding water, while mixing it, is how the coke and baking soda turned pasty. It's now ready for heat. Flames under the glass pot cooked the coke until it raised the oil. Hastily, I removed the hot glass pot from off the stove in order to place it inside of the sink. A hand blender had been used to break down the chunks. Water and ice forced bubbling crack to drop. After that, I poured out the excess water and melting ice. Upside-down the glass pot was held over the newspapers as the crack got banged off with a small rubber hammer.

I was about to work on batch number two, when Pro came into view, so I set forth directives, "All right, I need y'all to hold me down today as security. Brothers are coming through to pick up good weight. Switch positions every hour—one plays the inside and the other outside. Incense must be burning at all times. Niggaz, do what you do best and smoke as much bud as possible. The kitchen is out of bounds for everybody. It'll be a shame if someone with sticky fingers gets slumped in my living room."

It is five p.m. and a dog has been cooking crack for seven hours. I am only on my sixth joint. No matter how many incense sticks and blunts were lit up, all you could smell was crack. On time, Wolf showed up. He wasn't wettin' the cook-up, especially for the price of twenty-seven thousand dollars. I listened to manito put me on about his hood being on fire because Izzy and a Blood nigga named Pistol Po robbed and shot this white guy that ended up being an undercover Chelsea Police officer. Wolf presented for action, if it's within a realm of possibility, for him to buy himself in as a partner regarding any of the three businesses. I explained how we already had things functioning on point, and moreover, that if Mizery passes away, Felix is taking half ownership of Magik Entertainment, Maggie of Royal Rydes, and Amandria of Diamond Kutz. Even so, withal I advocated for an assemblage with Gambino, who would more than likely be holding down Tsunami Rekordz.

Almost an hour after Wolf left, I was banging out another seven hundred and fifty grams of crack, when Gladiator, Gambino, and Loski came through. They were in a rush, so transactions were quick. My brothers were not feeling the cooked-up product, besides; they hesitated till I lowered the numbers to twenty-four thousand dollars and thirty-eight hundred dollars.

Upon the Three Musketeers leaving, I scrambled back into my laboratory to weigh out another five hundred grams of powdered cocaine, two hundred and fifty grams of baking soda, and thenceforth unloading it all inside of the crowd-pleasing glass pot. Once I changed about, Eddito standing right there caught me off guard. Eddito is an ex-crackhead and dope fiend. The man's track marks are hidden in his Puerto Rican brown skin. He is a short and skinny dude with a pushback hairdo. At fourteen-years-old, I used to serve him twenty-rocks. The old man has been clean for two years. A recruited soldier. An exchange took place with no complaints.

"Jerry, your boy should be sold out by tomorrow. It's time for a whole thang?" this nigga exposed my government. *Jerry?* Then the ancient one held up his twork on some weirdo shit, before heaving it inside of a Timberland box and hence into a Blockbuster bag.

"I'll see what's up, because I need to re-up too," I retorted, while quickly thinking about the Asians and tomorrow's introduction.

"Who's your connect?" he cross-questioned.

What the fuck? This nigga is acting outlandish. "I have a Columbian connect. Why did you ask that?" I fed him some bullshit and awaited his comeback.

"I'm just curious, manito," he responded normal, so I shook off my rat alarm.

"So is this crack fire? How does your connect get it into the United States?" he quizzed, in front of spinning toward the living room.

Something is up with this nigga. My rat alarm kicked back in. "I don't know, bro. But I'll def find out and put you on," one tried to brush off the conversation.

Eddito sat on the couch playing NBA Live on my Play Station 3. I poured water into the ubiquitous glass pot, carrying forward. It was nine sixteen p.m., when I finished the eighth brick.

"Projekt? Spooky and Ricknice are here, but Ricknice is not on the list," Looney made known.

"It's all good, manito. Tell Pro to let them in," Looney already had a .380 automatic handgun by his side, as he listened heedfully to me speak.

"Spooky, follow me," I invited him into my room.

As soon as we entered, Spooky spoke, "Is this the same fire that Mizery had?"

"It's the same nigga, except cooked-up. You know that Mizery and me re-up together," I revealed, while counting the money.

"My cousins don't care if it's cooked-up or powder. They are out there in New Hampshire killing it with those white boys," Spooky expounded, while holding up the bricks the same way that Eddito did.

The mulah looked fresh, as if it had just come from a bank. When Spooky rolled out, I high signed Looney over for a brief sit-down. Now it was back to my showroom, where only Ricknice and Eddito were sitting at holding PS3 controllers.

"Where is Spooky?" I asked both of them.

Ricknice kicked back, "He bounced."

"Y'all didn't come together?" I investigated.

"Nah. I came in a Chelsea yellow cab. Manito jumped out of an all-black tinted truck. Wasn't it one of your cabs?" Ricknice quested in confusion, as he trailed me into my bedroom. "Projekt, here is forty-five thousand dollars. Let me hold a half of a man? I'll be back in three days with the rest," Ricknice suggested.

Ricknice is Puerto Rican, 5'11", has a light-skin complexion, rocks a bald fade, and maintains a healthy body by working out. Homey got a scar on his face that he sustained at a young age. Mizery speaks highly of him, so there are no question marks above the brother.

"How about you come back tomorrow with three thousand dollars and we'll be good?" he mugged me in intricacy for a second after my offer, and then realized that I just looked out by giving him two joints for forty-eight thousand dollars.

"Good look, bro," Ricknice handed over nine neatly rubber-banded five-thousand-dollar packs, after thanking me.

"The only inconvenience is that you'll have to return tomorrow, in order to pick up the second one, because I am still cheffing. 357 and JP are coming by in an hour, so your shit will not be ready until the morning time. For now on, I'll make sure that it's that raw powder," I guaranteed.

"Fuck it, my nigga. Tomorrow it is," Ricknice agreed to the situation, before he jumped on his horn to call a cab. Manito stuffed the kilo into a sleeve to a black and yellow Boston Bruins leather bubble coat.

It's one forty-eight a.m. and I was on my last brick, when JP and 357 finally showed up. Everyone's eyes were concentrated on Pro and Eddito playing a game of Madden. They bet two hundred dollars. Pro selected the New England Patriots and Eddito chose the Green Bay Packers. Pro blew Eddito out—49 to 16.

When I banged out the finishing brick onto newspapers to desert, I started cleaning up. Looney even mopped the project hallway with Pine Sol. Anything to kill that crack smell. After cleaning, Looney and Pro were hit with three hundred and seventy-five grams of crack to split between them. Pro took responsibility on handling Ricknice tomorrow; therefore, he snatched up a whole joint as well. Looney and Pro popped Fives with everybody and then flexed.

JP and 357 were next. "I only have two cooked-up birdies left. What do you niggaz want to do?" I offered.

"Dog, fuck crack! Niggaz want that raw! We have thirty thousand dollars on deck!" JP vented, in the mix of flashing stacks of bills.

"Me too, manito. No crack. Straightdrop, nigga," 357 supported JP.

"Fuck it! Give me fifteen thousand dollars apiece? You niggaz can't go wrong," I proposed a deal that they could not refuse.

These last two joints have to go. Moreover, if my math is right, I should have two hundred and seventy-eight thousand dollars. Not including 357 and JP's thirty thousand dollars and the three thousand dollars that Ricknice owes me. That is one hundred and forty-three thousand dollars profit. I'm on that quick flip, stack, fold, and hold!

They accepted my offer by putting up the paper. 357 lit up two blunts of Mango Pina marijuana that he copped in New York last week while visiting his grandmother in the Bronx. I tried passing the blunt to Eddito. Homey denied it though, talking some shit about trying to acquire a job that takes urines. JP pointed to a set of snowbunnies from Somerville that made an allurement to a rave this weekend. Nothing but college bitches. I'm over there. Those college ho'z are freaky.

Last time that a nigga went to a college party, I seen all types of crazy shit. In an empty warehouse, techno, freestyle, and house music boomed. Three five-dollar hits of acid promptly took control. It felt like slow motion all night. While smoking a square in a gigantic bathroom, I got an earful from a white boy's voice spearheading someone to deep throat. The acid had a hallucinating thug chain-smoking until two men came out of that stall. Nasty shit! I ended up fucking two bitches that night. One had been a short and chubby Cape Verdean smut holding big titties. *What's her name?* Once we smashed in the girl's bathroom, it was on to the next. A dark-skinned and slim Haitian stunt named Nautica. I woke up in a small apartment somewhere in Burlington. Shorty looked fly. A married woman that used your boy as a jump-rope. The bitch respectfully kicked me out.

"Projekt! Yo! Projekt!" Eddito shouted. Damn, I must have fallen asleep.

"Where is 357 and JP?" I put forth an inquisition.

"Those niggaz been off this. You knocked out with the blunt in your hand. Come lock up. I'm out!" Eddito blasted.

Eddito stepped down a flight of stairs holding a Blockbuster bag and inattentively walked into the hallway. Murderously, two masked men bushwhacked him in front of his apartment door. Before Eddito could react, a sharp piece of metal opened up an unguarded throat. He attempted to attack an unfamiliar assailant, but ended up keeling over, gulping for air. The bloody shirt got lifted as the recording devices were removed. Even the Blockbuster bag faded away.

What a night! The Cathedral Projects erupted lava. I have never seen so many police agencies in one area in one's life. Law enforcement officers were looking for suspects. Ghetto birds had been shining their lights all over the projects. Off went a nigga's jack. Boston Police detectives commenced knocking on people's doors; they were trying to find a witness. However, no-one was opening up his or her doors. If somebody is going to snitch or volunteer information, it's going to be on a down-low movement. My door felt a few knocks as well.

When more than one body bag got carried out—Pito, Hitman, Teddy Bear, and Eddito—I turned panicky. I stayed up sleuthing on the boyz conducting their investigation until the birds started chirping.

Before the journey to unite with the Asians, one had noticed the taped off sections through my window. I was a cool resident riding down an elevator. Thereafter, strolling through a fizzing region. *What the fuck?* Looney and Pro were posted up on the block serving a fiend. These niggaz is gangsta! I popped the Fives with both of them.

"That nigga was a rat! We got the recording equipment!" Pro declared, all amped up. I did not say anything. I just acknowledged what he had said and kept it moving.

Two Asian men clad in black Tom Ford suits patiently awaited the replacement's arrival. Unhesitantly, the short dude frisked one's person as the door soundlessly shut behind me. "I'm JB and this is my partner Han. So you contacted us to begin where Mizery left off, right?" the bigger one out of the two queried.

"Correct," was my simple response.

"I can assume that you know the rules?" JB inferred.

"You already know. Mizery is my right-hand man," I put forth, and then eyed them seriously.

"First, let's get something straight. Your brother can never wake up from the coma. We put him there. The death of my sister rests in his hands. An avowal broken for greed. Laya's head was decapitated as a sign of revenge. Business can only be possible if you assure us that the plug will be pulled or that you'll complete the job?" JB set forth expressly and authoritatively.

If I had my burner on me this chink would have gotten stained right here. "I'm not going to sit here stuntin as if a nigga doesn't care about what you just said, but it's understandable, blood is thicker than water. Your request is not a problem," I ensured him, while all along picturing homeboy's wig peeled back.

"As a token of my appreciation, the first twelve kilos are on the house. Now, I invite you to dinner, so we may discuss bankrolls?" JB opened up, ahead of giving me a friendly shoulder pat.

We went to eat at a Japanese restaurant called *Ginza,* which is located on Harrison Avenue in Chinatown. It was scrubby like a fast-food place. I ordered a plate of white house rice, chicken fingers, and chicken wings. JB asked for a plate of pork-fried rice with pork chops. Han put in for a dish of sushi and as well as a kettle of sake.

"Projekt, as acceded, tomorrow you will derive a shipment. Every nine days, Han shall pick up the money and the following day you'll again receive another shipment. There can be no changes unless we agree upon it in person. Understand?" he made known.

I agreed to his ways with a nod.

"Really, truly, Mizery's buying and selling was respected. The man never owed me a dime. Laya loved him. But he must die!" JB expressed his true feelings.

No bullshit, I feel the nigga.

CHAPTER 28

HAVE FAITH
AMANDRIA

I can't believe it! One was just overhearing their little powwow and it all makes sense now. Laya's brother shot Mizery and Projekt accepted an offer to put in the finishing touches. Ten minutes have already passed by since they split, but this terror-stricken white girl still sits tight in a noiseless bathroom. *What should I do?*

I straggled over to Mizery's hospital bed to dandle unresponsive hands and talk, "Your best friend is fucked up. I am not going to let him or anyone hurt you. JB is Laya's brother. He wants you dead. Now Projekt is on that guy's side. Baby? Wake up! I do not know whom to trust. Angel misses you. The boy is crazy about Rocky and Terror. It took us a week to bring those dogs home. My love, I have a confession to make. Angel is your son. Miguel Angel Rodriguez, III. Conceivability date had to be at the Red Roof Inn. A night of pleasure. In one's eyes, I believed that you fucked me and moved on. Nevertheless, when the truth had been explicated that you had gotten locked up, shame ate at your junior wifey. There is no justification for these wicked actions. I am sorry that I never told you. Angel knows. Our little man loves the fact that you are his father. You cannot say that a father-and-son affinity isn't felt when Angel visits. Mizery, I emptied out your safe. What do I do with all of that stuff? I know that I'm a square. Drugs weren't this do-gooder's choice of profession. We all have faith that you will breathe new life into. Your grandmother said that the priest and nuns from Saint Rose Catholic Church came to pray for you yesterday."

As I was making emotional love to Mizery, someone lightly knocked on the door. Gambino, Tizzy, Pluto, and Klover waited on a gesticulation for admission. Klover and Tizzy are blood brothers whom I met one time at a cookout last summer. Klover is a funny person. He's a short and stocky leprechaun-looking guy. Tizzy is skinny and taller, who always has a serious visage and doesn't speak too much. They are both white-colored Puerto Rican's with braids.

Pluto is cool. At first, one's impression of him had been a mean person because of the titan's intimidating character. He's 6'3", Puerto Rican, tan-skinned, 320 pounds, has short braids, and rakishes a body full of tattoos. He is the only one that rocks a five-point star on the face like Mizery. One day, a different side to the individual came to light. At his daughter's birth, the big gangsta was all smiles while snuggling and kissing her. They stayed for a little bit. Yet, before Mizery's brothers left, Gambino understood the salience to hookup.

Mizery's brother Danny and sister Priscilla flew down on an emergency leave from the United States Marine Corps. Danny slipped away from Japan and Priscilla turned aside from Quantico, Virginia. Danny is like a brother to me. He's Mizery's twin. Maybe not in the physical, but beyond any doubt, in character. There is a family rumor that Danny enlisted into the marines to escape a homicide investigation where he got identified in a photo array as a hitman that shot and killed two men. Back then, Danny was known as Danger.

As a teenager, I loved watching them perform at shows. They had a rap group called *TNP,* which stood for Top Notch Posse. It used to be Mizery, Danger, Black Riz, Hershel, Fat Kenny, Norma, Ritchie, Ant, Driskid, Waves, Little Keith, and Big Mike. TNP buzzed in the surrounding cities.

I have never met Priscilla until today. She is a very pretty girl with a macho attitude. I got one hundred dollars that says that she's a lesbian or bisexual. What a sweet girl though. Our connection had been instant.

They both started shedding tears as soon as they saw Mizery hooked up to all of those machines. Priscilla held his hand while lost in her own thoughts. Danny stood frozen, and in due time, demanded answers as to what had happened. His eyes told it all. Even so, I played the I-don't-know role.

The two were enlightened about their nephew's existence. We made plans to meet back here tomorrow for introduction to Angel. While gossiping with Priscilla pertaining to the show *Love In Hip-Hop,* and while walking down the corridor toward the elevators, I took notice of Loski, Maniak, Firu, and Spooky passing us in the opposite direction.

Later that evening, I was pacing back and forth in my living room, while anticipating Gambino's arrival. He had phoned me two hours ago, claiming to be on his way. Angel has been stuck in that room playing Modern Warfare online with some friends from school. Rocky and Terror began growling and barking. That's when I knew that Gambino was at the front door.

"Wait a minute! I have to put my dogs on the balcony!" I yelled, so Gambino could hear me.

I opened the door to spot Gambino standing there next to some short and thick, longhaired black girl, who was full of swag. She had been dressed in Louis Vuitton from head-to-toe. He broached this girl as Toya, his son's mother. *Does Gambino think that I invited him over on a hanky-panky level? And that's why this female is with the muddle-headed kid? To pomp loyalty toward Mizery?* Oh boy, this young fellow has it all wrong.

"Do you guys want something to drink?" I did not even wait for their response. I brought each one of them a good-sized cup of Hennessy with ice. They both thanked me.

"You got dogs?" Gambino enquired.

"I have Mizery's two puppies. Well, they're not exactly puppies anymore. They are seven-months-old. Do you want to see my babies?" I offered with a smile.

"Nah, I'm good. I heard those animals wilding when I knocked on the door. They don't sound too friendly," Gambino mocked good-humoredly, and then took a sip of his drink.

"I do?" Toya entreated. I brought her inside of my bedroom to show off Rocky and Terror through a sliding glass door connected to the balcony.

"Gambino? Look at them?" Toya called over to him.

"Those niggaz are beast mode," Gambino said, surprised at their size at seven months.

"They don't fight with each other?" Toya questioned.

"They did once, over food. Now we feed them apart. Other than that, they're good dogs and are very protective of Angel and me," I proudly put forth.

"I want one, Gambino?" Toya nagged.

"I want one too," Gambino replied.

"Do you guys smoke?" I invited Gambino and Toya.

"What kind of question is that? Matter-of-fact, roll this dour up," Gambino tendered, and thenafter handed me a bag of smoke.

"So what's up, Amandria?" Gambino queried, putting me on the spot as I began breaking up the bud.

"I don't know where to begin. Today, I was using the bathroom in Mizery's hospital room, when two guys talking in an Asian language entered. I got fearful. Projekt eventually came inside and then they all acquainted themselves. JB is Laya's brother that is actually blaming Mizery for his sister's casualty. He acknowledged being behind Mizery's attempted murder. What's more, is an ultimatum to Projekt to finish him off or no business would be conducted. Project accepted. JB and Han are part of the Asian Mafia," tears flowed from my eyes, after threshing out a problematic happenstance.

Gambino looked at me outraged and thereafter spoke, "Amandria, tell me that you are sure that you witnessed this?"

"I'm positive, Gambino. I wouldn't make this shit up," I communicated genuinely.

I lit the blunt and then passed it to Toya. Gambino lowered his head for a few seconds, before raising it back up and speaking, "I'll take care of this. Don't tell anybody else, okay?"

I nodded in agreement, all the while wiping my tears. Gambino is rock solid according to Mizery, so I'm following suit. We smoked in hush-hush, until I handed over some paperwork to Gambino, which gave him full ownership of Tsunami Rekordz if anything shall happen to Mizery. Soonafter, I hit the kitchen to refill our drinks.

"What the fuck? Mizery is like my dad. I love that man," Gambino gratefully expressed.

"Now moving on to the next subject—how much does a kilo of cocaine go for?" Gambino looked at me mystified, as if to question my incentive.

"It depends, if it's powder or crack, pure or cut. The prices vary," he expounded, while still trying to read my mind.

"How much for the stuff that Mizery was getting?" I asked, and then took a big sip of my drink.

"Mizery's product is one hundred percent pure in powdered cocaine. He charges thirty thousand dollars a kilo; but of course, the big homey gets it cheaper than that," Gambino went into detail.

"I have a proposition for you. I will give you three kilos of what Mizery gets for forty-five thousand dollars? That's half off," I proffered, while in the act of digging out the cocaine from a laundry bag, in order to settle the kilos on my coffee table.

"Thirty thousand dollars is on deck right now. I can bring you the other fifteen thousand dollars in a few days," after speaking, he looked at Toya, as if giving her a mental signal to go get the hard cash.

"I trust you, Gambino. Tomorrow, just stop by and drop it off, and when the rest is made, I'll be here," behind dictating the movement for a quick second, I felt like a real drug dealer.

The evening turned out delectable. Three sheets in the wind demolished a half of a gallon of Hennessy and smoked three more blunts of Sour Deez. The cards had been put on the table bearing on Mizery and Angel. Toya is good peoples. The two of us get along good. She showed me pictures of Lil' G-Man, who has beautiful blue eyes. A ladies man in the making. We exchanged numbers and promised to hang out next weekend.

The next day, I met up with Danny and Priscilla at Boston Medical Center. I brought along Angel. Maggie, Mizery's grandmother, and Felix arrived as well. Angel's family tree embraced him candidly. It's like every person knew, besides Angel and Mizery. Mizery's grandmother took this opportunity to lead us all in prayer.

Just as we finished adjuring to God for a miracle, Doctor Strom vagabonded inside. "How is everyone doing?" he courteously asked. Our positive feedback reflected a strong unit. "Well, unfortunately, Mr. Rodriguez still remains in the same condition. However, if he happens to awake, as we all hope that takes place, there are no permanent injuries, either physically or mentally. He's a strong man, who is healing very well," Doctor Strom reported.

CHAPTER 29

BEHIND METAL
BABY WISE

"**O**pen the fucking cells, bitch!" I was rashing on this rookie correctional officer taking his sweet-ass time to let us out for rec. These COs be testing niggaz. I'm in P-2, a gang block in Walpole State Prison, officially known as Cedar Junction State Prison, which houses nothing but UK Gangstaz. It consists of forty-five cells in total.

Last night, my battery died from listening to the *Launch Pad* and *Tropical Blends.* The Launch Pad is a two-hour hip-hop show that is hosted by DJ Hussell Simmons on Jamm'n 94.5 on Sunday nights between ten p.m.—twelve a.m... He's a DJ who shows mad love to prisoners. He termed us the *Headphone Crew* and we hold him down in high regards by loyally tuning in. The show goes hard with New England's finest local artists. Mizery's *Ryde or Die* and Gambino's *Behind Metal* tracks were played for three weeks straight. To launch on, forward clean tracks through an email to launchpad94.5@gmail.com.

Tropical Blends is two hours of reggaeton and reggae. It starts right after the Launch Pad and ends at two a.m... DJ Ray Barbouza and DJ Puff Dog be doing their thing. Last night though, Tropical Blends played trash. Too many commercialized reggaeton joints. They need to go in on that raw Boricua movement straight from Puerto Rico. Like my shit. Niggaz can't fuck with me!

Meanwhile, while waiting for the gate to slide open, one decided to put together a cup of coffee. Drinking gasoline before working out gives me a burst of energy. I placed a peanut butter jar full of lukewarm sink water inside of a big white Fluff container containing H_2O. A battery hitched to wires inserted inside of a light socket got sloshed into the aqua to heat up the jar full of pure liquid hydrogen and oxygen. The purpose of this process is to avoid contact between your swallowing water and stinger. Rumor has it that you can encounter Hepatitis C by these means. Bubbling liquid, two Sugar Twins, two scoops of Columbian coffee, and three spoons of creamer were mixed around inside of one's mug. Thenceforth, I took a baby sip of my steaming coffee. Finally, rec time! With coffee mug and Walkman in hand, I was off to workout.

After the light workout, a trip into the rainbox was mando. A laundry bag full of hygiene products and a change of clothes got tossed over my shoulder. In twenty minutes flat, behind getting fresh, I found myself jogging up a set of stairs to the third tier. I went to go kick it with Heavy, a big white-skinned Puerto Rican muscle head that shot and killed a member of the Latin Untouchables at a Zion concert, which resulted in a natural-life sentence. He is an Unknown from Springfield. *The Jerry Springer Show* was illustrating on his color television about sixty-year-old twin sisters, who unashamedly were staging saggy titties and no teeth. They were fighting over a twenty-three-year-old man. Absolutely ridiculous.

"Are you really watching this, comrade?" I said, more than asked.

"Ain't shit else on. Plus, I'm not really paying attention to it. A nigga is stressing over my appeal," Heavy ventilated.

"You good, bro. Just have faith. Your lawyer went hard and hit many strong points. By you sitting here all tensed up isn't going to change whatever decision the court is bound to make. Anyways, hable con Projekt. Shit doesn't look right for Mizery," I uttered, changing the conversation.

"I hope that nigga overcomes darkness. Ever since Mizery came home, those brothers in eastern Massachusetts turned back up. It's undisguised on how they are on fire, when you got the IPS saying little slick comments touching on outside events," Heavy mentioned.

"I feel you. Instead of Inner Perimeter Security, they should be called Inner Pussy Slaves. You right though. Chelsea and Boston are red-hot. But word to Mami, those niggaz is shined up and protected legally. Did you see them in the pics that Projekt sent? The brothers are posing beside supermodels, draped up with big jewels, stuntin in baja pantys, and flashing real count. Can I live?" I kept it one hundred in one's drollness.

"No bullshit," Heavy agreed, and then laughed.

"What's up with the insecto? Are we going to lay him down or what?" I probed with uncertainty.

The man that is going to set it up is Heavy's connect. Pee Wee Herman brings in a finger of dope, an ounce of loud, a carton of Newport's, and two eightballs of cocaine every two weeks for two thousand dollars. We provide it and he delivers it.

"Relax. You know that Gecko always comes through. Plus, fifteen thousand dollars more is sureness," Heavy disputed.

As you can see, Heavy and I have different nicknames for Sergeant Castro. Sergeant Castro is this short and scrawny, light-colored Venezuelan guy that became a correctional officer for only God knows why. He's like a hood nigga with a badge. Heavy roped the turnkey in by plugging him in with this hoodrat bitch named Italy. From there, he was our private courier.

"How much cheddar do the white boys owe?" I canvassed.

"Three thousand dollars for a half of a finger, three hundred dollars for three packs of cigarettes, and they are still behind two hundred dollars," Heavy validated.

"How about the Vice Lords, Bloods, Muslims, Crips, and Netas?" I further delved into. We did business with all.

"Everyone already paid. I need to holla at Perro from the Immortal Outlaws. He ordered a half of a rope of bud and two packs of cigarettes," Heavy let me know, as the brother calculated prices in his head and thenceforward scribbled some numbers down.

Two cells down, Squeeze tatted away on Mexican Rico, a Tango representative from the east side of Dallas, Texas. A portrait of his deceased mother was coming to life. Shading seemed effortless to him. Squeeze is also a lifer. He's a short and built, lightskinned Puerto Rican brother with a baldhead. Right behind me, Chicken made an entrance with music blaring out of a pair of Sony ear buds.

"Who's cooking tonight?" Chicken directed to no-one in particular.

"You are," Squeeze volunteered him, while concentrating on the tattoo.

"La linda. I cooked yesterday. But fuck it, I'll cook again. I'm going to chef up a Nacho Meal. So make sure that everybody brings me what they are going to throw in by dinner," Chicken enunciated.

Chicken makes a bomb-ass Nacho Meal with Ramen noodles, white rice, sliced pepperoni, pieces of summer sausage, melted herbanero cheese, chopped up pickles, hot chili beans, and nacho chips. Chicken is this short and thin, tan-skinned Puerto Rican cat with a low haircut. He also vamps a tiny teardrop underneath his left eye. He's from my hood, Sergeant Street in Holyoke. That's a UK block.

As I continued watching Squeeze tat away on Rico, I began memorializing about the day that I caught this murder case—it was one a.m. and a nigga had been trappin'. Daze and Smurf, two light-skinned sizable Puerto Rican Unknowns that stand at 5'10", sparked up a blunt of Creepy, when five pretty females pulled over in a pink and black Lexus. It took about twenty minutes before the ladies felt comfortable enough to get out of the car. Three of them were Spanish and two were African-American. I started spitting game to Tanisha, who resembles Stacy Dash but without the green eyes. Shorty familiarized me about how she is in college studying engineering to become an IT Tech for a high-profile mortgage company.

Two hooded people creeping on bikes had heckled our communion. One of them unshielded a dark-colored handgun. Before I could say anything, they both started dumping. Bullets blew out a car window and as well as hit the house that we were standing in front of. I ducked behind a truck and thenceforth shot back. The skinny kid fell off the bike. Nonetheless, the fat nigga just kept it moving. Daze gunned at him pedaling away. I remember thinking, *Where's Smurf?* Yet, my heedfulness swiftly vanished, bethinking how he had taken off hugged up on one of those Spanish girls.

At that moment, Tanisha started screaming. She dwindled to the ground next to one of her friends that was leveled out. The other girls joined in likewise. Daze and I began running when the police sirens were heard closing in. What an ugly situation.

For months, I laid-low at my baby-momma's crib in Springfield. Word was that the niggaz that shot at us were from Flatbush, some bitch-ass hood. The Spanish shorty and the kid that fell off his bike had died. *Are those girls going to snitch?* Were one's unending thoughts.

One night, an argument occurred between Destiny and I. I went overboard and smacked her a few times. Destiny is a short and dark-skinned, Native American girl with Brazilian hair and a sexy figure. She forced it by throwing an iron at the kid, which crashed through the living-room window. It accidentally landed on a neighbor's car's windshield. Springfield Police showed up asking for our information. My cousin's name came back with a warrant. I got arrested. Moreover, at the police station, fingerprint data uncovered one's true identity. A person wanted for first-degree murder. I guess dude that dodged the shots chose me out of a ten-picture photo array as the shooter. All four of the females stated that they had never seen any of the shooters. Daze was not even mentioned.

At trial, a jury returned a guilty verdict solely on the rat's testimony. A judge then sentenced me to natural life. You know what's crazy? After four years of being caged up, Tanisha surprised a nigga at a visit. She inquired as to why my attorney never phoned any of them as witnesses. Shorty additionally unfolded how they had made statements to the police officers that I had shot back in self-defense. On top of all of this, the girls claim to have been threatened by law enforcement officers into not testifying on one's behalf, in fear of being charged with joint venture.

Attorney Jessica Carter is on it! She filed two motions. One is a Motion for a New Trial based on newly discovered evidence. Our argument is a miscarriage of justice. The second one is a Motion to Reduce the Verdict, pursuant to Massachusetts Rule of Criminal Procedure 25 (b) (2) 378, Mass, 1976. Because at trial, my attorney requested jury instructions on second-degree murder, manslaughter, and involuntary manslaughter. Nevertheless, the judge refused to do so, ruling that the number of shots fired were excessive.

For the last six months, Tanisha has been ryde-or-die by one's side by faithfully visiting, writing, and cash sending. There are feelings involved. Matter-of-fact, I'm about to lock in my cell and finagle a letter:

Dear Tanisha,   4/30/13

I'm sorry that I have not written you back. I have been busy doing research on the motions that Attorney Carter filed. I really want to thank you and your friends for trying to help get my freedom back. I thought about you wanting us to be together and possibly getting married. Don't get me wrong, I want to be in a relationship with you. Even so, I am not a selfish person and wouldn't want your life to be put on hold just because mine is. I want to keep our relationship on a friendship level, until

I come home, because if I don't come home, what then?
I want you to be that friend that I can talk to about
anything. Thank you for the pictures. You look sexy as
hell in that all-white see-through bikini. What beach
was that on? Florida? Well beautiful, I'm going to end
this letter, but never the love.

A True Friend,
Baby Wise

One's eyes opened up to rattling bars. It's now lunchtime. The
cellblock came alive with convicts running around trying to get into
something. I grabbed two bags of nacho chips, two pickles, and a
summer sausage to give to Chicken. Today's lunch was triangle fish,
mashed potatoes, two slices of white bread, vegetable soup, plus watered-
down juice. I don't eat that bullshit, so I swung it to Fever, who is
originally from Bragdon Street in Dorchester. However, when the young
buck moved to Chelsea, he got G-Fived by Maniak, his right-hand man.
Fever is Puerto Rican, lean, yellow-skinned, small in height, and has
longish braids. Manito only has to serve three months to wrap up. He's
good money, an official nigga from eastern Massachusetts. The pothead
violated a light parole for a dirty urine. We were put on to what it is in
our UK family.

I was zigzagging through a crowd of hungry cons, till Heavy, "Ooh-
Ooh!" G-roared me over.

"Let's go, nigga. We're about to go clean 10-Block," Heavy pronounced, and then grinned.

As soon as we entered 10-Block, brooms kicked off sweeping. At Cell #7, lower left, Inspector suspiciously pried into, "What are you niggaz doing?"

"Where's that insecto at?" I pumped, remaining focused on our mission.

"He's in Cell #39, right next to Pretty Tony. They are both on protective custody status," he revealed. I smiled to myself, knowing that we were about to kill two birds with one stone.

Heavy and I preceded sweeping, popping up at random cells showing that Five love. Brother Most broadcasted his marriage to sister Malcria. Buba told us that he wanted to holla at Projekt over a misunderstanding concerning Teddy Bear being G-Fived into our UK family. Many brothers asked about how Mizery was doing, but they were brushed off with simple answers.

I even saw my Blood homey Flock from Bridgeport, Connecticut, a tall and skinny black guy that reps the Marina Village Projects. Niggaz labeled him Firearm, because the dog gets busy popping that metal. Nevertheless, buzzy caught an ugly case in Worcester, while in the mix of copping a few K'z off some Columbians. Flock shot and killed three people over bricks of flour. The paperwork is crazy. He wild out by putting to death one of those Columbians with a headshot. Firearm then tied up two panicked non-English-speaking motherfuckers and demanded the bricks. The nutcase went left by placing two frying pans full of corn oil on a flaming stove. Every question that was answered with, 'I don't know,' hands were forced into sizzling oil. Only bone and white meat survived. In addition, when that shit didn't work, faces got submerged into the liquid as well, instantly peeling off skin.

Testimony made in front of a Grand Jury described both victims looking like zombies from the movie *Resident Evil*. When it was all said and done, bullets from a .40 caliber handgun ended everyone's life. The problems came about, because he never seen the two young females hiding in a tiny pantry.

At upper-right, I G-roared, "Ooh-Ooh!" The brothers went bananas by shouting; banging on the cell bars; throwing objects on the tear; and lighting towels on fire. I pushed my broom to Fat Cheese's cell.

"What's good, fam? Do you want to buy a few stogies? I got three Newport's," I offered Fat Cheese.

"How much?" Fat Cheese investigated, as he walked over to the bars.

"I'll give you—" I never got the chance to finish giving an explanation. Heavy's ten-inch sharpened steel, which got taped to a broom handle, forcefully slid into the Roach nigga's eye. Through the bars, I rammed my spear into his ribs, hoping to puncture a lung. Metal continuously penetrated flesh, until a limp body dropped. When I shut the solid door, it was on to Cell #40. However, nobody lived there. Just an empty cell. He is one lucky motherfucker!

CHAPTER 30

DISASTER & DISAPPOINTMENT
MICHAEL H. SIELANDER

"**W**hat the fuck is going on with this investigation? One federal agent dead, two cooperating witnesses dead, the main target is in a coma, and there is numerous unsolved shootings and murders! It is a known fact that they are connected to the Unknowns and their rivals, but yet, we still have nothing! Nothing Delta has touched can be used! Any defense team will easily get it thrown out, based on a defendant's right to cross-examine an accuser! And that won't be possible! Why? Because he's dead! Our remaining CW, Eko, has executed control buys from Mizery, Eks, Wolf, Looney, and Firu! This is not enough! Operation Royal Ruin II budded on January 20, 2013! I want to hear positive updates!" I strongly said, showing my disappointment in the nonprogress.

"Agent Sielander, I begin by reporting the following information about Operation Royal Ruin II. We began staking out Projekt as a person of interest two weeks after the dismissal of the indictment. His movements were being monitored from a distance. Information attained bare purchases of three to four kilos every two weeks from random drug suppliers all over Boston. The big guy's actions had been unpredictable. A GPS tracking device was latched onto an Acura TL, in order to keep us aware of all of the locations that he traveled to.

"We tapped his cell phone and monitored recorded calls, unofficially of course. Overheard conversations brought Projekt out into the open organizing meetings, drug transactions, and a whole bunch of street crap. Even discussions when Mizery phoned from jail are saved on a CD in a top-secret file available only for our team to review.

"On May 31, 2012, Mizery's not-guilty verdict shocked us all. Two weeks after his release, Projekt and Mizery finally made contact. That same night, June 16, 2012, a celebration took place at King Author's, a strip club in Chelsea. A shooting occurred, but no-one was injured. Witnesses informed law enforcement that the UNLV Rebels were responsible for it. Because of our Supreme Court's recent decision mandating warrants to be obtained for tracking devices, it is now extremely difficult to keep constant surveillance on anyone. In addition, wiretaps are becoming intricate as well. These punks place confidence in switching cell phones on a monthly basis," Agent Deraney took a few sips of a cup of coffee and forged ahead.

"We know that a couple of days succeeding the King Author's shooting, unidentified members of the Unknowns shot and killed two UNLV members on Grove Street. Withal injuring several others. Additionally, that same night, Gambino and Loski invaded Fat Cheese's apartment on Shurtleff Street with Fat Cheese's mother and sister hostage at gunpoint. They made it known that Grove Street is now the Unknowns' territory. No-one reported this incident to authorities, clearly indicating that they were afraid to do so. An entire family just simply moved out of Chelsea.

"From this milestone, UK gang members took control of the drug trade in Chelsea. Fat Cheese also informed us about Don Cuba's jealousy and madness over losing business. Hitman charted to bump off both leaders. Fat Cheese holds to being entrapped by means of physical harm to family members and including himself. On September 30, 2012, an unsuccessful attempt on Mizery's life instead befell the murders of Dready and Kaos. It all went sour when Lady Roam erased Ice. Fat Cheese has also manifested on who helped them sneak into the DJ booth.

"Hitman went missing for over five months, before authorities happened upon his dead body inside of a basement located at the Cathedral Projects. During this breakthrough, Pito and Teddy Bear's dead bodies were also discovered. Boston Municipal Police corralled the bodies, while searching for witnesses and evidence that might have led us to track down Delta's butcher. Officers entered a basement tenants complained smelled like dead bodies. Maintenance workers assured BMP that it was dead rats and feces, but upon passage, Teddy Bear, Pito, and Hitman laid dead. According to Fat Cheese's implications to Hitman's premeditated attacks, one can assume that these assassinations were carried out on the same day.

"Only a few days passed, when eleven UNLV Rebels were taken out, including six who had been shot on Lexington Street in East Boston. This bloodbath has even raised the attention of our United States president. White House officials are demanding United States Attorney Carmen Cruz to gain control of this gang violence. Now Assistant United States Attorney Robyn Blatt is applying the pressure," Agent Deraney stated, as he inhaled a few drags of a Winston cigarette.

"What has me puzzled is how Don Cuba's wife and son had been chopped up and discarded inside of two separate trash bags. Not to mention thrown into the water underneath the Tobin Bridge. Half-mile away, Massachusetts State Police divers recovered a snub-nose .357

revolver, which ballistics confirmed to be Hitman's homicide weapon. Our theory reached Mizery being Don Cuba's wife and son's perpetrator, up until further investigation revealed that Don Cuba's wife, Maliya, is actually Mizery's ex-girlfriend, and Maliya's son, Mizhai, yes, the son of Mizery.

"Following these gruesome hackings, Don Cuba's body turned up dead on Franklin Avenue in Chelsea. Chelsea Police officers and Northshore Gang Taskforce investigators reported an observation of brain matter bespattered across Don Cuba's steering wheel, front passenger seat, dashboard, and windshield. A blood trail along the concrete signified that our victim had been dragged to the middle of the street, where he was shot two more times. A breathless man died with all of his belongings, quickly eliminating a robbery theory.

"Foul play never ceased. On February 15, 2013, an Asian woman's guillotined head sat openly inside of a Nissan Maxima. She was identified as Laya Lee. Her brother JB and cousin Han are suspected to be Asian Mafia bosses. They iron-jawed to have Ms. Lee cremated. By speaking to coworkers at World Line Computers in Chelsea, we learned that Ms. Lee had been involved in a relationship with Mizery. According to Eko, Mizery and Projekt were purchasing ten to fifteen kilos of pure powdered cocaine once a week from an untold root," he set about, painting a clear picture with his presentation.

"The Town Line Inn Hotel bloodshed is knotty, where two deceased females and an almost dead Mizery were recovered. No weapons were sighted, though we lifted heavy traces of gunpowder from Mizery's right hand and a dead female's left hand. Two spiritless females were tagged as Tiana Flores and Rosa Sanchez. Logan Airport's records show that five women came to the United States from Santiago, Cuba on October

10, 2012. Don Cuba's sister was among this group. DNA testing affirms that Mizery had intercourse with Ms. Flores and Ms. Sanchez. At some point, Mizery's right hand got handcuffed to the post of a bed railing, in addition to the handcuff being shot off. My hunch points to known visitors shooting to kill. A hotel manager heard muffled gunshots and thenafter caught a glimpse of a black Porsche calmly driving away. End of report," Agent Deraney debriefed, and then passed me four bulging manila envelopes titled *Operation Royal Ruin II.*

"Agent Deraney? Do we have any witnesses or evidence conjugating any suspects? There are way too many murders, shootings, home invasions, blood, and body chopping for no witnesses or evidence! Unbelievable! Only on the big screen and best sellers! I want confirmations! I want suspects! I want these scumbags singing like canaries! I want convictions! I want to hand out death penalties like candy!" I clamored in an aggravated tone.

"Well, Fat Cheese's testimony can be used to charge Gambino and Loski for armed home invasion. I am sure that Fat Cheese's mother and sister will testify as well. That is a definite double-digit sentence. They will be sitting up in USP McCreary sharing war stores next to their pal Pistol.

"On the early morning of Don Cuba's slaying, homicide detectives interviewed two elderly women that heard the gunshots. They claim to have been looking out of their windows, when they witnessed some chubby person dressed in black, shoot the victim before cutting loose. My guesswork says that it's Mizery, but without anything else, we have nothing. According to an UNLV member, who luckily faded out of the Lexington Street massacre, it was Blackrob behind the machine gun's trigger. However, when our witness was shown a photo array, the craven suddenly caught amnesia. Bullshit! No-one wants to be dubbed a snitch!" Agent Deraney's knee-jerk reaction echoed throughout.

"Agent Deraney, follow up on what we have. I want you to put faces to these crimes," I instructed, while looking at the other two agents who were listening attentively.

"Hello," I answered a ringing cell phone.

"Hi. This is Brian Murphy, the superintendent at Cedar Junction State Prison. Your federal witness, Justin Suarez, a.k.a. Fat Cheese, got murdered brutally," the man unfolded, as if nothing was wrong.

"Are you fucking serious! You're a fucking moron! Why wasn't he segregated in protective custody?" I screamed into the cell phone.

"Inmate Suarez resided in 10-Block, where the cooperator had been locked down twenty-three hours a day on rec alone status," Mr. Murphy responded, knowing that he was in the hot seat.

"So tell me how he ended up dead, genius?" I fumed.

"Mr. Suarez was found dead yesterday morning at approximately eight seventeen a.m., resulting from thirty-two stab wounds. His cell bars and solid door had been closed. An autopsy report discloses a person bereft of life for at least four days, before correctional officers blew the trumpet. The inner-perimeter security investigators believe that some of our employees may have been involved," he reported an obvious specification.

"Do you think so? You stupid motherfucker! Don't do anything! Don't touch anything! Don't interview anybody! Don't do shit! We are sending in a team to investigate this state of affairs! Everyone is a suspect, including you!" I hung up in his face, behind almost popping my voice box.

After translating everything to Agents Deraney, Lazar, and Slater, they were off to Walpole State Prison. The agents immediately moved out, understanding our current situation as a possible break in this investigation. I just settled behind my desk contemplating, when it hit me, the perfect plan to bring down the Unknowns.

It has been two months of interviewing new recruits straight out of the police academy from different states. One has yet to find the right two officers. Today, I hosted five sound outs and still not one qualifier. Wrong attitudes, flip-side characters, just not, what I am looking for. A careful evaluation is in order, because if anyone is somehow exposed, lives will be at risk.

"Agent Sielander?" my secretary announced her presence by softly knocking on the door.

"Yes, Mrs. Watson?" I acknowledged her, an old grouchy lady that mirrors Chewbacca from the *Star Wars*.

"Your ten a.m. appointment with Officers Nieves and Fuentes is in ten minutes. They have already been waiting for fifteen minutes. Should I send them in?" she asked.

"Sure, Mrs. Watson," I replied.

In the process of organizing a hodgepodge desk, both officers filed in. *On the button!* Now I had to pick at their brains. After shaking hands, a curtailed scan followed. Officer Nieves has blue eyes and reddish hair styled in a short cut. He is 6'1", white-skinned, and has an athletic build. Officer Fuentes is 6'2', medium built, has a tan complexion, brown eyes, black hair in a short fashion, and steps with a cocky swagger.

"Sit down, gentlemen," I said, and then mimed toward two empty chairs that were directly in front of me. "Gentlemen, I have a special operation, in which two officers are needed to go deep cover, in order to infiltrate an organized gang. My reason for wanting to select new recruits into a FBI investigation is to avoid officers that have been broken into a cop's mentality. Before details can be explained, an interview must take place, to even consider if either of you are adequate for this operation," I implied, knowing deep down inside that I had hit the jackpot.

"Officer Nieves, can you please tell me a little bit about yourself and how you grew up?" I put through the wringer.

"I am twenty-years-old and grew up in the Albany Projects in Brooklyn, New York as an out-of-control teenager in love with the street life. I am from Puerto Rican decent. One sold drugs for the OG'z, up until the age of fourteen, when I was arrested for three hundred grams of heroin. A judge sentenced me to three years in Spotford Juvenile. During the incarceration, my mother and father were murdered in what police categorized as a drug deal gone wrong. Upon release, I moved to Buffalo, New York with Auntie Maribel, a kindergarten schoolteacher. After graduating high school, I enlisted into the police academy," Officer Nieves gave a brief rundown.

"Officer Fuentes, can you please tell me a little bit about yourself and how you grew up?" I put the screws to him as well.

"I'm nineteen-years-old and was born and raised in Chicago, Illinois. I am one hundred percent Puerto Rican. At age eleven, I killed an abusive stepfather one night, when he came home drunk and started beating on my disabled mother. An attempt to stop him resulted in a bloody nose. Anger led a young boy to a calling .38 Special. Three bullets had been fired out of its chamber, ripping through the owner's chest cavity. I spent five years in a juvenile facility, before being committed to a mental health institution for a year. At seventeen-years-old, freedom had been a reality. Because of one's no-family subsistence, one of many counselors, good-heartedly let me stay at her house. She encouraged an absentminded young man to graduate high school. The decision to become law enforcement came about one day, when I stopped two crackheads from robbing an old lady for an empty pocketbook," Officer Fuentes finished his story.

"Okay gentlemen, both of you are exactly what I have been looking for. For the next twenty-four months, infiltration into the Unknowns' criminal enterprise in Massachusetts is our ground zero. This special operation is to be kept top-secret. You will become Unknowns by any means necessary, which involves gang bangin', selling drugs, murder, and anything else to prove your loyalty to their supremacy. Any illegal activity will be protected under full immunity. You guys have thirty days to say goodbye to home," were my determined words. This was the beginning and end to an obnoxious organization.

CHAPTER 31

MA$$A$HOOT$HIT
GAMBINO

"**Y**up, yup, I'm Loyal 2 Da Hood, left side, black flag, Five what's good," I rapped out. I had just finished laying down the hook to a new track called *Loyal 2 Da Hood*.

I had been sweating in the booth perfecting this track for two hours. One of Mizery's verses got mixed in as well. Raffito is a beast producing music. Lyrikote, baby! I am going to send the 'Loyal 2 Da Hood' track to Jammin' 94.5 on the Launch Pad, so Hussel Simmons can bang my shit.

Ever since Tsunami Rekordz opened up, it has been all about the music. *MA$$A$HOOT$HIT* has twelve tracks so far. Five solo: (1) Behind Metal (2) People's Anthem (3) Ready Or Not (4) I'm A Dog (5) I Don't Luv U Bitch. I also have a few collaborations: (6) Da Gambino Family featuring RayDog, Loski, Stiz, and Born (7) Redrum featuring Styles P (8) Fuck Da Police featuring Jeezy (9) Deep Throat featuring Lil' Kim (10) Loyal 2 Da Hood featuring Mizery. Lastly, accentuating two of Mizery's joints: (11) Roachkilla featuring Stiz (12) Ryde Or Die featuring Raffito & Joshua. The expectation release date of my album should be in three months. A record release party is on the verge of being planned with live performances from Raffito & Joshua, Rihanna, French Montana, and yours truly, Gambino.

Real talk, I tried to get in Rihanna's belly on the night that I recorded the *Deep Throat* track with Lil' Kim. It had been the first time that we had met and your boy almost piped it. All of us were popping bottles of Ciroc and smoking that ewe-wee. It was surprising to see Lil' Kim and Rihanna chilling together. I guess they must have squashed their beef. By the time that Lil' Kim had finished recording her verse, Rihanna and I were in the bathroom kissing and feeling on one another. Every time that my hands rubbed on that pussy through those tight Sergio Valente jeans, she teased away. That bitch is mad sexy. Lil' Kim continuously hated by knocking on the door and wanting to leave. Lil' Kim didn't give Raffito or Joshua any type of play. The two of them bounced without anyone exchanging numbers. Nevertheless, one day, out of the blue, Raffito tells me how Rihanna phoned the studio, volunteering to perform at the record release party.

While concentrating on this music, my money has been flowing in slowly. A nigga is still sitting on those bricks that Amandria hooked me up with. I fell back a little after all of the craziness that went down. Now that things are quieting down, I'm about to get back on top of the bird game. What's fucked up is that I have no connect. Fuck Projekt! He is the true definition of a Judas. *Money over family, huh?* That nigga deserves five to the head!

"Gambino? Fire, nigga!" DJ Lucky Charms complimented me, while saving the track. DJ Lucky Charms is average-height and chunky, white-skinned, Puerto Rican, and has short dark hair. He was born and raised in Chelsea.

"That's what it is, my nigga. We're a dream team, baby!" I gave credit to all.

"I'll be done with mixing it down by tomorrow. Right now, Raffito and Joshua are going to bang out *Bien Loca,*" DJ Lucky Charms promulgated, and at that moment, blasted a reggaeton beat as Raffito and Joshua got ready to step into the recording booth.

"Do y'all thang; I got some shit to handle," I shot back, and then gave everyone dap and left.

It has been hot and muggy all day. You know how the sun stays beaming in July. I set off to San Andreas, where Firu, four-Five-six, Loski, and Maniak were posted up, looking like crooks. "Weight on deck," was my announcement.

The name Maniak fits the brother perfectly. He's El Salvadorian, 5'7", bulky and thick, has yellowish-brown skin color, short hair, and wears glasses. This insane gangsta has numerous bodies under that UK belt. I remember the day that I got G-Fived. The both of us were driving around in a stolen Pathfinder hunting for some UNLV Rebels. The truck pulled up in front of Grove Park, where it had been swarmed with grey bandannas. Maniak called over that Roach nigga Havoc, some tall Bosnian chump, who hesitantly walked over with a gloved left hand reaching for something inside of a pouch to a hooded sweatshirt. When Havoc touched the street and began treading toward our vehicle, Maniak stepped on the gas. Before we knew it, Havoc was being dragged from block to block. By the time that the hot mobile reached Hawthorne Street, Havoc had to be nearly dead. His body could be seen skinned raw. Two bullets to the cranial from my .40 caliber High Point ended dude's life.

Firu told me that he needed two hundred and fifty grams of crack. The nigga suggested that the two of us get up after I visited Mizery. four-Five-six began jewelling a Thunder 5. It takes .44 shells, shotgun shells, and some other shit. The hammer wasn't even that big either, maybe a little bigger than a nine revolver. I drove away and then stopped at the bottom of San Andreas to let two pretty El Salvadorian bitches cross.

"Vaya, mami? Ese culo de papi?" I holla'd at both of them.

The duo threw up their middle fingers while smiling at me. As they walked, my two 15'inch JL Audio woofers banged a reggaeton mixed CD straight from Puerto Rico. Those crazy-ass bitches started dancing right in front of the whip. I hopped out to gorilla pimp.

Both of those ho'z are from East Boston. Myra is a short and thick tan-skinned chick with short dark hair. She goes to college and works. Shorty kept playing with my braids. Claudia is a short and thick tan-skinned chick too. The quiet one that doesn't speak unless spoken to. Her light-brown hair is ridiculously long, literally touching a bubble ass. Their cell phone numbers had been logged in, right before two hugs and two kisses were given to your boy. You know, pimp am I.

I hopped back inside of the whip and quickly chirped around the corner of Shurtleff Street; merged left; took another left at a stop sign across the street from the Chelsea Fire Station; cruised down Broadway rumping some LOX; and lastly banged a Fifth Street right in the direction of Diamond Kutz. Once out front, I popped the Fives with Quest, Born, Shine, Rizzo, and Pluto. "Weight on deck," was my announcement.

My man Quest is all skin and bones. A tiny-ass Puerto Rican yellow nigga with a low cut whose unpredictable when it comes to that paper. Despite the fact that he is forever fucking up people's bread, his obedience makes up for it when it's code red.

Born is a jailbird for real. He has done more prison time than I have been alive. This six-foot milk-colored and beefy Portuguese brother is a true definition of a UK Gangsta. The OG styles a short hairdo and bears a mean swagger. He's continuously the first warrior volunteering to put in work.

Shine can be a very conniving person. One time, Wolf accused manito of stealing a half-kilo of powdered cocaine that he had stashed in manita Leesy's house. However, Shine denied it, claiming death before dishonor. Yet, not even a week later, the homey was in the hood pitching weight. Since then, it has been all eyes on him. Shine is a lightskinned mulatto cat that stands at 5'8". He's muscular, has a bald fade, and is nice with his hands.

Rizzo is an official OG and had been part of the Unknowns' foundation in Crack City. It was he, Mizery, Trizsmacks, Danger, Ricknice, and Emo. They were a force to be reckoned with. There isn't anybody that can fuck with Rizzo when it comes to stealing cars, trucks, or motorcycles. The brother is an animal behind the wheel. OG Rizzo stands at 5'9", is Puerto Rican, tan-skinned, weighs 180 pounds, has short dark hair, and forever thinks that he's a pretty boy.

I stepped inside of the barbershop to show Fats some love as he was giving Mecca a lineup. Big boy Mecca is 5'8", heavily-built, Italian, has light-colored skin, and a bald fade. An aggressive man that is feared when angry. Just the other day, Babyface and him had a fistfight over a play. A black crackhead came wandering up Chestnut Street looking for six twenty-rocks for one hundred dollars. They both approached the fiend displaying the product in their hands. The woman chose Baby face's crack because the sizes were bigger. Mecca got upset and disrespected Babyface by calling the bro a bitch. A tussle took place, which brought about raccoon eyes for Babyface and a bloody nose for Mecca. The next day, they got drunk together at King Author's, as if nothing ever happened.

Packed as always, a crowd had been playing Madden for money and all of the chairs were full with niggaz getting haircuts or braids. Once back outside, two Asian females bought bud off Quest and thenceforth jumped back into a Royal Rydes' Escalade truck. They have to be ho'z working for Magik Entertainment. Around the corner on Chestnut Street, Spooky, Babyface, and Wolf were sitting on some steps drinking a fifth of Hennessy.

"Weight on deck," I announced, as we popped the Fives. Soonafter, I headed back to a vibrating Vhop to behold blue and white.

That same night that Babyface and Mecca got drunk at King Author's, after their little scuffle the day before, Babyface received an emergency phone call. His little sister, who was a four-month infant at the time, stopped breathing and had been rushed to the hospital. Behind a traumatic wait, doctors published that she lived and suffered from a mild asthma attack. Babyface is short and tubby, longhaired, light-skinned, and full-blooded Puerto Rican.

"Next time that I hear your music that loud, I'm going to give you a ticket!" the bitch-ass Spanish cop said, all the while acting tough.

"Suck my dick, you fucking bitch!" I blurted out, right before leaving Fifth Street smoking.

A left had been taken onto Chestnut Street and thenafter I hit fifty in my 2001 souped-up black Honda SI; another left on Fourth Street; a quick right at Broadway; and thenceforward the system got turned back up as I sped toward Hawthorne Street. Only Mexicano and K-Rock were chillin' on Tiesha's steps, one more whore working for Magik Entertainment. *What happened to that fatty?* Now she is mad skinny, looking like her lips have been sucking on that glass dick.

Black-ass K-Rock is an African-American man that resembles the actor Danny Glover from the movie *Lethal Weapon*. He is another hot-tempered brother, especially when the lush is intoxicated. He's at least six feet tall, well-developed, and has a taper with waves.

"Where's everybody at?" I asked them.

"Everyone is at Koka's house getting bent. Ghost bailed out. He beat his drug case on illegal search and seizure. Niggaz put up ten stacks on the probation matter. So while everyone is partying, we're out here paperchasing," K-Rock replied, while all along looking hazed out.

"I dig it. Weight on deck," had been my repetitive announcement, and then I was off.

At Mizery's hospital room, three men stood next to his bed. I clicked the safety off the .380 automatic pistol, which was inside of my Gucci jean pocket, and thereupon stormed inside, ready to clap shit up. Amandria jumped up right in front of me. Damn, I didn't even see her and Angel.

"Relax, Gambino. That's Mizery's father, his little brother Alex, and friend-brother Black Sosa," Amandria explained.

"My apologies for the disrespect. Things have been crazy around here lately. It's hard to trust anyone," I looked all in their eyes, to let them know that my words were sincere.

"No need for the apology. Your loyalty to my son is thought of highly," Mizery's father rendered, as he popped the Fives with me.

Mizery's dad is 6'3", white-skinned, fat, bald, and strikes as a mean person. The big guy was wearing a long black leather Versace trench coat matching a Pedro Navaja hat. He's an old-school mobster. Alex is 5'8", light-skinned, clean cut, maybe in his early twenties, and is a skinnier version of Mizery. Black Sosa grew up with Alex and is considered family. He is Puerto Rican and Dominican, 6'1", dark-skinned, skinny, and rocks a short haircut.

Popdukes told me that Mizery used to live in Waterbury, Connecticut on Williams Street for about a year. Moreover, that Black Sosa, Alex, and Mizery became Baby Unknowns trying to assume his role. A story had been recounted bearing on the three brothers that entered a pet store and robbed it at gunpoint for a six-count litter of Bluenose pitbulls and dog food. This robbery made headlines. One day, Popdukes overheard them talking about how they had six puppies in the basement, which resulted in an ass whipping. And the dogs—history. Right after Mizery graduated the eighth grade at Wallace Middle School, he moved back to Massachusetts. Now I know where Mizery's set of Unknowns came from. We were all in conversation when Doctor Strom walked inside.

"How is everybody doing this evening?" Doctor Strom politely asked. The six of us nodded, as to say, 'we were fine.' "Mr. Rodriguez still remains in the same condition. Then again, yesterday a nurse reported that while cleaning the trachea and checking his vitals, a leg moved from one spot to another. Researching similar cases exemplifies a possibility of Mr. Rodriguez regaining consciousness," he communicated, and then smiled.

Doctor Strom continued explaining Mizery's progression more in detail, but then excused himself after receiving a page to the emergency room. His potentiality was needed, pertaining to a car accident involving a drunk driver that crashed into a pregnant woman's Toyota Corolla. I heard Doctor Strom saying that a woman would be arriving promptly in a helicopter. Before making my exit, Black Sosa flagged me over.

"I know that you niggaz are getting money. When you want to step it up, holla. Our team gets it straight off the boat, papa. We can even work out a business plan, where I throw you like ten raw joints on consignment, in order to help a brother organize your empire. Trust is not an issue on the strength of Mizery. Amandria told us that Mizery loves you, as if blood," Black Sosa said, while staring into my eyes without blinking.

"Your offer is appreciated, but right now, there are too many things going on in one's life. My concentration is on music," I spoke with truth.

"Honestly twin, whenever, I got you," he assured me, as we popped the Fives and exchanged numbers.

I shot a glance at Popdukes and Alex, who both winked at me, knowing exactly what our confabulation had been about. *I wonder why Mizery doesn't fuck with them?* They are the perfect connect. I jumped into the SI to hit up Firu regarding the two-fifty pack, but his impatient-ass went ahead and grabbed it from Projekt. Mentioning that name got a nigga's temperature boiling. He has to die!

CHAPTER 32

GOD SENT ME AN ANGEL
AMANDRIA

"**C**an you please pass me the corn, Auntie Rachelle?" Angel respectfully asked my sister.

"Sure, honey," Rachelle responded, in the mix of reaching for a bowl of corn.

"Thank you, Auntie Rachelle," Angel thanked her, and then scooped up two spoons of corn to sprinkle it onto his plate.

"How is Miguel doing?" my mother questioned.

"He is still in a coma. However, the other day a nurse reported that Miguel moved his leg. The doctor advised us how that is a good sign of him possibly awakening," I explained to Ma.

"Amandria, do you want another piece of chicken?" Rachelle offered, while pouring herself a glass of milk.

"No, thank you. I'm really not that hungry," I declined, and thenceforward I eyed my plate of food that was barely touched.

"No-one knows who shot Miguel yet?" Rachelle popped a question.

"The police have no suspects, so they claim," I replied, while all along staring at the picture of Miguel that was on Ma's refrigerator.

"Amandria? I am not a stupid bitch. I'm talking about on the streets," Rachelle rudely stated, before giving me a dirty look.

"None of Miguel's friends are going to tell me things like that," I retorted in an upset tone.

Rachelle and I are like oil and water. She is like 5'6", half-Haitian, thicker than I, has coffee skin color, long dark hair, and thinks that she's the toughest girl in the world. But that's my bitch. One's bestie. We have different fathers. Both of them have passed away.

"Ma, can you please pass me more mashed potatoes?" Angel hungrily desired, as he finished his first plate of food.

"Wow. You are really hungry today, huh? Did you eat lunch?" a concerned mother queried, because normally this kid would be rushing to take a shower, so that he could get the full two hours of playing Xbox 360 before his eight p.m. bedtime rule.

"Today was Sloppy Joe, Ma. I hate Sloppy Joe," he rejoined, and then piled more mashed potatoes, corn, and two pieces of chicken onto his plate.

When Angel finished gobbling down a second plate of food, Ma, Rachelle, and I cleaned off the dinner table. Rachelle washed the dishes and Angel went to take a shower. I couldn't wait to stretch-out on my bed and light up a blunt. What a frustrating day at work. An elderly patient, which I frequently visit, had a sudden outburst by throwing feces over an accusation against me for trying to induce heart failure with pain medication. Sometimes, patients can be so sweet or they can be the cruelest people.

"What time are you going to visit Miguel tomorrow?" my mother inquired.

"After work, around four O'clock," I returned.

"Rachelle and I are going to meet you there," Ma spoke to me, as she gathered her belongings.

I love my mother. She's a very supportive person that has set family values into two daughters and a son. Ma is a towering hefty white lady with short dark hair that can give someone the wrong impression because of the woman's feisty voice. Nonetheless, she is a big sweetheart that would give the shirt off her back if you needed it. Mom just got over a stage of depression. She and James, a short scraggy black man, ended a twenty-year relationship, which gave rise to James and Junior, one's gigantic brother, moving to Atlanta, Georgia.

Rachelle and Ma said their goodbyes and promised to return next week for dinner. Mizery loves when Ma comes over to cook Italian meals. His favorite dish has to be stuffed shells, meatballs, and that soft delicious garlic bread. Our family treasures him.

Dwelling upon when I first met Miguel—Rachelle just hit the seventh grade at Williams Middle School. I was a junior attending Chelsea High School. Miguel and Rachelle were in homeroom together. They actually became best friends. Miguel used to hang out with our crowd of sidekicks at Volk Park drinking forty ounces of malt liquor. The first time that his lips touched mine had been in Rachelle's friend Vanessa's house. Both of us were piss-drunk off Private Stock. Kissing almost led to going all the way. We were virgins, even though Miguel acted as if he wasn't.

From that day on, we were inseparable, officially boyfriend and girlfriend. Mom and her boyfriend James hated Miguel, a spic hoodlum. I used to beg them to give the kid a chance. One time, Miguel and I hung out at a minor-league Chelsea Mall, only to bump into Auntie Lynn shopping. She must have blown her whistle, because fifteen minutes later, James stormed in like a raging bull. He grabbed Miguel by his throat and threatened to kill him. Of course, that didn't stop us from sneaking around.

It took about six months of begging Mom and James to get to know Miguel before they finally agreed. Rachelle also helped persuade them. Miguel had been invited to dinner on several occasions. It didn't take long for Ma and James to gain affection for him. Even Baby, our Chow Chow, accepted Miguel. Even though Baby bit his leg one late night while he was trying to tiptoe through our kitchen. Mom and James eventually allowed a spic to move in.

I loved Miguel so much that I decided to lose my virginity to him. It was an awesome experience in Rachelle's bedroom. His fingers gradually teased a wet clit, making me yearn for that hard dick. A pair of jeans and panties slid off, to welcome pain, thus pleasure. Rachelle's nosey-ass walked in to walk out. In ten minutes flat, a glob of cum spurted onto Rachelle's bed.

Then came what seemed to be the worse day of my life. Miguel herald relocating to his father's house in Waterbury, Connecticut. God stabbed me in the heart with a sword. When he left, a good-for-nothing world went upside-down. I could not eat, sleep, or concentrate on anything. It took months for me to get over it.

About a year later, Mizery retreated. My stomach formed in knots, as little fat Miguel hugged me, kissed me, and swore that he loved and missed me. And just like that, we were a couple again. But Miguel rotated a different person. This mimic was older, taller, mature, plus heavily involved in a gang. Mr. Thug always carried a gun, as if the youngster were John Wayne or something. Miguel quit school to drink liquor and smoke weed every day. A straight mess. Fighting became a constant thing over showdowns to spend time with his friends rather than with a loving girlfriend. I secretly caught him cheating, but never said anything about it. Our puppy love relationship ended the minute that Miguel got cuffed up for a shooting—

"Ma! Ma!" Angel had to shout, in order to snap me back into reality.

"I'm sorry, Angel. I was just stargazing," I wisecracked, as we laughed together.

"You were thinking about Dad, huh?" Angel asked, already knowing the answer.

"Yes, Angel. I miss your father," were my truthful words, as tears trickled down one's face.

"Don't worry, Ma. Dad is strong. He'll wake up," Angel vented. His confidence had made me feel much better.

"Son? Where is your homework?" I inquired, moving on to another subject.

"It's on the kitchen table. Homework was simply a drawing for art class. Whoever has the best one wins an extra bag of chips for lunch," Angel riposted, full of self-reliance.

"Angel, please bring Rocky and Terror inside. Feed them apart and then change their water. You can stay up playing Xbox until ten p.m..." I surprised Angel.

"Thanks, Ma," Angel uttered, and then sped off.

"Daddy? Wake up? I miss playing Madden and Modern Warfare with you. Rocky and Terror are huge. Both dogs try to bite everybody except for Ma and me. When I feed them, I have to separate the two. Because one day I had been giving those dogs boneless spare ribs and they started fighting. Terror bit Rocky on his stomach. We had to take Rocky to the animal hospital," Angel was lying next to Mizery in the hospital bed talking to him.

Mom and Rachelle began bawling as soon as they caught sight of Mizery. My mother had to sit down to drink some water. Rachelle stood there, dazed out, not being able to believe the situation. Mizery's grandmother and Aunt Maggie set foot inside of the hospital room to greet us. As always, Mizery's grandmother gathered everybody around Mizery to join in worship.

"Let's go get something to eat at the cafeteria before it closes. It's on me," I invited everyone, when our prayer concluded.

"Sounds like a good idea," Maggie agreed, sounding hungry.

"I don't want to eat, Ma. I'll stay with Daddy," Angel sadly said, wanting to remain next to his father.

"Okay, Angel. But I'm buying you something to eat," I declared, and then had to turn around, because I almost broke down right there.

"Angel loves his Daddy, huh?" my mother supposed, as we were scooting down the corridor.

"Ma! Ma!" Angel came out of the room screaming. "Daddy is awake! He woke up!"

I ran in the direction of Mizery's hospital room with my anxiety at an all time high. As I reached the bed, one could observe that Mizery was still arranged in the same position that he had been in when we left. I seen no movements. But as I ambulated close by, Mizery slowly turned his head and then smiled at me.

CHAPTER 33

DEATH BEFORE DISHONOR
PROJEKT

OOM! BOOM! BOOM! "Open the fucking door! FBI! Get on the fucking floor! Now! Before I blow your fucking brains out!" FBI agents shouted, ahead of throwing me onto my face, in order to lock handcuffs around both of one's wrists.

"You are never going to fuck again!" Looney yelled in a clear English voice. He was wearing a bright-orange FBI jacket.

"Here is a warrant for the murders of Hitman, Teddy Bear, Diamond, Booty, and Negra," Chrisrock alleged, showing me photos of dead bodies on an autopsy table.

"Sign this search warrant, scumbag! Or we are going to tear your apartment apart! If you have anything in here, let us know and charges will not be filed!" Amandria yelped.

What the fuck is going on? Feds? I cannot even think straight. *Is anything stashed in here?* I was handcuffed and facedown on my living room floor, until 357 lifted me up, and before long, smacked an addled face. As I shook that off, Gambino strolled over holding a Carolina Hurricanes hockey bag.

"Jackpot, buddy. Looks like fifteen little birdies, balla!" Gambino smart-mouthed, and then laughed, as he swayed a walkie-talkie in his left hand.

"That's not it, agent. Here is the murder weapon used for Diamond, Negra, and Booty," Wolf presented, as he seized it inside of an evidence bag.

"You actually thought that I died, huh?" Eddito impudently remarked, while standing there holding the front door open.

As Babyface escorted an arrestee to an awaiting elevator, I peeped Shizauto and Pro disconnecting cameras. They mocked me with a nod. My lips tried to say something, but the words just wouldn't come out. It's like I had no control of myself.

BOOM! BOOM! BOOM! I woke up to someone really banging on my front door.

"Who is it?" I squawked, while shaking off that horrible dream.

"Abre la puerta, cabrón! Es Looney!" Looney sounded like he was banging on my door for a grip.

I unlocked the front door in order to pop the Fives with a goony. Thenafter, he inquistioned, "Tu vas a capiar hoy, verdad?" Looney tossed me rubber-banded stacks in a sneaker box, while all along remaining in the hallway. Thenceforward, the bro headed toward the elevator. Yet, before the elevator doors opened up, the nut clearified, "Esos son chavos de parte de Pro y Yo que pusimos juntos." I respected Looney's hustle.

It's nice out today, so I kept it simple with a pair of dark-blue True Religion jeans with a white Polo shirt, construction Timberland boots, a black Red Sox fitted hat, and black Moncler Lunettes. A 24K rosary chain synchronized one-carat diamond studs freshly. I splashed on some Burberry Touch and got right. Cutup hotdogs mixed inside of scrambled eggs were smoothly washed down with a cup of orange juice. Twin nine-millimeter handguns were tucked into my Truey's on the way out, but one had to stop short, because I almost forgot the backpack that was gwuaped up.

While bumping some underground shit from Jeezy on the ride to get up with JB and Han, I spotted a goldish car stalking a nigga. On the Tobin Bridge, a left had been made toward Chelsea. I ghosted in my GT Bentley, hitting one hundred and ten miles per hour, until I got off the Chestnut Street exit. Our UK hoods were dead, but then again, it was only eleven thirty-nine a.m... Niggaz were probably still hung over from clubbing last night. I coasted to the city of Lynn and then parked two streets down from the Blue Notes bar. Once inside, Han greeted me. Thenceforth, he escorted a dog to the back office.

"How are you doing, my friend?" JB asked.

"Business couldn't be better," it was a simple answer, in the mix of handing the backpack to Han.

"There are five extra as a bonus," JB made known, as he pointed at two Heineken boxes resting on a brown couch.

"I appreciate the love. Your request will be handled when the correct moment arises," I let him know.

"The time is now! Mizery gained consciousness! He must die!" JB squalled, trying to intimidate me.

"Who put you on that Mizery awakened? I would have been the first person to know this!" I said, just as tough.

"Obviously not! My connection informed me last—"

"Connect this!" I vociferated.

BLAM! BLAM! BLAM! BLAM! BLAM! BLAM! BLAM! BLAM! And the other nine-millimeter pistol perforated Han. *BLAM! BLAM! BLAM! BLAM! BLAM! BLAM! BLAM!* I thenafter stood over Han aiming the burners at him. *BLAM! BLAM!* JB tried to crawl as blood regurgitated in gobs. *BLAM!* They were both dead now.

I strapped the backpack back on my back and then picked up two weighty Heineken boxes. A nigga stretched two blocks until reaching the Bruce Wayne. *Why didn't anybody call me about Mizery?* In the process of scrolling down to Amandria, my actions were frozen. One thing learned in federal cases is that your location can be tracked by cell phone towers. On the other hand, I can't complain. I'm sitting pretty. Wait until Mizery finds out that those Asians got bodied.

With everything on me, I navigated myself through ghostlike projects. Upon entering my project building, one pressed the Down arrow to an elevator, while all along neglecting a vibrating cell phone that loaded hands could not pull out. When I reached the fourth floor, in nothing flat, keys jingled to open a locked door. Ill-fated, I never saw the triggerperson creep behind me; firing five bullets into an accessible cranium. A UK Gangsta was on his way to embrace Lucifer. I guess that's the price that you pay for being...

!!Loyal 2 Da Hood!!

EPILOGUE

P rojekt attired an all-black three-piece tailored Giorgio Armani suit combining a gold silk shirt and tie. The nigga freaked it with gold-bottom midnight GA shoes. The 14K Cuban Link chain accommodated a Jesus piece that was flooded with yellow VVS diamonds. It hung down to the dead man's dick. El cordel coordinated 2K stud earrings and a two-finger UK ring. His right hand flossed ten stacks while gripping a MP5 machine gun left-handedly. A black bandanna that had been neatly tied dangled from the left wrist. Projekt gaped at everyone through Ferragamo shades as he leaned on an onyx casket. Projekt's wake got set up at the crime scene apartment in the Cathedral Projects. La Familia del flew down from Loiza Aldea, Puerto Rico and strong-mindedly chaired the wake like they do for the bichotes in PR. Straight gangsta! Projekt stood there, as if to say, 'If it don't make dollars, it don't make sense.'

Projekt's wake was full to capacity, looking like the Puerto Rican Festival at Franklin Park. No bullshit! Mizery had been present, but had to be pushed around in a wheelchair. Things seemed confusing—tearful to say goodbye to Projekt, but in high spirits to see Mizery alive. Many discussions took place between Gambino and Shizauto, Looney and Loski, Young Gunna and Gladiator, and a few others. The exchanges were positive and full of energy to rebuild the UK family.

Ten days passing Projekt's initial funeral, Spooky was traversing down Fifth Street about to get a lineup when someone uttered, "What's good, homey?" Spooky turned around and took notice of two niggaz masqueraded by helmets sitting on a white Triumph Supersports motorcycle.

The passenger racked-back and aimed a sawed-off 12-gauge shotgun, and thenafter blustered, "Suicide!" *BLABOOM! BLABOOM!*

Spooky lifted off his feet and thenceforth hurtled right through the front window of Diamond Kutz. *ZOOOOOOM!* The assailants throttled away in the mix of a crowd forming around the barbershop. Spooky trembled from two enormous holes to the chest and stomach as blood upchucked out of a defunct mouth.

HOOD GLOSSARY

360'n: 1. A face slash that consisted of three hundred and sixty stitches.

about that life: 1. A street-orientated person heavily involved in the street life.

Abre la puerta, cabrón!: 1. Open the door, motherfucker!

Abuela/Abuelita: 1. Grandma or Grammy.

aight: 1. Okay.

aired him out: 1. Attempted to shoot him. 2. Shot him.

AK-47: 1. A machine gun. 2. Marijuana.

alphabet boyz: 1. Law enforcement.

ants-in-pants: 1. Anxious.

arroz blanco: 1. White rice.

arroz con dulce: 1. Rice candy.

arroz con gandules: 1. Yellow rice with pigeon peas.

así me gusta, mami: 1. That's the way I like it, baby.

Ay papi, así: 1. Oh baby, like that.

babygirl: 1. A nickname for a female.

baby-momma: 1. A mother.

bag: 1. To self-introduce, in order to catch the other's interest.

baja pantys: 1. Lower panties. 2. Amazing cars.

balla: 1. A person making serious money.

ballin': 1. Making serious money.

bananas: 1. Crazy.

bang: 1. To fight. 2. To represent a gang.

bangin': 1. Representing a gang. 2. Fighting. 3. Something well liked.

bankrolls: 1. Money.

base: 1. Pure crack.

Bean: 1. Boston.

Beantown: 1. Boston.

beast: 1. Beyond good in something; impressionable. 2. Very big.

beat-down: 1. Rugged. 2. Physically assaulted.

beat'em in the head: 1. To win over.

beating that shit up: 1. A male giving hardcore sex.

be easy: 1. To relax. 2. Calm down. 3. Be careful.

beef: 1. Problems.

belly: 1. A vagina.

belly of the beast: 1. Prison.

bendición: 1. An asking for blessings.

bent: 1. Intoxicated.

be off this: 1. Leave.

bestie: 1. Best friend.

bid: 1. Serving a jail sentence.

bien loca: 1. A crazy female. 2. A female in heat.

big faces: 1. Money.

big homey: 1. A gang leader. 2. An elder.

bird: 1. One thousand grams.

bitch: 1. A derogatory term toward a female. 2. A positive remark toward a female. 3. A disrespect toward a male.

blood: 1. A gangsta.

blow: 1. Powdered cocaine.

blowjob: 1. Oral sex.

blown-up: 1. Reduced from its pure form and mixed with a substance for greater weight.

blow-up: 1. Reduced from its pure form and mixed with a substance for greater weight. 2. To succeed.

blue: 1. Marijuana.

blue and white: 1. Local law enforcement.

blunt: 1. Marijuana rolled inside of any type of cigar paper.

body shit: 1. Kill.

bomb: 1. Extremely good.

bomb sloppy: 1. Extremely good sex. 2. Oral sex.

boner: 1. An erect penis.

boohooing: 1. Crying. 2. Complaining.

Boricua: 1. Puerto Rican.

Boss One: 1. A gang leader.

bounce: 1. To leave.

boyz: 1. Law enforcement.

box: 1. Solitary confinement. 2. A vagina.

brain game: 1. A person's reputation for giving oral sex.

bread: 1. Money.

breezing: 1. Moving fast.

brick: 1. One thousand grams.

brickhouse: 1. A location used to hide illegal materials.

bricks: 1. Housing projects. 2. The streets.

broad: 1. A female.

Bruce Wayne: 1. An amazing car.

brushed my shoulders off: 1. Pay the situation no mind. 2. Disregard the situation.

bubble: 1. Shapely buttocks.

bucked: 1. To shoot. 2. To be shot.

bud: 1. Marijuana.

bugged me out: 1. To be confused.

buried the hatchet: 1. Came to an agreement.

burner: 1. A Firearm.

bust a nut: 1. Ejaculate.

butterfly: 1. A kiss.

butter-pecan Rican: 1. A light-brown Puerto Rican female.

buzzy: 1. A cousin.

caking it: 1. Making serious money.

call girl: 1. A high-class prostitute.

cálmate: 1. Calm down.

came: 1. Ejaculated.

camel toe: 1. A vagina.

came-off: 1. A very quick achievement.

came-up: 1. A very quick achievement.

Cancer stick: 1. A cigarette.

cannon: 1. A high-caliber firearm.

castle: 1. Home. 2. Prison.

cat: 1. A person.

caught-up: 1. To get caught.

cheddar: 1. Money.

cheese-eating-faggot: 1. An informant.

chef: 1. To cook. 2. To mix drugs.

Chef Boyardee: 1. To cook. 2. To mix drugs.

chefmatik: 1. Someone who is extremely good at handling drugs.

chick: 1. A female.

chillin': 1. Hanging out. 2. In a comfortable mood.

chink: 1. An offensive term toward an Asian person.

chips: 1. Money.

chirped: 1. Screeching tires.

chopper: 1. A machine gun.

chuletas: 1. Pork chops.

clap: 1. To shoot with a gun.

clear as a bell: 1. Obvious.

clocked: 1. saw; viewed.

code red: 1. A time of danger.

coke: 1. Short for çocaine.

cokehead: 1. A cocaine addict.

Columbian Gold: 1. Marijuana.

comfy: 1. Comfortable.

comma-throwing: 1. Spending thousand of dollars.

Como estas, papi?: 1. How are you doing, baby?

con: 1. Short for convict.

concrete jungle: 1. A neighborhood. 2. Housing Projects.

confab: 1. Short for confabulation; a conversation.

connect: 1. Short for connection.

connection: 1. A supplier.

cooked-up: 1. Powdered cocaine transformed into crack.

cookie: 1. A vagina.

cool: 1. All right.

cooling: 1. Comfortable; untroubled.

cornrows: 1. Braids.

count: 1. Money.

countinghouse: 1. Bank.

crack: 1. Powdered cocaine cooked with baking soda and transformed into a hard substance; smokeable cocaine.

cracker: 1. A white person.

crackhead: 1. A crack addict.

crackhouse: 1. A location used to distribute or smoke crack cocaine.

cracking up: 1. Laughing.

creeping: 1. Cheating. 2. Sneaking up on someone; moving slowly.

Creepy: 1. Marijuana.

crib: 1. Living quarters.

crook: 1. A criminal.

crushing: 1. Having sex.

cuff: 1. Something given on consignment.

cum: 1. Sperm.

curving mini bat: 1. A penis.

cut: 1. A hidden area.

cuz: 1. A gangsta.

cuzzo: 1. Cousin.

dap: 1. A handshake.

deep: 1. Many.

deep-six: 1. To end a relationship. 2. Murder. 3. Throw away.

deep throat: 1. Sliding a penis in someone's esophagus.

def: 1. Short for definitely.

dime: 1. An attractive female.

dinky: 1. Small.

Dios te bendiga: 1. God bless you.

dipping: 1. Going fast.

DMX: 1. Crack cocaine.

dog: 1. A gangsta. 2. A friend.

dogged it: 1. Ran.

dogged-off: 1. Oral sex.

doggy: 1. A gangsta.

do-gooder: 1. A well-intentioned person who assist/interfere in matters and situations that they don't fully understand.

dogtrottin': 1. Jogging.

doing the one-two: 1. Being involved in the subject at hand.

doing us: 1. Spending time together.

dome: 1. Oral sex. 2. A head.

don: 1. A gangsta.

dope: 1. Heroin.

dope fiend: 1. A heroin addict.

dope-fiend: 1. A chokehold.

do the math: 1. Analyze.

dough: 1. Money.

dour: 1. A nickname for Sour Deez marijuana.

down-low: 1. Undisclosed.

do y'all thing: 1. Proceed in your movement.

drama: 1. Problems.

draped up: 1. A person with nice jewelry on.

Duérmete niño mió, que sueñes con los angelitos. Te quiero con todo mi corazón y que Dios te bendiga: 1. Sleep son of mine, and dream with the angels. I love you with all of my heart and may God bless you.

dulce: 1. Candy.

dumping: 1. Shooting.

dying: 1. Laughing.

eager beaver: 1. An intensely energetic, enthusiastic person.

ear-hustling: 1. Listening to someone else's conversation.

eat cheese: 1. To cooperate with law enforcement.

eating: 1. A person making serious money.

eight ball: 1. Equivalent to 3.5 grams.

erased: 1. Murdered.

Eso es mió.: 1. That's mine.

Esos son chavos de parte de Pro y Yo que pusimos juntos.: 1. This is money that Pro and I put together.

esta bien: 1. It's okay.

Estas perdido, cabrón?: 1. Are you lost, motherfucker?

evening lady: 1. A high-class prostitute.

ewe-wee: 1. Marijuana.

expressing friendliness: 1. A smile.

expressing tenderness: 1. A smile.

fall back: 1. Relax. 2. To no longer be involved.

fallen woman: 1. A prostitute.

fam: 1. Short for family.

fatty: 1. Shapely buttocks.

finger: 1. Ten grams of heroin.

fire: 1. Superb.

flag: 1. Bandanna.

flagged up: 1. Displaying a bandanna on one's body.

flaming: 1. Appealing. 2. Dressed all in red. 3. Bringing unwanted attention. 4. Shooting.

flexed: 1. To leave a location.

fly: 1. Attractive. 2. Well dressed. 3. Cunning.

fly-by-night operation: 1. A business. 2. An illegal business.

food: 1. Enemy. 2. Ammunition.

fool's paradise: 1. The neighborhood.

forced it: 1. Exaggerated.

four-pound: 1. A .45 caliber handgun.

fresh: 1. Clean and well dressed.

from the gate: 1. From the beginning.

fuck with me: 1. Interact with me.

fuego: 1. Fire.

funny-money: 1. A suspicious person, thing, or situation.

fuzz: 1. An informant. 2. Law enforcement.

G: 1. A gangsta. 2. One thousand dollars.

GA: 1. Giorgio Armani.

game: 1. The drug business. 2. Words to persuade.

gang bangin': 1. Representing a gang. 2. Rival gangs warring.

gangsta: 1. A street-orientated person. 2. A gang member.

gasoline: 1. Coffee.

gassed: 1. Self-assured.

gate: 1. A cell door.

G-check: 1. Investigate. 2. To put someone in their place.

gear: 1. Clothes.

get-high: 1. Drugs.

get-right: 1. Get it together. 2. Cocaine.

getting me tight: 1. Making me mad.

getting money hard: 1. A person making serious money.

getting raped: 1. Being taken advantage of.

get up: 1. Meet.

G-Fived: 1. Initiated; officially a member.

ghetto birds: 1. Police helicopters.

ghost: 1. A dead person. 2. To leave a location.

gimmy-beaver: 1. A greedy person.

goes sour: 1. Goes wrong.

going down: 1. Happening.

golden: 1. Content.

good-good: 1. Expressing the subject at hand to be liked.

good look: 1. Thank you.

good stead: 1. Money.

goony/goonies: 1. Warrior(s).

got'em coach: 1. Victory.

got right: 1. Got it together.

got shit on murder: 1. Having things under full control.

got shitted on: 1. Disrespected. 2. Humiliated.

got smoked: 1. Punished to the fullest extent of the law. 2. Suffered from a gunshot wound. 3. Murdered.

Grand Daddy Purp: 1. Marijuana.

greenback: 1. Money.

greenery: 1. Money. 2. Marijuana.

grimy: 1. Sneaky; all for self; a person who cannot be trusted.

grip: 1. A long time.

G-roar: 1. A UK Gangsta call.

G-spot: 1. A sensitive spot in the vagina.

Gucci: 1. Content.

guerillas: 1. Gangstaz.

gunclapper: 1. A known triggerperson.

gun game: 1. A person's reputation with a gun.

gunner: 1. A known triggerperson.

gunnin': 1. Speeding. 2. Shooting.

gwuap: 1. Money.

habed: 1. To be brought into court from a prison.

hable con: 1. I talked to.

hammer: 1. A firearm.

hammered-up: 1. Being armed with a gun.

hamponas: 1. Female gangstaz.

hanky-panky: 1. Sexually fooling around.

hard: 1. Acting tough. 2. Acting selfish. 3. Crack cocaine.

hatchie: 1. A hatchback motor vehicle.

hating: 1. Jealously.

hazed out: 1. High off marijuana.

head: 1. Oral sex.

headlock: 1. Under control. 2. Kept to oneself.

held me down: 1. Assisted me when in need.

hip: 1. To already know.

hipped: 1. Placed in one's waist.

hit'em up: 1. To shoot him.

hit him up: 1. Call him. 2. To shoot him.

hitter: 1. A gangsta.

ho/ho'z: 1. Whore(s).

holla: 1. Call. 2. Talk to.

homeboy: 1. A gangsta. 2. A friend.

homey: 1. A gangsta. 2. A friend.

hood: 1. Neighborhood.

hoodie: 1. A hooded sweatshirt.

hoodrat: 1. A neighborhood whore. 2. A neighborhood female.

hoodrich: 1. To be wealthy.

hook: 1. A chorus line to a song.

hooptie: 1. An old vehicle.

hopped: 1. Moved. 2. To get involved.

horn: 1. Phone.

hornballs: 1. Sexually excited and desirous people.

hot: 1. Superb. 2. Bringing unwanted attention. 3. Informer.

hot mess: 1. Out of control.

hush-hush: 1. Quiet.

hustle: 1. To make money by any means necessary.

Hydro: 1. Marijuana.

ice-grilling: 1. Staring excessively.

I got you: 1. To assure someone.

ill: 1. Intensive. 2. Superb.

illest: 1. The best.

illmatik: 1. Intensive. 2. Superb.

insecto: 1. An insect. 2. Enemy.

jack: 1. Phone.

jakes: 1. Law enforcement.

jewelling: 1. Showing off; displaying.

joint: 1. Referring to the subject at hand.

jumpoff: 1. A whore. 2. The subject at hand.

jump-rope: 1. To use someone to affect another person.

junior wifey: 1. A childhood girlfriend.

K/K'z: 1. Kilo(s).

kablooeying: 1. Exploding.

keep it one hundred: 1. To be honest.

kept it moving: 1. To have left.

kicking it: 1. Conversating.

kicks: 1. Sneakers.

kid: 1. A person.

kilo: 1. One thousand grams.

kite: 1. A letter.

kitty cat: 1. A vagina.

kooky: 1. Crazy.

kracking: 1. Started. 2. Happening.

Kush: 1. Marijuana.

la familia del: 1. His family.

la linda: 1. Yeah right. 2. Sarcastically saying, "I don't think so."

lamping: 1. Relaxing with style.

la mujer: 1. The woman.

left-titty: 1. Heart.

legal tender: 1. Money.

lickety-split: 1. Quickly; briskly.

like a bat out of hell: 1. Quickly; briskly.

lineup: 1. A facial haircut.

little man: 1. A male child.

live wire: 1. Someone recklessly out of control.

llamo: 1. Called.

lo mismo: 1. The same.

looked out: 1. To help someone.

loud: 1. Marijuana.

love-love: 1. Good.

LV: 1. Louis Vuitton.

mad: 1. Large amount.

magic: 1. Marijuana.

making it rain: 1. Spending a great deal of money.

mami: 1. Mother. 2. An attractive female. 3. Baby.

man/men: 1. A kilo(s).

Mango Piña: 1. Marijuana.

manhood: 1. A penis.

manita: 1. Sister.

manito: 1. Brother.

math: 1. Phone number. 2. Number(s).

metal: 1. A knife. 2. Gun. 3. Prison.

mi amor: 1. My love.

Mickey Mouse: 1. An informant.

milf: 1. A mother I'd like to fuck.

minime: 1. A child. 2. Follower. 3. A penis.

minute: 1. A long time. 2. A short time.

Mirar, hijo.: 1. Look, son.

Morir Soñando: 1. A Latin orange fruit drink; which means to die dreaming.

move: 1. To proceed with action.

mulah: 1. Money.

my man: 1. Boyfriend. 2. Friend.

my people: 1. People one places confidence in.

nena: 1. Girl.

nice: 1. Good.

nigga: 1. A person.

noassatall: 1. A female having no shape to her buttocks.

nut: 1. Sperm.

nutted: 1. Ejaculated.

off'd one: 1. Murdered someone.

off-the-chain: 1. Astonishing; taken aback.

off-top: 1. First.

OG'z: 1. Original Gangstaz.

old boy: 1. A person.

old school: 1. From the past era.

on deck: 1. To already have it available.

one hundred: 1. Honest.

one love: 1. A signification of respect.

onion: 1. Twenty-eight grams.

on point: 1. Focused; observant; always aware.

on the strength: 1. Just because.

overlaps: 1. Big lips.

pancaked: 1. Laid out flat.

papa: 1. Father. 2. A man.

Papa Dios: 1. God.

paper: 1. Money.

paperboy: 1. A person making serious money.

paperchase: 1. Trying to make money.

papered up: 1. Having money.

papi: 1. Father. 2. An attractive man. 3. Baby.

Papi, tu quieres esto?: 1. Baby, do you want this?

peddles: 1. Sells.

pernil de cerdo y pasteles: 1. Pork shoulder and a Spanish meat pie.

pesos: 1. Dollars.

piedra: 1. Rock.

piff: 1. Marijuana. 2. A nickname for Purple Haze. 3. Impressive.

pig: 1. Law enforcement.

pigeon: 1. A whore.

pimp: 1. A person who prostitutes people for money. 2. A womanizer.

pink panther: 1. A vagina.

pipe: 1. A penis.

piped: 1. To have had sex.

pits: 1. Short for pitbulls.

plátanos: 1. Plantains.

play: 1. A drug transaction. 2. Action.

plug: 1. A supplier. 2. To introduce.

poppin' the Five: 1. A handshake.

pops off: 1. Happening.

Por favor ten cuidado.: 1. Please be careful.

posted up: 1. Frisked by the police. 2. Hanging out in the neighborhood.

potato accounts: 1. Small accounts.

pothead: 1. A user of marijuana.

pound: 1. A male thrusting hard during sex.

PR: 1. Puerto Rico.

PR-80: 1. Marijuana.

presidents: 1. Money.

pro: 1. Short for prostitute.

pull: 1. To self-introduce, in order to catch the other's interest.

pump: 1. A shotgun.

Purple Haze: 1. Marijuana.

pusher: 1. A drug dealer.

put in work: 1. Malicious violence that a person is willing to administer towards their enemies when necessary or mandatory.

put me on?: 1. Help me out?

quick flip: 1. To make fast profit.

rack: 1. One thousand dollars.

Raekwon: 1. Powdered cocaine.

rainbox: 1. The shower.

rat: 1. An informant.

raw: 1. Pure.

raw dog: 1. Unprotected sex.

ready assets: 1. Money.

real talk: 1. Being truthful.

redrum: 1. Murder spelled backwards.

reppin': 1. Short for representing.

reps: 1. Short for represents.

re-up: 1. Purchasing more drugs.

Roach: 1. A disrespectful term toward a rival gang member.

Roachkilla: 1. A disrespectful term toward a rival gang member.

rock: 1. A piece of crack cocaine.

rocking: 1. Wearing. 2. Using.

rope: 1. An ounce; twenty-eight grams.

rubber-bands: 1. Money.

rubberneck: 1. Staring excessively.

rubber-stamped: 1. One's signature.

rumping: 1. Loud music with bass. 2. Selling drugs. 3. Busy.

ryde: 1. To be involved.

ryde-or-die bitch: 1. A loyal female.

Scarface: 1. Powdered cocaine.

scram: 1. A lame; a nobody.

screwball: 1. Crazy.

second-string: 1. Small.

set: 1. A gang. 2. A subdivision to a gang.

shook: 1. Scared; petrified.

shooting shit up: 1. Shooting.

shorty: 1. A female.

shotta: 1. A gangsta.

shotty: 1. A shotgun.

si: 1. Yes.

sidekick: 1. A friend.

Si papi, esto es tuyo. Enséñame lo que tu quieres?: 1. Yes baby, this is yours. Show me what you want?

sitting pretty: 1. In a comfortable position.

Si tú sufres, Yo sufro, si tú lloras, Yo lloró, si tú botas sangre, Yo boto sangre, somos uno!: 1. If you suffer, I suffer, if you cry, I cry, if you bleed, I bleed, we are one!

sleeping: 1. Not paying attention.

slick: 1. Cunning.

slumped: 1. Dead.

smacked-up: 1. Reduced from its pure form. 2. Intoxicated. 3. High.

smash: 1. To have sex; intercourse. 2. To hit.

smashed that: 1. To have had sex.

smut: 1. A whore.

snitching: 1. Cooperating with law enforcement.

snow: 1. Powdered cocaine.

snowbunny: 1. A white girl.

snug as a bug in the rug: 1. Comfortable.

solid: 1. A standup person. 2. Favor.

sour: 1. Not good.

Sour Deez: 1. Marijuana.

spic-and-span: 1. New; fresh.

spit: 1. To shoot. 2. To rap. 3. To talk.

spit burger: 1. Oral sex.

spot: 1. Location. 2. Center of attraction.

square: 1. A cigarette.

squash: 1. Resolve; come to an understanding.

squealer: 1. An informer.

stack: 1. One thousand grams. 2. To save money.

stain: 1. Murder.

stash: 1. A hiding place.

stepped-on: 1. Reduced from its pure form.

stiff one: 1. An erect penis.

stinger: 1. A prison-made hotpot used to boil water.

stogie: 1. A cigarette.

stool pigeon: 1. An informer.

straightdrop: 1. Pure.

straight off the boat: 1. Imported drugs.

streetwalker: 1. A prostitute.

stuck like Chuck: 1. Not being able to move.

stunt: 1. A whore. 2. A deceiving act.

stuntin: 1. Showing off. 2. Living glamorously. 3. Making pretend.

sucker: 1. A passive person; a wimp.

sweet, nasty, gushy stuff: 1. A vagina.

team: 1. A group of people.

Te amo.: 1. I love you.

teensy-weensy: 1. Tiny; very small.

telly: 1. A hotel.

thang/thangz: 1. The subject at hand.

thingamajigs: 1. Items.

third degree: 1. To question intensively.

thou: 1. Short for thousand.

throwaway: 1. A dispensable object.

throwback: 1. Old; out of style.

tight: 1. Mad; upset. 2. Cheap.

tightfisted: 1. Greedy. 2. Desiring excessively.

tio: 1. Uncle.

titi: 1. Aunt.

Todo esta bien.: 1. Everything is okay.

Toma tú bandera, toma tú machete, vamos a seguir peleando para la liberación nacional de Puerto Rico!: 1. Here is your flag, here is your machete, let's continue to fight for the national freedom of Puerto Rico!

Tony Montana: 1. Powdered cocaine.

top me off: 1. Oral sex.

tornado: 1. Oral sex.

to the face: 1. For self.

touch down: 1. To arrive at its destination. 2. To be released from prison.

trap life: 1. The drug trafficking life. 2. Jail living.

trappin': 1. Selling drugs.

trick: 1. A prostitute. 2. One who pays for a prostitute.

trippin': 1. Acting out of order.

trophy: 1. An appreciated female. 2. Wife.

truckin': 1. Moving.

true-blue: 1. Faithful; honest.

Truey's: 1. True Religion clothing.

Tu no tienes respeto.: 1. You don't have any respect.

Tu oísteis esos tiros?: 1. Did you hear those gunshots?

turnkey: 1. A correctional officer.

turn up: 1. Ready for action. 2. To proceed with action.

Tu vas a capiar hoy, verdad?: 1. You are going to re-up today, right?

twerp: 1. A wimp.

twin: 1. Brother or sister.

Twinkie: 1. A disrespectful term toward a rival gang member.

twisted: 1. Intoxicated. 2. High. 3. Braided. 4. To have had rolled a blunt.

twork: 1. Drugs.

two-stepped: 1. Walked. 2. Danced.

two-timing: 1. Being unfaithful in a relationship.

unstepped-on: 1. Pure.

upchucked: 1. To vomit.

Vaya con Dios!: 1. Go with God!

Vaya, mami? Ese culo de papi?: 1. What's up, baby? Is that ass mine?

wack: 1. Not liked.

Watermelon Kush: 1. Marijuana.

wave: 1. Style. 2. Fashion.

weasel: 1. An informer.

weight: 1. A great amount of drugs.

weight is up: 1. Clout.

weight on deck: 1. To have a great amount of drugs on call.

went hard: 1. Above and beyond.

wettin': 1. Paying mind to.

wet-wet: 1. A vagina.

What's good?: 1. What's happening?

What's poppin?: 1. What's happening?

What's the deal?: 1. What's the situation?

wheels: 1. A vehicle.

whip it, whip it, real hard: 1. To transform cocaine into crack.

whipped out: 1. To brandish something.

whipping: 1. Driving fast.

white: 1. Powdered cocaine.

whitegirl: 1. Powdered cocaine.

White Widow: 1. Marijuana.

whooping: 1. Hurrah; laughing.

wifey: 1. Wife.

wig: 1. A head.

wig this bitch: 1. To shoot someone in the head.

wilding: 1. Acting crazy.

word to Mami: 1. I swear on my mother.

worm: 1. A penis.

wrist work: 1. To mix or cook drugs.

X: Ecstasy pill.

yayo: 1. Cocaine.

Yo entiendo.: 1. I understand.

Yo tengo hambre.: 1. I am hungry.

Yo tengo hambre también.: 1. I am hungry as well.

Yo te voy a romper ese bicho a besos limpio.: 1. I am going to break your penis by clean kisses.

You feel me?: 1. Do you understand me?

young buck: 1. A young person.

ILLMATIK CREATIONS

STILL
LOYAL 2 DA
HOOD
MIZROK

Outside the Box Connections (OTBC) mission is to keep inmates connected with everything happening in the world and bridging the connection between family and friends. With millions of incarcerated people having spouses, children, mothers, fathers, siblings, and inmates having such limited resources to stay connected, we recognized the dire need of bridging the gap and that's when Outside the Box Connections was formed.

We are proud to play a role in helping inmates stay connected and informed.

We offer many affordable products and services to inmates to help stay connected such as our personalize gift boxes for family and loved ones, social media packages, updates of current news and events happening around the world, magazine services, book services, gift cards, local numbers, calendars, picture copying and printing services, and much more.

Our motto is quite simple: Quality in a service or product is not what we put into it. It is what the client or customers gets out of it. Let us keep you connected affordably while providing excellent customer service - nothing less.

We look forward to your future business with us.
Outside the Box Connections; where we do the shopping for you!

Outside the Box Connections
P.O Box 900785 Homestead, FL 33090
Phone: 276-299-0545
Email: customers@outsidetheboxconnections.com
Website: www.outsidetheboxconnections.com